Applause for L.L. Raand's Midr

The Midnight Hu...
RWA 2012 VCRW Laurel Wreath ...
Night Hunt
The Lone Hunt

"Raand has built a complex world inhabited by werewolves, vampires, and other paranormal beings...Raand has given her readers a complex plot filled with wonderful characters as well as insight into the hierarchy of Sylvan's pack and vampire clans. There are many plot twists and turns, as well as erotic sex scenes in this riveting novel that keep the pages flying until its satisfying conclusion."—*Just About Write*

"Once again, I am amazed at the storytelling ability of L.L. Raand aka Radclyffe. In *Blood Hunt*, she mixes high levels of sheer eroticism that will leave you squirming in your seat with an impeccable multi-character storyline all streaming together to form one great read."
—*Queer Magazine Online*

"*The Midnight Hunt* has a gripping story to tell, and while there are also some truly erotic sex scenes, the story always takes precedence. This is a great read which is not easily put down nor easily forgotten."—*Just About Write*

"Are you sick of the same old hetero vampire/werewolf story plastered in every bookstore and at every movie theater? Well, I've got the cure to your werewolf fever. *The Midnight Hunt* is first in, what I hope is, a long-running series of fantasy erotica for L.L. Raand (aka Radclyffe)."—*Queer Magazine Online*

"Any reader familiar with Radclyffe's writing will recognize the author's style within *The Midnight Hunt*, yet at the same time it is most definitely a new direction. The author delivers an excellent story here, one that is engrossing from the very beginning. Raand has pieced together an intricate world, and provided just enough details for the reader to become enmeshed in the new world. The action moves quickly throughout the book and it's hard to put down."—*Three Dollar Bill Reviews*

Acclaim for Radclyffe's Fiction

2013 RWA/New England Bean Pot award winner for contemporary romance *Crossroads* "will draw the reader in and make her heart ache, willing the two main characters to find love and a life together. It's a story that lingers long after coming to 'the end.'"—*Lambda Literary*

In 2012 RWA/FTHRW Lories and RWA HODRW Aspen Gold award winner *Firestorm* "Radclyffe brings another hot lesbian romance for her readers."—*The Lesbrary*

Foreword Review Book of the Year finalist and IPPY silver medalist *Trauma Alert* "is hard to put down and it will sizzle in the reader's hands. The characters are hot, the sex scenes explicit and explosive, and the book is moved along by an interesting plot with well drawn secondary characters. The real star of this show is the attraction between the two characters, both of whom resist and then fall head over heels." —*Lambda Literary Reviews*

Lambda Literary Award Finalist *Best Lesbian Romance 2010* features "stories [that] are diverse in tone, style, and subject, making for more variety than in many, similar anthologies...well written, each containing a satisfying, surprising twist. Best Lesbian Romance series editor Radclyffe has assembled a respectable crop of 17 authors for this year's offering."—*Curve Magazine*

2010 Prism award winner and ForeWord Review Book of the Year Award finalist *Secrets in the Stone* is "so powerfully [written] that the worlds of these three women shimmer between reality and dreams…A strong, must read novel that will linger in the minds of readers long after the last page is turned."—*Just About Write*

In **Benjamin Franklin Award finalist** *Desire by Starlight* "Radclyffe writes romance with such heart and her down-to-earth characters not only come to life but leap off the page until you feel like you know them. What Jenna and Gard feel for each other is not only a spark but an inferno and, as a reader, you will be washed away in this tumultuous romance until you can do nothing but succumb to it."—*Queer Magazine Online*

Lambda Literary Award winner *Stolen Moments* "is a collection of steamy stories about women who just couldn't wait. It's sex when desire overrides reason, and it's incredibly hot!"—*On Our Backs*

Lambda Literary Award winner *Distant Shores, Silent Thunder* "weaves an intricate tapestry about passion and commitment between lovers. The story explores the fragile nature of trust and the sanctuary provided by loving relationships."—*Sapphic Reader*

Lambda Literary Award Finalist *Justice Served* delivers a "crisply written, fast-paced story with twists and turns and keeps us guessing until the final explosive ending." —*Independent Gay Writer*

Lambda Literary Award finalist *Turn Back Time* "is filled with wonderful love scenes, which are both tender and hot." —*MegaScene*

By Radclyffe

Romances

Innocent Hearts

Promising Hearts

Love's Melody Lost

Love's Tender Warriors

Tomorrow's Promise

Love's Masquerade

shadowland

Passion's Bright Fury

Fated Love

Turn Back Time

When Dreams Tremble

The Lonely Hearts Club

Night Call

Secrets in the Stone

Desire by Starlight

Crossroads

Homestead

Honor Series

Above All, Honor

Honor Bound

Love & Honor

Honor Guards

Honor Reclaimed

Honor Under Siege

Word of Honor

Code of Honor

Justice Series

A Matter of Trust (prequel)

Shield of Justice

In Pursuit of Justice

Justice in the Shadows

Justice Served

Justice for All

The Provincetown Tales

Safe Harbor

Beyond the Breakwater

Distant Shores, Silent Thunder

Storms of Change

Winds of Fortune

Returning Tides

Sheltering Dunes

First Responders Novels
Trauma Alert
Firestorm
Oath of Honor
Taking Fire

Short Fiction

Collected Stories by Radclyffe
Erotic Interludes: *Change Of Pace*
Radical Encounters

Edited by Radclyffe:
Best Lesbian Romance 2009–2014

Stacia Seaman and Radclyffe, eds.:
Erotic Interludes 2: *Stolen Moments*
Erotic Interludes 3: *Lessons in Love*
Erotic Interludes 4: *Extreme Passions*
Erotic Interludes 5: *Road Games*
Romantic Interludes 1: *Discovery*
Romantic Interludes 2: *Secrets*
Breathless: *Tales of Celebration*
Women of the Dark Streets
Amor and More: Love Everafter

By L.L. Raand

Midnight Hunters
The Midnight Hunt
Blood Hunt
Night Hunt
The Lone Hunt
The Magic Hunt

Visit us at www.boldstrokesbooks.com

TAKING FIRE

by

RADCLY*f*FE

2014

This Trade Paperback Original Is Published By
Bold Strokes Books, Inc.
P.O. Box 249
Valley Falls, NY 12185

First Edition: July 2014

CREDITS
EDITORS: RUTH STERNGLANTZ, STACIA SEAMAN
PRODUCTION DESIGN: STACIA SEAMAN
COVER DESIGN BY SHERI (GRAPHICARTIST2020@HOTMAIL.COM)

Acknowledgments

When I was five I wanted to be a space commander like Captain Glendora, who "manned" the spaceship SS *Glendora* on a local TV show. By ten I had switched to alternately being a soldier—I faithfully watched *Combat!*, a WWII TV drama, every week—or a sheriff, à la *Gunsmoke*. I had the various toy guns, hats, helmets, badges, and patches to go with every persona. No one mentioned I might not be able to be those things seeing as how I was a girl, although I occasionally had problems convincing my friends (all boys in my neighborhood) that I should be in charge. Contrary to popular criticisms, those shows didn't instill a tendency for violence or disregard of life in me, but rather a deep appreciation for honor, justice, valor, and self-sacrifice. I love to write heroes because I think the world needs them—whether they be military, law enforcement, firefighters, medical, or unsung family and friends. The First Responder series lets me write about a variety of heroes, and this one was a challenge on many levels. Having never been to Africa, I had to do a lot of Google mapping; having never been in a Black Hawk—ditto fact searching; having never seen death in war, I had to read about it. I am indebted to Phil Klay, whose book *Redeployment* offers an unflinching and soul-shattering view of the war in the Middle East. I apologize for any factual errors in this work and hope that I have done justice to the many heroes who have experienced what I have not.

Thanks go to senior editor Sandy Lowe, whose patience is limitless; to editor Ruth Sternglantz for refining my work; to Stacia Seaman for keeping me honest; and to my first readers Connie, Eva, and Paula for constant encouragement.

Sheri got the cover exactly right—thank you for fourteen years of amazing artwork.

And to Lee, my own personal hero–*Amo te*.

Radclyffe, 2014

For Lee, for taking chances

Chapter One

Djibouti, Africa

Four more days before she punched her one-way ticket out of hell. New York City wasn't exactly Max's idea of heaven, but it would be an improvement over Djibouti and nirvana compared to Afghanistan. The life she'd left fourteen months ago hadn't consisted of much more than work, but no matter how empty the rest of her existence might be, no one would be shooting at her in Manhattan. Maybe.

Max lay on her cot in the twilight watching the sand swirl in random eddies through the half-open door of the containerized living unit. The other compartment in the ten-by-twenty sand-colored metal box was empty, as were most of the other CLUs in the neighborhood. Only one thing could empty the hundreds of identical boxes in CLUville so completely—chow time. She couldn't be bothered to traverse the heat and the flies and the hundred-yard trek to the chow hall even though the food at Camp Lemonnier was a thousand times better than what she'd grown immune to at the forward operating bases. Half the time the pre-packaged meals at the FOBs tasted about like the cardboard they were shipped in. Besides, calories were calories, and drinking them had its advantages. The bottle of no-label whiskey tucked under her mattress provided fuel for the engine with the side benefit of a few hours' oblivion. If she couldn't sleep, she'd take what she could get. At least the alcohol blanked the dreams—a civilized term for the images that haunted her, awake and asleep.

A shadow fell across her face and a blocky form filled the doorway. "Yo, Deuce—you gonna grab some chow?"

"Hey, Grif. You go ahead." Max had told the corpsman a thousand times to call her Max, but the closest he could get to ignoring her rank was the nickname she'd gotten the first time she'd set foot on the sand. Lieutenant Commander Max de Milles, US Navy Medical Corps. *MDM, MD* fast became *MD2* and from there just plain Deuce.

"You sure?"

She could hear his frown, although his face was lost to shadow. "Yeah, I'm good. Just going to catch some sleep before my next duty shift."

"Won't be long before you can do that with both eyes closed instead of just one," he said. "When's your ride out?"

"End of the week." She tried to sound casual, like it didn't really matter, but she hated to even talk about the end of this tour. She'd always been a little superstitious—most surgeons were, but war had a way of honing everything down to the sharp, bright core, and superstition had become a religion. She'd learned pretty quickly on her first tour that talking about something was a sure way to jinx it. Or worse, bring your nightmares to life. Everyone knew the consequences of breaking the unwritten rules: never discuss the danger of going outside the wire, never brag about the girl waiting back home, never count the days until end of tour. If you did, you might mistake that buried IED for a rock, or log on to the Dear John email, or get the last-minute change in your separation orders.

"Man," Grif sighed. "A few weeks on a ship and a day's flight—you'll be home before Labor Day."

"You won't be far behind me." She didn't want to make small talk. She didn't want to hear about Ken Griffin's high-school-sweetheart-now-wife or his three kids back in Kansas City, or how he was going back to his job as an EMT. She didn't want to imagine him with his family or hear about his dreams—not when all that could end in a millisecond. After tending countless troops with shattered bones and battered bodies and devastated lives, she'd finally managed to wall herself off from the human beings who depended upon her. Her brain and hands functioned mechanically to fix their torn flesh as efficiently as ever, but her emotions had disconnected. When she failed, when she lost one, she no longer thought about the suffering of the husband or wife or kids back home. She just moved on. Until she fell asleep.

Grif grinned the soft, loopy grin he got when talking about his family. "Yep—maybe I'll bring Laurie and the kids to New York City and look you up."

"Sure," Max said. *Just shut up. Just...don't say any more. Don't you know it only takes a second, one misstep, to change everything forever?*

"Right then." His tone held a little uncertainty, a little concern. Grif was worse than a girl sometimes—his feelings played across his face like images on a marquee in Times Square. He worried and fretted and most of his anxiety was directed at her. Not because *she* was a girl, but because she never unloaded. Never got drunk and trashed her tent, never shot off her mouth about the fucking Taliban, never joined in movie night and hooted at the lousy porn, even though plenty of the female troops did. She burned inside like a boiler about to blow at the seams. She knew it and so did he. What he didn't know about were the nights she walked outside the wire until the lights of the FOB faded and there was just her and her constant companion, death. Or how she sat in the sand in the still, dark desert with her bottle and watched the stars revolve overhead and dared the gods of war to come and get her. None ever did.

No one knew. No one ever would.

"I'll email you my number," Max lied. "You give me a call and we'll meet for dinner."

"Awesome. 'Night, Deuce."

"'Night." Max waited until he moved away, leaving a patch of black sky and a haze of dust in his wake, and reached for the bottle.

❖

Juba jungle, Somalia

The tent flap twitched aside and Amina peered in. "A Skype request came through for you to call back soonest."

Rachel frowned, closed her laptop, and tucked it under her arm. She wasn't scheduled to use the camp's satellite hookup and wasn't expecting any communication from Red Cross headquarters. She joined the dark-haired interpreter, who had started out as her liaison with the Somali Red Crescent Society and had soon become a friend, on the walk through camp to the base station. "Who was it, do you know?"

"It was from America. A pleasant blond woman requested we have you call. She did not say why. Only that you're to use official channels."

"Oh." Rachel was glad the weak illumination from the solar lights strung at intervals along the perimeter of the encampment hid her blush. She hated having attention drawn to her special status, one she tried very hard to downplay if not erase. Blending in at the field outpost with Somalis from the Red Crescent Society, the multinational delegates from the Red Cross, and the French medical team from Doctors Without Borders would have been a lot simpler if she didn't have special diplomatic status on top of being one of the few Americans. "I'm sorry I'll be using up someone else's airtime."

"No one here has anyone at home who can afford to have Internet, or if they do, they're too busy to use it."

Amina's smile lightened her voice, and the affection in her nut-brown eyes and the teasing expression on her elegant face showed even in the almost-dark. Rachel was thankful for the hundredth time she'd found a friend who didn't care about her family or her status. "I thought you said your fiancé was a techie."

"He is, and he spends all his waking hours working with or playing on his computers—not Skyping me."

"Then he's crazy."

Amina slipped her arm through Rachel's. "Something tells me you could teach him how a betrothed should act."

Rachel laughed. Amina had been educated in England and was far worldlier than the other Somali women on the Red Crescent relief team, but she doubted Amina would have made the comment if she'd known Rachel's preference for partners. The subject had never come up—why would it out here in the jungle where there were so many more important things to think about, like how to stem the measles epidemic that was devastating the nomadic populations, or how to get food and shelter to the displaced herders and farmers in the wake of the famine and devastation brought on by recent tropical storms, widespread flooding, and attacks from marauding rebels.

Anyone's sex life or, in her case, lack thereof, was way down on the list of pressing topics. When she and Amina spoke of personal things, she simply said she had no one waiting at home. Technically true. She doubted Christie was pining away and would have plenty of women to entertain her among her rich and powerful friends. Of course, to be fair, Rachel had told Christie not to wait for her, and although Christie had been gracious enough to protest, she was sure Christie had moved on as soon she'd left for Mogadishu. At least she hoped she had.

If the circumstances had been reversed, Rachel would have done the same. She'd dated Christie Benedict exclusively for six months because she found Christie's company preferable to the alternatives. Women who moved in her family's circles—or more specifically her father's—rapidly lost interest when they discovered she had no desire to swim in the shark-infested waters of Capitol Hill or, worse, pretended they didn't care while subtly urging her to use her influence to further their personal agendas. At least Christie had her own access to influence and power. She was beautiful, cultured, and good in bed. She should have made a perfect partner, but even in their most intimate moments, Rachel never felt a spark. Not a flicker of true desire, let alone passion. She'd observed her parents' perfectly serviceable marriage for twenty-five years—far longer than needed to recognize the signs of a union sealed not by love and passion, but by mutual convenience. Her father needed a wife to complete his image, and her mother needed a husband to fulfill her desire for family and status. They probably even loved each other, in some way, but not in the way she wanted for herself. Not with a fire that burned in their hearts. So leaving Christie had been easy and a secret relief. No doubt Christie felt the same.

"I'm sure you can handle whatever lessons he might need," Rachel said as they neared the headquarters tent, the largest in the encampment other than the huge hospital tent. The smaller two-person sleeping tents ringed the flat central area where they took their meals and met with villagers and nomads who ventured into the camp for medical care or other assistance. In recent weeks, the stream of Somalis in need of aid had grown into a river of sick, injured, and starving people.

Amina sighed. "He does not like me doing this work, but I feel I must." She swept an arm toward the dense jungle, rapidly darkening into a solid wall of blackness. Out there somewhere, thousands of men, women, and children were homeless without food or basic resources. "Who else will help them if not us?"

"We're here and we won't leave them." Rachel squeezed Amina's arm. "When you tell him how bad it is out here and how important this work is, he'll understand."

"I hope so." In the light slanting through the netting covering the door of the tent, Amina's face brightened. "But you're right. We won't abandon them."

"No," Rachel said, lifting the netting aside, "we won't."

"Do you want me to wait and walk back with you?" Amina asked.

"No, I'm fine." Rachel wasn't worried about being alone in the camp—she knew all the team members, and despite constant reports of armed rebels in the surrounding jungle, none had ever been spotted by the guards posted around the encampment. "Get some sleep. I'll see you at breakfast."

"Good night then," Amina said and slipped into the night.

Rachel crossed the sparsely furnished sixty-foot square tent to the trio of folding tables that made up the communications center—a few laptop computers, a satellite radio hookup, a shortwave radio for communicating with the ATVs, and three metal camp chairs stationed in a snaggletoothed row. The sidewalls were high enough to accommodate her five feet ten inches without her having to stoop. Squares of netting formed windows at regular intervals and allowed enough air to circulate to counteract the faintly musty smell of well-used canvas. The chairs were empty, as was the rest of the admin center. She was likely the last one up and about other than the sentries on the perimeter and the medical personnel in the hospital tent. Someone was on duty there around the clock.

Satisfied she was alone, Rachel settled onto a narrow metal chair, plugged her secure laptop into the outlet in the generator under the table, and connected to the sat line. The signal strength was good for once. Low cloud cover. She hurriedly brought up the scrambled video link and typed in her password.

The screen flickered, and a few seconds later her father's face rippled into view and settled into the familiar lines of his craggily handsome face, thick dark leonine hair, and bristling brows. He wasn't at the office—no seal preceded his connection. That might not mean anything—he often called her at odd hours from some place he was traveling. She didn't know his itinerary. Or he could be calling from an unofficial location because he didn't want their conversation on record. She'd long ago ceased asking or wondering.

"Rachel," he said in his deep baritone.

"Hi, Dad." She hoped she didn't sound as wary as she felt. A call from her father was rare. Usually any contact came from his assistant, and those messages were relayed through Red Cross headquarters in Geneva or the local counterpart in Mogadishu. In the two months she'd been in-country, she'd heard from him once. "Is Mother all right?"

"Your mother is busy with a fundraiser at the museum at the moment and perfectly well. This concerns you, and I'll be brief. I'd appreciate it if you'd hear me out before arguing."

Rachel's chest tightened. So it would be that way, would it? Her father preempting any discussion with an order. That used to work when she was fifteen, but she wasn't fifteen any longer. They didn't have much time for the call, and rather than protest and waste more of it, she just nodded.

"Your location is no longer secure. A team is flying in to evacuate you before morning."

"What? What kind of team? From where?"

Her father sighed audibly. "Navy personnel from Lemonnier. The details aren't important."

Rachel stared at the image of her father, flattened and faded by distance and time. His eyes were still easy to read—hard and certain and unswayable. Some theorized he would be president one day. He would probably be tremendous in the role, but she didn't even want to imagine what that would mean for her. "Why?"

"That's classified."

"I think you're safe in telling me—I'm hardly a security risk out here."

His mouth thinned. "You are a security risk by virtue of who you are. I was against you taking a field assignment and this is why."

"You're saying someone wants to kidnap me?" Her voice rose as incredulity won out over anger. She'd used her middle name as a surname in all her professional dealings since college just so she could avoid special treatment or the presumption of privilege. "Oh, come on. No one knows who I am, other than I have diplomatic status like half the other Americans on the continent."

"There are no secrets in our line of work, you should know that by now. If you were to be captured—" He shook his head as if annoyed he'd said too much. "There's no point in having the discussion now. Just be ready at zero five hundred."

"What about my team—and the others? Are they—"

"Plans are still being finalized, and until they are, any discussion with anyone could jeopardize everyone's safety. You are not to disclose this information to anyone."

She glanced at the timer on the lower corner of the screen. Just over two minutes had elapsed. Much longer and they ran the risk of their transmission being picked up by someone randomly monitoring satellite feeds.

"What do you mean no longer secure? What's the emergency? I can't just leave—"

"This is not negotiable. Your safety comes first. Please don't argue—the decision has been made. Just be ready. I'll speak to you again when you're in a secure location."

The screen went blank. Rachel could almost believe she'd imagined the conversation. She was on a humanitarian mission for the Red Cross—they were a neutral delegation protected by the internationally recognized agreements of the Geneva Conventions. She was safe, or as safe as anyone in the jungles of a nation that was ravaged by natural disaster and generations-long civil war could be.

Her father couldn't honestly believe she was just going to walk away from her responsibility and her colleagues because he ordered her to, and if he did, he was very wrong.

Chapter Two

The bird rocked as the concussive blasts from rocket fire buffeted them like leaves in a windstorm. Flaming red tongues cleaved the night. The air, heavy with soot, tasted of acid and gasoline and terror. The pilot nuanced the lift and thrust and kept the rotors spinning, and they descended through billowing clouds of greasy black smoke into chaos. The armored truck, once tan like the desert sand, lay on its side, a mangled mass of blackened metal half submerged in a huge crater in the center of a narrow dirt road that twisted into the barren mountainside.

The Black Hawk lurched to the ground and wraithlike shapes raced out of the dark, faceless phantoms silhouetted against the pyre like refugees from a nightmare. Max jumped out and ran past the troops carrying wounded to the Black Hawk. She had to reach the truck, get to the survivors before snipers or fire beat her to them. Thunder roared and the earth shuddered. Max flew through the air and landed hard on her right side. Rocks and metal rained down on her. Head spinning, she picked herself up off the ground and stumbled across what was left of the road, tripping into holes and over smoldering bits of debris. Blood ran wet and warm down her cheek and she blinked the sweat and sticky fluid from her eyes. Automatically she felt for her first aid kit. The canvas IFAK still hugged her shoulders, although her numb hands could only register the bulk of it banging against her back as she half ran, half staggered toward the forms littering the ground around the burning truck.

The thunder of the IEDs pounding against her eardrums slowly dwindled to a throbbing roar. Screams and shouts floated through her confused mind like words shouted underwater. Her legs wouldn't move fast enough, her lungs burned from sucking in air so hot her nasal passages cracked and bled. Specters, their features obliterated by grime and blood and smoke, beckoned to her.

Medic medic medic. Always the same. *Medic medic medic.*

They needed her and she couldn't reach them. Her leg plunged into a blast hole and she fell, pain lancing through her thigh. She caught herself on outstretched hands and muffled a moan. Her pain was nothing compared to theirs. She pulled herself free and tried to stand. Her leg buckled and she fell again. This time she couldn't smother the cry of agony.

No matter. Pain was her penance. They depended on her and she was too slow. She had to be strong. She dragged herself forward on her forearms, pushing with her uninjured leg, dragging the other.

Up ahead, they were dying. Everywhere around her, they were dying. She wasn't fast enough, she wasn't strong enough, she wasn't good enough. Wasn't good enough. Another crack of thunder and the world exploded. Hell on earth had arrived.

Max jerked awake in the dark. Breath rushed from her chest as if she'd been punched in the solar plexus. Her olive drab T-shirt clung to her torso, black with the sweat drenching her hair and body. Her fingers cramped, and she forced her fists to loosen their grip on the thin mattress under her. She mercilessly ordered her muscles to relax and ordered herself to lie still when all she wanted was to get up and run. She laughed, and the desperate sound echoed in the metal box like so many mocking voices. Run to where? There was no escaping her dreams. She'd tried tempting fate outside the wire, but exchanging one hell for another never worked.

She was alive, and the price she paid was guilt. She didn't need a shrink to tell her that. She pressed her thigh where shrapnel had penetrated when a buried IED exploded on a twisting road in Afghanistan. They'd dug it out in the field hospital, patched her up, and she'd gone back to her unit a few days later. A few inches higher, an inch to the left, and her femoral artery would have been severed and she would have bled out on the road like so many had done before her eyes. She had lived and the man next to her had died. The woman behind her had lost a leg. She descended into hell again and again to atone, but it was never enough.

No matter what she did, no matter how hard she fought the images, struggled to deafen the screams resounding in her head, she couldn't escape. She slid her hand under the mattress, found the smooth outline of the small flat glass bottle, and pulled it out. She unscrewed the cap with shaking fingers and took a swallow. The whiskey burned like the air that had scorched her lungs, but the fire in her belly promised to settle her nerves in a minute or two even if it didn't cleanse her sins. She took another swallow, recapped the bottle, and pushed it back out of sight. She held up her wrist and read almost twenty hundred in the luminescent numbers on her watch. She was due for her last twenty-four-hour shift in another six hours.

Even though the medevac callouts this far from the hot zones of Iraq and Afghanistan were far fewer than they had been, she couldn't risk being less than 100 percent functional. Soldiers, marines, airmen, sailors, and allies still got injured and shot and blown up. She still had a job to do. She'd have to tough out the rest of the night without the momentary help of the whiskey.

She curled on her side, drew her knees up, and closed her eyes. All she had to do was hang on for four more days and she'd be back at NYU, where even the most horrendous cases would seem simple compared to the inhuman carnage of war. She was alone, and thankful no one had witnessed her nightmare. CC, a machinist specialist who shared her CLU, wouldn't be back until after Max left for her shift. Sharing ten by thirty feet for months on end would be unimaginable to most people, but out here, these accommodations were among the best. They had a window air-conditioning unit, a partition between their sleeping areas, and mattresses that weren't bug infested or grimy with filth. They had hot showers and decent food. She had it good.

She and CC weren't overly personal, but they shared more than either of them did with those they'd left behind. CC would keep Max's secrets even if she knew, but Max guarded her privacy ferociously. Her demons were her own.

A sharp rap sounded on the metal door of her CLU, and Max swung upright on the side of her cot.

A voice called, "Commander de Milles?"

"Yes."

"Captain Inouye wants you."

Max pushed her hands through her hair, found a plastic bottle of water and splashed some on her face and neck, and strode to the end of the container. She pulled the door open and stepped out onto the top of the two metal steps leading down to the ground. An ensign saluted and she returned the salute.

"Sorry to disturb you, ma'am. There's a briefing at twenty thirty hours in the com center."

"Right," Max said, her mouth suddenly as dry as if she were breathing burning air. *Never talk about what might happen outside the wire. Never brag about the girl back home. Never count the days until end of tour.*

Anything could happen. Anything was about to.

Shivering with a ripple of anxiety, Rachel quickly skirted the two large fire pits in the center of the camp they kept burning day and night. They didn't need the heat, not when the average temperature ranged above 100°F every day and didn't fall much lower at night, but they conserved their propane for the generators by using the open fires to keep water boiling and coffee, endless coffee, constantly available. The dozen sleeping tents ringing the encampment, forming a barrier between the jungle and their living space, were dark except for one, where a dim light within silhouetted the hunched form of a man sitting on the side of his cot, perhaps reading or composing a letter. The canvas sides glowed like a giant jack-o'-lantern, and Rachel had the uncomfortable thought that the oblivious occupant made an easy target. Pushing the disquieting image firmly aside, she slipped inside the tent she shared with Amina as quietly as she could. Their days were long, starting before sunrise, and if that wasn't exhausting enough, fighting dehydration was a never-ending battle. By suppertime, everyone was drained, mentally and physically, and bedtime came early. The first few nights after they'd arrived, everyone on the disaster recovery team had stayed up well past dark, sitting around the fires, getting to know one another, eager to undertake the challenge of their mission. After two months, faced with the endless deprivation of the Somalis caught in the crossfire of a war they did not understand or welcome, the diseases that had long been eradicated in more prosperous countries, and the seemingly endless task of restructuring a society devastated by enemies natural and manmade, their enthusiasm had transformed into weary but dogged determination. No one stayed up late imagining great victories. Everyone went to bed early to conserve their strength for another day in the endless battle.

She'd been in the field twice before as a disaster relief coordinator—once after the hurricanes that devastated Haiti and again following the massive flooding in the central United States—but she'd never been this far from the life she had known in miles or in experience. She could barely remember what it was like to sleep in a bed, to wake to hot showers and brewed coffee, and not to be cut off from the rest of the world for long stretches of time. The constant connectedness of the electronic world was a memory. Here she was as detached from her past life as she could possibly be, and yet she had never felt more herself. Her needs, her goals, her pleasures had been stripped down to the core. Out here what she did mattered, her life had meaning. She made a difference every time she fed a child or gave a bag of seed to a farmer or a loaf of bread to a tribesman. Her work wasn't done, and if she left before it was, she feared she'd be haunted by the faces of those she'd failed to help.

Rachel sank onto the edge of her cot and, resting her elbows on her knees, buried her face in her hands. She had promised not to leave. What would she do in ten hours when the helicopter arrived for her? None of this made sense. If she thought her father would be more forthcoming, she'd call him back, but she knew him. He'd said all he was going to say and expected her to obey him. Rachel sighed, wanting to pace, furious at her father for leaving her in the dark. He probably never even considered how his authoritative bearing affected her. He was used to everyone in every sphere of his life doing as he wished without explanation. Even her mother rarely challenged his decisions or desires. Her older brother, groomed since childhood to follow in her father's footsteps, had never seemed to mind. He'd finished law school and had already entered local politics. Rachel had been the only one who refused to follow his orders without question. She had been the only one to challenge his authority. When she'd been old enough, she'd demanded to choose her own path.

"Bad news?" Amina whispered from the darkness.

"I don't know," Rachel said, her father's words echoing in her mind. *Do not discuss this.* Why? Did he think the doctors, the engineers, the teachers and epidemiologists and translators were spies? His fundamental distrust of everyone's motives was fueled by a lifetime of immersion in politics and the manipulation and maneuvering that went with it. Even though she'd been only too happy to leave that world behind, she wasn't foolish enough to discount her father's warnings. He might be exaggerating the danger for some agenda of his own, but what if he wasn't? She considered her words cautiously. "Have you heard any news about…anything affecting our security?"

Amina pushed aside the light sheet that covered her and sat up. Now that Rachel's eyes had adjusted, she could see the glint in Amina's eyes and the faint glow of her caramel skin in the little bit of moonlight slanting through the folded-back flaps of the mesh screens. She centered herself in Amina's steady, honest gaze and grew more certain of the rightness of what she was doing.

"I have not heard anything," Amina said, "but Dacar handles security and receives briefings by radio almost every day, I think. We only are informed about ordinary things—supplies and medical deliveries, when the trucks will arrive to transport patients, that sort of thing."

"No one has mentioned evacuation?"

Across from her, Amina drew a sharp breath. "No. Not that I've been told. Is there something we should tell Dacar?"

Amina didn't ask what Rachel knew, only waited, not because she was passive or intimidated, but because she trusted Rachel to tell her what she could. Her trust in Rachel, in Rachel's commitment to their mission they shared, meant more to Rachel than all the feigned interest or attention of Christie and the other women she'd been involved with.

"I don't know what's happening—if anything at all is *really* happening," Rachel said, "but I've been told we are to be evacuated. All of us. Something about a security issue, but I don't have any details."

"But the patients. What of them? We are not scheduled to send anyone to meet the trucks for another two days. What of those who are not ambulatory?"

"I don't know. Maybe there are other plans to move them."

The patients, who usually numbered around twenty, were mostly children, pregnant women, and the elderly of both sexes. Their illnesses ranged from dehydration and malnutrition to febrile convulsions accompanying a measles infection. Rarely they'd see someone with a gunshot wound—a victim of a run-in with the al-Shabaab rebels who continued to wage their decades-long war to overthrow the African Union–backed government. The team from Doctors Without Borders had a rudimentary operating room for emergencies, but most of their efforts were focused on public health issues. The rest of the Red Cross members concentrated on long-term rehabilitation or relocation of the civilians who found their way to them in increasing numbers every day.

"Then someone should have told us by now, no?" Amina's voice vibrated with tension. "Should we talk to Maribel?"

Rachel felt a breath of hope. Certainly Maribel Fleur, the head of the Doctors Without Borders team, would have been informed if evacuation was imminent, but there was no activity beyond the usual at the hospital. Everything at the camp seemed normal. If they were in danger, there was no sign of it. But she couldn't afford to be wrong. The lives of her colleagues and those they had all come to help might be in danger if she kept silent. And if she didn't, if she revealed what little she knew, perhaps she would endanger everyone even more. Waiting was not in her nature, but this time she'd have to.

"The camp seems secure, and there's nothing else we can do tonight. Let's wait until morning." She might have no choice but to wait, but she had a choice about going. When morning arrived and she made it clear she wasn't leaving, she'd find out what was happening.

CHAPTER THREE

Max entered the briefing room at HQ, a larger rectangular version of her sleeping quarters, and edged around the long table covered with maps and reports that took up most of the space. The windowless walls were lined with shelves holding field manuals and thick folders. Captain Inouye, an average-sized middle-aged guy with short sandy hair and a square boxer's build, stood by a projection screen at the opposite end of the room. Dan Fox, a Black Hawk pilot she'd flown with a number of times before, slumped in his flight jacket on one side of the table next to his wingman, Ariel Jordan, a young African American with sleek dark hair long on the sides and gathered at her nape into a short tail. The bird's crew chief, Ollie Rampart, a big blond Iowa farm boy who spoke slow and moved fast in a firefight, and several junior officers from Inouye's support staff made up the rest of the group.

"Commander de Milles," Captain Inouye said by way of greeting when she walked in.

"Sir." Max saluted.

"Have a seat, everyone, please." Inouye turned to the screen and someone dimmed the lights.

Max sat opposite Fox and regarded the screen where an ensign projected a map of the Horn of Africa, showing Djibouti, Somalia, Kenya, and the adjoining countries.

"We're here," Inouye said, unnecessarily tapping his finger on the city of Djibouti on the coast just north of Somalia. "We're the biggest expeditionary force left out here with the exception of the troops at the forward bases in Afghanistan." He slid his finger in a straight line down to Mogadishu in southern Somalia. "We've got a small advisory force here. Their main objective is to help coordinate the National Army's response to the ongoing civil unrest and escalating terrorist activity in the area. I stress the word *advisory*."

Inouye's sarcasm was subtle, but Max's stomach roiled uneasily. She already didn't like where this was going. Somalia was an unstable hellhole, and every US involvement in the last twenty years seemed to escalate from support to intervention, whether the politicians called the situation advisory or not. They'd lost troops there more than once when the line between support and combat had blurred. Birds had gone down and troops had died. This time around, the rebels were reported to have joined forces with al-Qaeda, which meant better arms, better intelligence, and better organization. All those things made for a stronger, more dangerous enemy. She kept her eyes to the front and her posture relaxed. Fear was a luxury she couldn't afford.

"Down here," Inouye way went on, moving his finger south of Mogadishu and drawing a circle on the southernmost part of Somalia, "is the Juba jungle area. It's believed the rebels are gathering in force in the jungle where their bases are hidden from aerial surveillance and from which they can launch surprise attacks into neighboring areas." He tapped Kenya. "Most recently, a suicide attack at a Kenyan mall killed a number of civilians, including Americans."

Inouye managed to look commanding without being aloof. He always seemed to be holding a conversation rather than relaying orders, but Max wasn't fooled. Whatever was coming, she'd have nothing to say about it. Her job was to follow orders, and she accepted that nothing they did would succeed if that simple premise was ignored. She had no doubt Inouye was leading up to a special mission of some kind, and the image of Manhattan that had been slowly gathering strength in her mind began to fade. She might still get home, but maybe she wouldn't. The other side of a mission was always a question mark—a blank space in the future where it was best not to dwell. Her hands had been clenched, but now they relaxed. Her shoulders settled against the back of the seat. The familiar, even when it brought danger, was oddly comforting. All that mattered was that she do her job. The future was an indulgence not meant for warriors. Only the here and now mattered.

"And right about here," Inouye went on in his conversational tone, pushing a red pin into the map in the middle of the jungle, "is an International Red Cross emergency response station. A dozen people—six from the Mogadishu division of the International Red Crescent Society, all Somalis; three French medics from Doctors Without Borders; and an American and two Swiss, including their team coordinator, an engineer, and a water and irrigation specialist. About twenty-five clicks away"—he swept his hand in a crescent behind the red pin—"is the bulk of the rebel encampment. We estimate a force of several hundred."

Max heard the next words before he even said them. She figured everyone else in the room knew what was coming too. No one said anything. No one coughed or even moved.

"We need to go get these folks and bring them out of there," Captain Inouye said. "Simple extraction. In and out. We're sending two birds—extraction at zero five hundred." He paused and took a breath. "There's one more thing."

The map disappeared and a head shot of a woman with a list of stats next to the photo took its place. Clear gray-green eyes, auburn shoulder-length hair with scattered gold highlights. A broad, sculpted mouth with the barest hint of a smile. Strong nose with a tiny bump on the bridge beneath a faint crescent scar. Tension in the long smooth jawline, a few frown lines creasing the otherwise creamy forehead. Serious, intense. Not beautiful. But striking. The text identified her as Rachel Winslow, age twenty-eight, nationality American, occupation Red Cross disaster response coordinator. Max focused on Rachel Winslow's eyes. Her gaze was direct and confident, like the eyes of a woman who knew what she wanted.

"She is your priority," Inouye said. "You will transport out the others if possible, but in the advent of resistance or other unforeseen conditions forcing you to abort, you will do so only after she is secured. You do not leave without her. Any questions?"

Max looked at Dan Fox. The Swampfox was known for getting in and out of hot zones when no one else would even chance touching down. This was right up his alley. He'd be team leader once they took to the air. He'd maintain contact with the mission controllers and relay situation updates as events played out, but when everything went sideways—and on a mission like this it was bound to, he'd determine their actions in the field. As if on cue, Fox said, "What can we expect from ground resistance?"

"Short answer, we don't know. The rebels move their weapons

stores constantly. They might have surface-to-air missiles, they'll certainly have small arms, but how much and where they might be, we don't know. Surprise is on our side. Fast run in, quick extract, out again."

That approach had worked before. Small teams could penetrate even highly fortified areas more quickly than larger forces with their columns of support vehicles and heavy armaments. Six months before, an American diplomat and a Danish reporter had been extracted by a US Navy SEAL team from a city under siege in Kenya. No one asked Inouye why they were making this trip. It didn't matter. Orders were orders.

"You'll travel light—essential personnel only—to leave room for the civilians and any patients who require transport."

Max wasn't expendable—and tonight she'd be doing double duty as medic and combat troop. Every team carried a medic—either a regular soldier also trained as a medic or a corpsman or flight surgeon, like Max. Once the assignment of medics to combat missions had become routine, the mortality rates of even the worst injuries were drastically lowered, and now their presence was critical to troop morale. Troops faced the dangers of combat and the possibility of mortal injury with more confidence if they knew medical assistance was close at hand. If the troops believed they would survive if injured, their performance was sharper, mentally and physically. Max's job was to keep them and their belief alive.

"Who is the target?" Fox asked.

"You know what I know," Inouye said, waving toward the screen. He narrowed his eyes. "But someone pretty important wants her out of there."

"Shit," someone muttered.

"Handle with care," Inouye said flatly. "Anyone else?"

Max said, "I'll need at least one more corpsman with that many civilians at risk."

Inouye nodded. "Griffin will be riding along. That it?"

No one else had anything to say.

"Very well then. Lieutenant Fox can take over from here."

The captain left and Swampfox walked to the map. He studied it for a moment and turned to the rest of them. "Flying time's a little less than two hours, depending on headwinds. We'll leave at zero three hundred. Anybody have anything to add?"

No one did. Max left without speaking to the others and headed directly to the Black Hawk to check the medical supplies. This would be her one and only chance to be certain she had what she needed in the field. This bird was not a medevac helicopter like the ones she usually rode in when picking up wounded. This bird wasn't marked with the identifiable red cross of a noncombatant helicopter, although in this war the neutrality of medics and their machines, on the ground or in the air, had been ignored to such an extent that many medevac birds now carried defensive armaments. Medics carried assault rifles and sidearms too in case they needed to defend themselves or their wounded. This bird wasn't going to have the full complement of medical equipment, and she planned to supplement what was there with her individual first aid kit. She relied more on her IFAK when treating injured anyhow—she always knew what she had on hand and could find it in the dark. She was going through the IV bags, checking labels and drugs, when Grif spoke from behind her.

"Thought I'd find you here."

Max glanced over her shoulder. "Guess you heard, huh?"

He shrugged, his big oval face with its dusting of freckles calm as usual. "Got tapped for a ride along. Not much else to know. Sorry your nap got trashed."

"No problem. Too hot to sleep anyhow." Max grinned, the adrenaline anticipation of the upcoming mission having burned off the lingering melancholy and dulling effects of the alcohol. Nothing put the brakes on guilt and self-recrimination like the imminent threat of mortal danger. "At least we'll be cool up there."

"Need a hand?" Grif climbed into the belly of the Black Hawk.

"Yeah, now that you're here, can you check the med boxes for me and stock as much extra antibiotics and IV opiates as you can find room for in your IFAK? Field bandages too."

"Sure thing. Expecting trouble?"

Max smiled faintly. "Always."

When she was satisfied they had the bird set for their mission, she told Grif to go get some sleep and headed back to her CLU. CLUville was quiet, or as quiet as it ever got in the middle of the night. The streets were never empty, but most of the admin buildings were dark, the DFAC was dark—late-night suppertime having come and gone. Anyone who wanted food now would have to make do with whatever they could find in the vending machines scattered around the base until the dining facility opened again at zero five hundred. Just about when most troops were sitting down to eggs and bacon, she'd be dropping out of a Black Hawk onto the jungle floor.

The photo of Rachel Winslow flashed through her mind. Whoever she was, she wasn't just a Red Cross worker. Someone wanted her out of harm's way and had enough power to make it happen. Max wondered what was really happening in the Juba jungle that these aid workers needed to be pulled out now. They'd been there for a while, so what had changed? She didn't need to know, any more than she needed to know what had brought Rachel Winslow to the darkest part of a lost land even God had forgotten.

Max detoured to the communal showers and stood under the hot water for a long time, letting her mind empty. When she set out on this mission she wanted her reactions to be sharp and nothing in her head but the objective. Back in her CLU she changed into clean field camos, checked her gear, weapons, and IFAK. When she was satisfied she was prepared, she set her watch and stretched out on her cot in the dark to wait.

The night was never silent. After the humans settled into their tents for the night, the animals ruled. The susurrus of insect wings on canvas, the hacking cough of a hyena, the deep-throated roar of a lion. And always, beneath it all, the soughing of the canopy overhead that sheltered them from the sun during the day and shrouded them in shadow at night. At first Rachel had had a hard time getting used to the perpetual shade on the jungle floor, but she soon came to appreciate the protection the dense foliage provided from the relentless heat. Tonight, though, she felt as if the jungle were closing in, isolating them from the rest of the world. She wasn't naïve. She knew the dangers, environmental and civil, of this mission. She'd always been cautious and careful, but until tonight, she'd never been afraid.

She prided herself on choosing her own path, controlling her own destiny, and now she waited in the dark while events she didn't understand and couldn't control unfolded around her. Distant thunder boomed, then boomed again, closer this time. Rachel sat up.

Not thunder. Explosions.

Chapter Four

The Black Hawks crossed into Somalia at 2,000 feet, flying at an average cruise speed of 170 miles per hour. Max rode in the open left rear door, her legs hanging out as she watched the undulating contours of the slowly changing landscape. As the minutes passed, vast expanses of desert and low scrubland slowly gave way to the denser ground cover of the jungle. Reconnaissance images she'd seen taken in daylight showed sparse smatterings of small villages comprising no more than a few ramshackle huts, a parched acre or two of struggling crops, and scraggly goats running through twisting rutted paths; nomadic tribespeople in tent camps ringed by camels; and the ever-increasing masses of displaced natives sleeping on the ground next to their bundles of belongings. Now all was dark except for the reflection of the moon off the few streams traversing the high ground like silver ribbons. The deprivation and desperation of the land and its people were hidden in a shroud of shadows.

The second Black Hawk trailed behind them, gunners on both sides and six Hellfire missiles mounted underneath. Neither bird held a full crew. Besides Swampfox and his copilot, she, Grif, Ollie, and the second crew chief and gunner, Bucky Burns, were the only occupants of their bird. The other Black Hawk carried only four. With luck, they'd be able to transport everyone out, including patients. She understood their orders and that Rachel Winslow was their priority, but leaving anyone behind went against everything she believed in. Wounded or dead, no one was left behind, and those civilians were now her responsibility, just like the troops who ventured outside the wire on a mission. Everybody came home. No matter what.

Burns and Ollie scanned out the doors for signs of enemy activity with long-range night-vision scopes. The rebel forces had no airpower, but a vigorous pipeline of arms and ammunition from Yemen provided them with automatic weapons capable of firing rounds that could penetrate the bird's fuselage or windshield. Word had it that 400 surface-to-air missiles powerful enough to take out an airliner had been stolen by al-Qaeda forces during a recent attack on Benghazi. The rebels were mobile, at home in the jungle, and skilled after decades of strife. And a Black Hawk was a big target. Rumor had it there was a bounty on Black Hawks.

The wind, as dry and empty as the land, whipped her face below her goggles, an arid slap reminding her she did not belong in this country, but here she was. Here they all were, bound by duty and ideology and, some would say, trapped by the same. She didn't feel trapped or tricked or coerced into fighting this war whose goals had long since morphed into something far different than they had been a decade before. She and her fellow troops weren't even in the same country where it had all begun. In Africa, war was a way of life. Entire generations were born into it, lived in it, and died in it without ever knowing anything else.

She'd known when she'd signed up for the Navy to subsidize her medical training she might one day be sent to a place like this for reasons that were not hers to question. That was the way of war. She didn't regret her decision to get her medical training on the Navy's dime—she wouldn't have been able to afford it any other way, and she was willing to pay up on her obligation in any way the Navy demanded. She only regretted the consequences of the war for those she had pledged to serve.

The rhythmic drone of the engines and the whir of the rotors were hypnotic, oddly soothing, and all too conducive to introspection. Out here, where bursts of adrenalized excitement and fear alternated with hours and days of boredom while waiting for the next call, introspection was an all-too-familiar companion. Tonight, Max could do without the solitary voice of her own thoughts.

They'd been in the air almost two hours, with no sign of activity below, and she wasn't sure at first she'd actually seen the quick flare of orange that winked out almost as soon as it appeared. Max blinked, clearing her vision. Another flicker of light shot across her visual field. A trick of sight, brought on by fatigue or distraction. When it came again, she touched the radio mic at her throat. "Swampfox, did you see that? Ten o'clock. Light flares."

Roger that. Standby.

Fox would be calling in to base for a situation update. Max's skin prickled. Nothing was worse than heading into enemy fire, even though by now she should be used to it. Fox's voice crackled in her headphones.

Rocket fire in the vicinity of the LZ. Heads up.

Burns and Ollie shifted the machine guns into position and half leaned out the open doorways. Grif moved back out of the way. Max stayed put. She could use a weapon if she had to, but for now she'd just act as lookout. She flipped down her night-vision goggles, and the area of heavy vegetation off to her left where she'd first seen the momentary flare lit up with green fluorescent puffs of smoke that plumed and fractured, then drifted away like thin strands of seaweed undulating below the surface of a quiet pond.

The sight would have been eerily beautiful if it hadn't meant death had come calling.

❖

Rachel jumped up and pushed her feet into her boots. Across from her, Amina was hastily doing the same.

"What is it?" Amina asked in a high thin whisper.

"I don't know." Rachel answered automatically, but what else could it be? Unless some storm had unexpectedly blown up without warning, those thunderous booms were coming from a battle, and judging by their loudness, the fight was on its way to them. Whatever was happening, she did not intend to be trapped in her tent, blind and helpless. "I'm going to find Dacar."

"I'm coming with you," Amina said.

Rachel unzipped the tent flap, stepped out, and grabbed Amina's hand. The solar lights that usually lit the encampment were gone. A man with a rifle—one of Dacar's Somali security guards?—poured water on the fire. The camp plunged into darkness except for the dim glow of the propane-powered lights inside the hospital tent that burned day and night. Muffled shouts came from everywhere. Rachel couldn't recognize the voices or the words, only the tenor of fear and urgency.

She thought she heard Dacar calling orders, but she couldn't be certain. Another volley of explosions lit up the sky like perverted Fourth of July fireworks. Red and orange starbursts—bombs, not festivity.

The headquarters tent was at the opposite end of the camp, and Rachel saw only blackness in that direction. She'd long ago conquered her fear of the dark, or so she'd thought, but tonight the distant terrors of childhood crept back to taunt her. She didn't want to venture very far from the only bit of light and safety she could see, no matter how false the sense of security might be.

"Let's try the hospital." Rachel had to trust that Dacar and the other guards were looking after their safety, and she would be of no help to them in that. But she could help with the patients. She and Amina ran hand in hand over the familiar ground, made strange and somehow dangerous by the inky dark, to the big hospital tent. Inside, cots lined one side and stacks of supplies the other. A second smaller room in the rear, behind a canvas flap, served as an operating and treatment room. Maribel, Jean-Claude, and Robert moved among the cots, comforting the crying children and trying to calm the anxious adults. Amina instantly joined them, translating for those who did not understand and soothing those who were too terrified to listen.

Rachel smelled smoke, acrid and sharp. More shouts, closer now. Gunfire, rapid staccato cracks like hammer blows on steel. Her heart pounded so quickly she couldn't think. But she had to—the drills they'd practiced in case of emergency evacuation replayed in her mind. No drill had prepared her for this. The noise alone was disorienting. She forced her mind to focus. Gather necessary supplies—medicine, food, drinking water. Communication devices, flashlights. Weapons. God, they didn't have weapons. They were noncombatants. Neutral. Humanitarian. Did those words mean anything to whoever was out there, shooting? She feared they might not. Her stomach knotted. The overwhelming urge to run built inside her like pressure rising in a geyser. Sweat broke over her skin in a cold, sick wash of terror.

Patients panicked. Those who could move jumped from their beds, some of them barefoot in hospital scrubs, and rushed toward the exit, their eyes wide with dread. Several women grabbed children and, despite Amina's and the medical personnel's pleading, fled into the night. A pair of elderly patients, too ill or unaware to flee, remained along with a pair of toddlers who cried and cowered in their crib.

Amina spun around, her eyes stark. "They say it's the rebels. They say we'll all be killed."

Rachel took a deep breath, Amina's fear blunting her own. "We're noncombatants. We're no threat to them. If they come through here, they'll be looking for drugs or supplies or weapons. They can take what they want."

"Yes," Amina said, her voice shaking. "I do not think we want to be here when they arrive, but"—she looked at the frail old man with the infected leg and the blind woman with pneumonia and the children with raging fevers from measles—"we have no choice."

Rachel held her wrist close to one of the flickering lights. Almost five a.m. She thought of her father's instructions for her to be ready to leave. Did her father know this was coming? How could he have kept her in the dark and allowed everyone here to be endangered? She couldn't believe that of him. He was rigid and authoritarian, but he was not so ruthless as to ignore the safety of international aid workers and helpless civilians. Right now, she didn't care what he knew or what he expected her to do—she wasn't leaving without her friends and coworkers, and she wasn't abandoning those who depended on her.

"I'm going to headquarters. If Dacar isn't there, I'll try to radio the center in Mogadishu myself. Will you be all right here?"

"Yes," Amina said. "But hurry."

"Tell the medical staff to prepare the patients to be transported. You should grab anything you need too. I'll be back as soon as I can."

Rachel hurried toward the exit, paused, and turned back. Amina was staring after her, looking small and vulnerable in khaki pants and a loose white T-shirt. "In case I'm…delayed, there's a helicopter coming. Get the patients on there and everyone else you can find."

"But what about you?"

"I'll catch up." Rachel smiled. "I promise. Just take care of things here."

She slipped through the tent flap and quickly took cover in the shadows beyond the glow of the light filtering through the canvas. Keeping close to the edge of the clearing with the jungle at her back, she worked her way around behind the sleeping tents toward headquarters. The gunfire had stopped, and she didn't know whether to be happy about that or not.

Ten yards in front of her, three men burst out of the jungle. Rachel froze, the sound of her pulse pounding in her ears so loud she couldn't believe they didn't hear it. Each wore a scarf around his neck, a tunic-like shirt that came to the tops of his thighs, long loose pants, and boots. Two carried rifles. The third had some kind of tubular weapon about four feet in length balanced on his shoulder and a heavy rucksack strapped to his back. They were laughing. They didn't look her way.

Rachel didn't breathe for so long her vision dimmed and her head spun. When no one else came and the sounds of the men's voices disappeared, she crept forward again. Where had they gone? Most of the supplies were kept on a wooden platform under a tarp next to headquarters. If they were there, she wouldn't be able to reach the radio.

The wind picked up and she took advantage of the rustling to move a little faster. A streak of lightning shot across the clearing. Rachel stumbled and looked up.

Not lightning. Searchlights. Not wind—rotor wash. A helicopter slid into view like a huge black bird of prey. Rachel's heart lurched, and relief, so intense she almost cried out, surged through her.

Gunfire erupted from all around the camp, the sharp cracks making her jump and her legs tremble. Caught halfway between the hospital and headquarters, she had nowhere safe to run. She did the only thing she could. She sprinted into the jungle to hide.

CHAPTER FIVE

The sky lit up with tracer trails. The rattle of automatic weapons fire penetrated Max's protective ear coverings, concussive pops beating against her eardrums. Fox's voice, tight but controlled, announced, "We're taking fire. Hold on."

Max gripped the edge of the open portal. The bird pitched and rolled, an intentional maneuver to give those on the ground an even more difficult moving target. Below her, the jungle vegetation morphed from black into spurts of vibrant green relief as the light from muzzle flashes and rocket flares illuminated their surroundings for brief seconds. The fractured kaleidoscopic images of the trees and earth jumped and flickered as the helicopters descended with their noses and rockets pointed down.

Dawn was on the horizon. She wouldn't need the night-vision goggles any longer and was about to toss them aside when an uneasy sixth sense warned her not to count on anything, or to count anything out. She pushed them up, secured them to her helmet, and squinted down at the landing zone. The only place to land appeared to be right in the middle of the encampment—and right in the center of the firefight. A ring of small square tan tents came into view, bordering a clearing about half the size of a football field. Dense jungle vegetation crowded in around the perimeter, providing excellent cover from which to attack. Two larger tents sat at either end of the clearing like chaperones at homecoming, policing the exits. The place looked eerily deserted. Where was everyone? And who the hell was shooting at them?

In another second, the bird settled lower over the LZ and she had her answer. Three men carrying assault rifles and a grenade launcher knelt and started firing up at them. The pings of bullets ricocheting off the Black Hawk were followed by another round of communication from both birds.

Verify your targets. We've got friendlies down there.

Those aren't friendlies lobbing RPGs at us.

I hear you. Visually verify—rules of engagement.

They weren't to fire unless fired upon, but that seemed to be a foregone conclusion now. Beside her, Ollie fired out the side window and rounds kicked up dirt like deadly raindrops racing across the sand.

Ollie, Burns, stand by on the ropes, Fox said. *We're going in hot.*

Roger, Ollie said and Burns echoed him.

Cover fire, Romeo Two Four, Fox requested of the second Black Hawk that hovered above them.

Roger, Swampfox One.

Both crew chiefs fired the machine guns nonstop, round after round strafing the border between jungle and the clearing to force the insurgents back into the jungle and away from the LZ. Oil-scented steam rose from their weapons. Coils of three-inch-thick nylon ropes lay by their feet ready to be tossed out for a rapid descent. They would drop down and clear the immediate area so Max and Grif could deploy and find Rachel Winslow.

Max pushed the image of Winslow from her mind and sighted her weapon on the figures milling about on the ground. She had no idea who they were, and if they weren't firing directly at the birds, she wasn't about to fire on them. Some of them could be the Red Cross people they'd come here to protect. Clouds of sand whipped up by the rotors caked her nose and mouth. She tried not to breathe too deeply.

When they were fifty feet above the ground, a man and a woman carrying a litter made of two poles with sagging canvas strung between them erupted out of one of the large tents and ran awkwardly across the open ground toward them. She keyed her mic. "We've got wounded approaching. Get us down."

Roger that, Fox grunted. *Ollie, Burns. Go! Go!*

The crew chiefs tossed the ropes, pulled off their headphones, and jumped. Max fired toward the jungle, trying to keep her rounds above head height to deter anyone from shooting back, and hoping not to hit a friendly. Ollie and Burns slid down to the ground and crouched in the swirling red-brown dirt, firing at rebels who appeared and disappeared like wisps of smoke.

Grif crouched beside Max in the portal, waiting for the skids to touch ground. He squeezed her shoulder.

"Keep your head down, Deuce."

"Planning on it," Max yelled. She had jumped out of birds into hot zones plenty of times before, and she didn't worry about what might happen. She couldn't stop a bullet if it had her name on it. "You get those medics with the litter on board. That must be the hospital tent up ahead. I'll check it."

"Roger, Deuce."

Closer now, Max could make out the features of the woman at the front end of the litter. She wore plain tan hospital scrubs and field boots. Her thick blond hair escaped from a twist at her nape and thick curls flew about her face in the wind. Her eyes were wide, her mouth open, and she appeared to be panting in panic or exertion. Not Rachel Winslow.

Max brushed aside an unexpected twinge of disappointment and jumped the last five feet, landing next to Ollie. Automatic weapons chattered all around her. Another man and woman broke from the jungle twenty yards away and ran toward her, shouting, "We're Red Cross. Help us!"

"Get into the helicopter," Max shouted, waving them toward Ollie and Burns, and raced toward the people carrying the litter. A wizened old man, or possibly a very malnourished young one, lay on the litter, his eyes glazed. "Are you the doctor? How many more patients are back there?"

"Yes, I am Maribel Fleur," the woman said with a hint of a French accent. She gulped for breath. "We have another non-ambulatory and two children."

"We'll get them. You two get on board," Max said.

"You will need help. I will go back—"

"No! I'm a doctor. I'll handle it." Max waved for Grif to grab the litter, signaling him to get both the old man and the two French medics into the bird. "They'll need you to look after them inside. Go. Go."

She didn't wait to see that the woman followed her instructions. Grif would take over. She held her rifle close to her chest and sprinted for the hospital tent. Just as she reached it, another woman and man pushed through the opening bearing a second litter with a thin, white-haired woman on it. The woman carrying the litter was young and dark-haired with a smooth caramel complexion. The man with her was white, in his mid-forties with a day's worth of reddish beard and terror in his eyes.

"The children," the young woman gasped. "Two of them inside."

"I'll get them," Max said. "Where is Rachel Winslow?"

The woman shook her head. "I don't know. She went to the headquarters tent."

"Headquarters. Which one is that? The other big one?"

"Yes. Yes."

"When?"

"Ten minutes ago? Then there was shouting and more shooting. I was afraid to go after her." The woman's face contorted with fear and guilt. "I shouldn't have let her go alone."

Max pointed to the Black Hawk. "It's all right. I'll find her. Go to the helicopter. Hurry."

The man shouted something in French that was lost in the wind, and the two of them rushed toward the Black Hawk with the litter bobbing precariously with every step. Max shoved inside the tent, swept the room quickly with her weapon ready, and spied the two toddlers, a boy and a girl of about three, standing in a common crib. Their faces were smeared with tears and splotched with blisters, and both were wailing.

"All right you two, you're all right." Max slung her rifle onto her back and scooped up one under each arm. They grabbed onto her with surprising strength, their legs settling on either side of her hips. "We're gonna run for it. You'll be fine."

A boom sounded from somewhere close by. Big caliber rocket or shoulder-launched mortar shells. If one of those took out vital parts of the Black Hawks, none of them would be getting into the air again. They didn't have much time. Maybe none at all.

"Hold on! We'll be okay!" The kids wouldn't be able to understand her, but they'd know she wasn't afraid. She only hoped Ollie, Burns, and the gunners on the second Black Hawk had cleared the LZ because she couldn't fire her weapon and carry the kids too. Looking neither right nor left, she fixed on the belly of the bird and raced across the open ground, the air thick with dust and smelling of hot metal and death. The kids clung to her like limpets. Neither of them cried. The French doctor, hair flying and face set, jumped from the bird and rushed to meet them. She held out her arms. "Give them to me."

Max handed over the children. "Stay in the helicopter this time!"

The blonde pointed in the direction of headquarters where two bodies lay in front of the tent. "What about them? There are injured—the rest of our team is out there somewhere!"

Max's chest tightened. Was one of those bodies Rachel Winslow? Maybe all this was for nothing. No, not nothing. Two old people, the French medics, a couple of civilians, and two kids were safe. Almost safe, anyhow. If the Black Hawks got up into the air and out of there soon, they would be. "I'll see to them. You're out of this now."

The blonde looked like she might argue. She clearly was not afraid. Or not afraid enough. The little boy started crying again. The blonde hugged him and the girl to her chest, nodded curtly, and scurried back to the Black Hawk.

Fox's voice came over her radio. *Ground fire is getting heavy. They're firing RPGs. We need to get airborne.*

Max ducked behind a tent. The flimsy barrier would at least keep her from being a visible target. She touched her mic. "Five minutes. I can't find Winslow, and there may be more wounded."

We didn't plan on this, Fox said. *Burns took a round to the shoulder. We need to get him and these civilians out of here. It's too hot to land the other bird. I'll give you as long as I can.*

Grif skated around the corner of the tent with a collapsible litter balanced on his shoulder. His smile gleamed through a layer of camouflage paint and dirt. "Good day for a jog."

Max snorted and pointed toward the bodies in front of the big tent. "Rachel Winslow might be over there. Let's go."

Heads down, they ran across the clearing, skirting the smoldering fire pits.

Two men in plain khakis lay on the hard-packed earth. One was still breathing, and they rolled him onto the litter. Blood bubbled from a wound in his chest. Max knelt next to the other one. A large chunk of his neck was missing—probably torn away by a rocket grenade fragment. His eyes were fixed and staring, and he was beyond any help she could provide. She needed to get inside the big tent to search for Rachel Winslow. She called back to Grif, "Get him stabilized and give me one minute to check inside. If she's not here, we'll get him back to the bird."

"Go ahead. I'm good," Grif said, opening his IFAK with practiced efficiency and withdrawing bandage packs and an IV.

Bounding up, Max ran for the tent, shouldered her rifle, and burst inside, fanning the room with her weapon, half expecting to find the rebels pointing weapons back at her. A woman in a torn, grimy white shirt and black cargo pants spun around, her eyes wide with adrenaline and shock. She stared at Max's rifle.

"Rachel Winslow?" Max rasped. Her throat burned from the smoke and dust and her voice came out a low growl.

Rachel couldn't answer, her father's warning resounding in her memory. *If you are kidnapped...kidnapped...kidnapped.* The intruder's face was indiscernible beneath the layer of grease and grime that covered every exposed inch. The rifle pointed at her was quite recognizable, though. Rachel glanced past the soldier toward the opening in the tent. Could she get out? She would never make it across the camp, even if she did somehow elude this soldier. She searched the dirt-caked uniform for some kind of insignia. Rebels wore uniforms too. She couldn't make out a patch, a name, a flag—no, wait—a glint of gold at the collar. Rachel stared at the twin snakes encircling the staff. A caduceus. A medic. She drew in a breath, felt as if she had just surfaced after having been held underwater for hours. "Yes. I'm Rachel Winslow."

The rifle lowered. "Come with me."

"Who are you?"

The soldier—the woman soldier, Rachel realized as she calmed down and took a closer look—gave an impatient shake of her head and strode toward her in three long steps. A hand closed over her upper arm. "Commander Max de Milles. US Navy. Come on. There's no time."

"I'm not going anywhere." Rachel yanked her arm free. "I've got to get back to the hospital tent. Amina is over there. The patients, my team—"

"They're taken care of. You're the last one. Let's go."

Max tugged and Rachel stumbled outside. The encampment still looked very much the same at first glance. A few of the tents had been shredded and their torn canvas flickered in the wind like skeletal flags. She sucked in a breath and everything changed. Dacar lay on the ground a few feet in front of the tent. She grasped the hand gripping her arm and tried to break free. "Let me go. That's one of our people."

"He's dead. You will be too if you keep fighting me."

On the far side of the camp, a helicopter hovered a few feet off the ground. Gunfire clattered from a second one, circling higher up. Amina appeared from behind the closest tent and ran toward them. "Rachel! Rachel, I can't find the others! I think Mahad is dead!"

"That's one of our security team," Rachel said. "We need to check—maybe he—"

"There's no time." Max dragged Rachel toward another soldier who knelt over a wounded man. "Status?"

The medic looked up and shook his head. Rachel felt a hand in the center of her back pushing her forward, and Max said, "Get her into the bird, Grif."

"What about you," Grif yelled, jumping to his feet.

Max ignored him and said to Amina, "Show me."

"Deuce," Grif said, "forget it. It's too hot down here. We need to get out of here."

"We'll be right behind you. Get Winslow on that bird!"

Rachel tried to pull away, but Grif was bigger and stronger even than Max de Milles had been. "I'm not leaving until everyone—"

An explosion of gunfire and rocket bursts drowned her words. The ground kicked up around them, splattering her with bits of dirt and rocks. Her cheek stung and blood ran down her face.

"Sorry, ma'am," Grif said, practically carrying her now. "We'll come back for the others. You can count on—"

He grunted, stumbled, and fell, pulling Rachel to her knees beside him. Blood shot from his upper thigh in a brilliant red arc. Rachel instinctively pressed both hands on his leg. Crimson fluid, warm and thick, oozed between her fingers. She pressed harder.

"No," he groaned. "Leave it. Get to the helicopter."

"I can't! You're bleeding." So much blood. Rachel leaned down with all her weight, terror closing her throat.

Behind them, the roaring grew louder and dirt swirled in thick clouds. The helicopter rose, and a few seconds later a fusillade of gunfire filled the air with endless metallic clattering. The jungle on the far side of the camp seemed to disintegrate. Tree trunks splintered, leaves split into confetti-sized pieces, and mounds of dirt heaved upward. Rachel crouched over Grif, expecting to be struck by a bullet at any second.

"Get into the tent," Max shouted, pushing Rachel aside. "That's cover fire—they won't shoot at the tent."

Amina grasped Rachel's arm. "Come, come inside!"

"I can't," Rachel said. "His leg—"

"I've got it. Go, goddamn it." Max ripped open a hemostatic pack, pulled out a pressure bandage, and slapped both onto Grif's leg. She gripped Grif under the arms and pulled. His heavy body lurched forward slowly, and he groaned.

"Leave it, Deuce," he gasped.

"Shut the fuck up and push with your good leg. If I try to carry you, that bandage is going to give way."

Rachel pushed Amina toward the tent, ran back, and grabbed Grif's ankles. She looked up and saw surprise in Max's clear blue eyes. "Pull. I'll get his legs." Overhead, the helicopters grew smaller until they were just black smudges against a brilliant red sunrise.

Chapter Six

Max spared one quick look into the sky. Both Black Hawks lifted higher and swung away in sharp curves to the north, to safety. Good. The mission had gone to hell, but they'd managed to salvage part of it with only two casualties on their side—Burns and Grif. The civilians had not fared as well. Two Somalis dead and another injured or dead that she knew of. The other three were either dead in the jungle, captured, or hiding. She had an unknown number of rebel forces who might close in at any minute, and she had to keep Grif and the rest of them alive. The firing had stopped and the silence was like a vacuum, leaving the air thin and empty. She scanned the encampment. Nothing moved except the fluttering of torn canvas, weary banners celebrating a questionable victory. The battle was over for the moment but the mission objective had not been achieved. They'd failed to extract Rachel Winslow.

"You need to get to cover," Max said.

"You can't carry him alone." Rachel Winslow's gaze never wavered, locked on Max's face like a laser-guided missile. Her face was set in a mixture of defiance and controlled fear—pale lips slightly parted, teeth clenched, pupils so wide the black eclipsed the green Max remembered from the photo. Grif was a former Iowa State linebacker—six-five, two hundred and forty pounds of muscle—but Rachel held Grif's legs off the ground by the ankles as if he weighed nothing. Adrenaline strength.

Max should order her to get inside. Not that she had any faith Winslow would listen to her. She didn't have any choice but to give in.

Grif's life was in the balance, he was only intermittently conscious, and if she tried getting him up onto her shoulder, the leg wound was going to blow wide open. That fountain of blood spelled arterial tear, and a big one. He might still bleed to death at any minute. She needed help, Winslow wasn't going anywhere, and no place here was safer than the other.

"On my count," Max shouted. "Lift his legs and keep your damn head down."

Rachel nodded, keeping her focus on Max, on the sharp hard strength in her eyes. The pressure in her chest eased enough for her to breathe, and the scream that threatened to erupt from her raw throat faded. The horror was out there, a few feet away in the bodies of her friends and the still-echoing clatter of thousands of bullets crackling through the air, but she could push the awfulness back to the shadows if she just held on to the certainty in Max's eyes. "I'm ready."

For no reason that made any sense, Max felt a wave of calmness flow through her, calm she had no right to be feeling in the midst of chaos and carnage. Strength suffused her muscles. "Three. Two. One!"

Max lifted and so did Rachel, and between them they half carried, half dragged Grif's big frame the twenty yards to the headquarters tent and inside. As soon as they stretched him out on the packed-dirt floor, Max unslung her rifle and pushed it into Rachel's hands. "Guard the door."

Rachel looked from the rifle to Max and her expression widened in disbelief. "I don't know how to shoot this thing."

"You'll learn quickly when someone shoots at you," Max said, not looking up as she ripped open her IFAK and pulled out a bag of saline and the attached tubing. "If you see someone coming you don't know, point and pull the trigger. The weapon will do the rest."

"I am a noncombatant."

Max paused as she knelt in the dirt, while the blood of her friend seeped through her pants, and spared the woman a fleeting glance. She had no time to debate or reassure or explain. She needed Rachel to follow her orders. "We're all combatants now, or didn't you notice the people trying to kill us? The people who *were* killing us?"

Rachel's mouth set in a thin line but she turned, went to the doorway, and crouched behind the folded back flap. Something about the set of her shoulders made Max think she could handle what might come at her from out of the jungle, and right now she needed someone to watch her back. She'd have to trust her, and trusting anyone except one of her fellow troops didn't come easy. Resolutely, she focused on Grif.

Winslow's friend, the young woman with the dark compassionate eyes, approached and knelt on Grif's other side. She said softly, "What can I do to help you?"

"What's your name?" Max asked, cutting Grif's sleeve open from wrist to shoulder with her knife.

"Amina."

Max handed her the IV bag. "Hold this up in the air, Amina. As soon as I get the IV line in, squeeze it. He needs fluid."

"Yes. All right."

Max pushed a plastic catheter into one of the big veins on Grif's forearm. Fortunately, he had veins like tree branches and they hadn't disappeared despite his blood loss. She was in in seconds and slapped a piece of tape over the tubing. "Squeeze."

She checked his BP again—eighty over nothing. His pulse was thready and his color pasty. He was just this side of shock. She grabbed another bag of saline and shoved a second IV into his other arm. "Can you handle this bag too?"

"Yes," Amina said, and took the other bag.

The pressure bandage on Grif's thigh was saturated. Blood seeped from beneath it and ran down his leg in rapidly widening rivers. She needed to control the bleeding or she'd still be playing catch-up while he bled out.

"Keep squeezing." Max found an ampoule of broad-spectrum antibiotics, popped it into the accompanying syringe, and snipped Grif's pants from knee to hip. She plunged the needle into his ass and pushed the ampoule home. He grunted and his eyelids twitched open.

"Jesus Christ," Grif groaned. "What the hell happened?"

"You took a round in the thigh." Max loaded up another ampoule with intravenous Demerol.

"Fuck. What about my balls?" Grif fumbled for his crotch, stretching the IV tubing extending from his arm.

"Stop fussing. I haven't checked them personally yet," Max said flatly, "but from the location of the entry wound, I think you're safe there."

"Keep them that way."

"Trust me, your balls are my utmost concern."

Grif's mouth twitched into a grin. "Fuck, it hurts, Deuce."

"I know." She pushed the Demerol. The dose was calibrated for an average-sized man, but Grif wasn't average sized. The narcotic would help with the pain but it wouldn't obliterate it, and she couldn't give him any more. His BP was too low, and she didn't know how long they'd be out in the field. She didn't want to run out. "The Demerol will kick in shortly, but I'm going to need to get a look underneath this bandage. That's gonna hurt a lot more in a minute or two."

"Great." Grif turned his head, struggling to focus on Max. His pupils were pinpoint and divergent. The Demerol was starting to work. "What about the target? We get her out?"

"Not yet." Max glanced toward the door where Rachel squatted, staring out, the assault rifle held stiffly away from her body as if it were a wild thing that might bite her. A rare slice of sunlight illuminated the side of her face. Her shoulder-length hair had come loose from its tie and lay in soft tangles on her shoulders. Her jaw was long and shapely, her cheekbones delicately arched, her nose straight above the whimsical mouth. Her eyebrows were distinct and subtly arched. A laceration marred her cheek just below her right eye, and a smear of blood discolored the skin over her jaw. Even bruised, bloody, and dirt-smudged, her face was an arresting combination of strength and beauty.

Max had witnessed her strength, physical and emotional, seconds earlier when Rachel had insisted on carrying Grif despite the rounds whizzing by their heads. Unfortunately, Rachel was also stubborn and prone to ignore authority. Personally, Max would prefer Rachel be a little less brave and a lot more pliable, but she'd worry about that later. She realized the woman, the target, had become Rachel to her sometime in the last half hour, and she pushed that strange and unwelcome realization aside. She needed to concentrate on priorities, and the first was keeping Grif from bleeding to death. She didn't doubt for a single second that someone would come for them if she could keep them all alive. She just wasn't sure how she was going to do that.

"Anything out there?" Max asked as she broke open another pack of hemostatic gauze and a new pressure bandage.

"No. Not that I can see." Rachel blinked against the bright sunlight illuminating the center of the clearing. When had the sun come up? She strained to see into the shadows where the jungle canopy obscured the demarcation between the bare ground around the tents and the nearby undergrowth. She imagined she could see a hundred pairs of eyes peering out at her, the glint of sunlight off a hundred rifle barrels, and the menacing faces of enemies everywhere. Dacar's body and that of another guard lay not more than twenty feet from where she knelt, but already they seemed unrecognizable to her. Their features had not changed all that much, but the absence of life left them looking vacant and empty, as if they had never been vibrant human beings with goals and ambitions and fears and joys. How could this have happened? Of course, *rationally* she knew how it could happen. She was in the middle of a country that had been at constant war for more than two decades, in a continent where almost every country had a centuries-long history of internecine strife. She knew the risks, but her mind rebelled against the senselessness of it all.

The Red Cross was recognized around the world for its humanitarian goals and its careful neutrality. She and her coworkers had come to help the very people whom the rebels purported to represent—the native Somalis, the people of this land. She'd seen the briefing reports. She knew that Islamist extremists had joined forces with the rebels, strengthening and feeding their militant might and fervor. But why had they attacked the camp?

Her father had warned her the area was no longer safe, but if he'd known they were about to be attacked, he would have told her. Maybe he had, in his own way. He'd insisted she be ready to leave just before dawn. Maybe the attack had come early. Maybe he'd breached security to contact her at all. She wanted to believe that, but none of it really mattered any longer. She was here now, and her father and all his resources and power could not change that.

She checked over her shoulder to see how Grif was doing. Max knelt by his side, speaking in short curt phrases to Amina, her movements rapid and sure as she worked. She was more than just a soldier. The caduceus on her collar spoke to that, but how could a healer justify the violence of war? The two extremes were impossible for Rachel to reconcile. All the same, she was glad Max was here, because she suspected she and Amina would both be dead without her. They still might be.

"Where are they?" Rachel asked, almost wishing she could see someone. She didn't want to shoot anyone, but she didn't want to sit here waiting to be shot either.

"They're probably gone," Max said in her level, emotionless way. "The rebels are known for their hit-and-run tactics. Once the birds opened up on them, they probably decided they'd had enough of a fight for one day."

"Will they be back?"

"Possibly. Do you have anything here of particular value?"

"I don't know what they would consider of value."

Max smiled faintly and wrapped some kind of external pressure device around Grif's leg. "Good point. Weapons?"

Rachel shook her head. "Only what Dacar..." Her throat suddenly closed on the name. She didn't know him very well. He'd been a quiet, reserved man, but his smile had been friendly and he seemed competent and professional. She only saw the others briefly whenever they changed shifts and came in to eat before returning to their tents to sleep or talk quietly among themselves. She'd never known anything about them beyond their names. "Only what the guards were carrying. We have no money."

Amina spoke up. "We have the hospital. Equipment, medicine, drugs. And we have food."

Max grimaced. "Yes. And those are valuable commodities. If they're aware that you have these things, they'll be back."

"What are we going to do?" Rachel surprised herself with the question, realizing she had automatically assumed that Max de Milles would be in charge from now on. Why had she done that? She never looked to others to solve her problems or protect her. The answer was simple and unavoidable. She was completely out of her depth. She knew nothing about the waging of war, only the consequences.

"My team will be back," Max said.

"How can you be sure?" Rachel asked.

Max's brows, two heavy dark slashes above intense blue-black eyes, lowered. "They'll be back."

"But they don't know we're alive."

"It doesn't matter. We don't leave anyone behind—and we make no distinction between the living and the dead."

The way she said it, as if for her life and death were indistinguishable, chilled Rachel's heart. Was this what war did, crushed the emotions, obliterated the value of life? Or was it that in order to wage war, one must already have lost one's humanity?

Chapter Seven

I'm going to take this dressing off," Max said to Amina. "There will be more bleeding."

"I've seen blood before," Amina said, her voice almost sad.

"Okay. Just keep doing what you're doing." Max pulled on a clean pair of gloves and gently removed the old bandage, trying not to dislodge any clot that might have formed. Bright red blood spurted onto her sleeve, and she pressed a finger over the femoral artery above the inch-wide entrance wound in the center of the fleshy part of Grif's upper left leg. The wound was through and through, with a ragged exit hole four times as big on the back. His balls were fine, he'd be happy to learn, but from the nature of the bleeding, the round had nicked a branch of the big artery in his thigh. If they were lucky, it was just a branch. If the femoral was hit, they were in deep shit.

Grif had lapsed into semiconsciousness again, partly narcotic effect and partly blood loss. His vitals had stabilized, but he was rocky. The golden hour—the optimal time period to transport the wounded from the field to a forward hospital for definitive care—was about up, and she doubted they'd be extracted anytime soon. All she'd done so far was control the immediate threat, but that wasn't going to be enough if the bleeding continued.

Amina gave Max a worried glance. "How is he?"

"Better than he was. You don't need to squeeze the fluid in anymore." Max finished applying the new dressing and sat back on her heels. She capped one of the IVs and connected a fresh bag of saline to the line running into his left arm. Four liters in already. Much more and she'd need to start worrying about his lungs and fluid overload. "Could you bring one of those chairs over here? I'll hang his IV from it so you don't have to keep holding it."

"Of course." Amina retrieved a folding chair from in front of the long table holding the communication equipment and placed it next to Grif's shoulder. "I think there are blankets in the back. Should I get some to cover him?"

"That would be good. Thanks." Max propped up the IV bag and rubbed her face. Amina had been as steady while Max changed Grif's dressings as if she'd had battlefield experience, and maybe in her own way she had. Violence was a way of life in this place. "You did great."

Amina smiled almost shyly and went to retrieve the blankets. Max rose, stretched the cramps from her lower back, and checked her watch. Seven hundred hours. She felt as if they'd been inside the sweltering tent with its stale, oppressive air for a week already. Her shirt stuck to her back with cold sweat despite the heat, and she loosened her clamshell body armor and set her equipment belt on the floor next to Grif. Now that he was stable for the moment, she had to deal with the rest of their situation. She joined Rachel at the door and looked out.

"Everything quiet?"

"Yes, but I keep thinking I see things. And then I don't."

"That's pretty common the first few times on watch. Don't worry about it. If there's someone out there who doesn't want you to see them, you won't. And when you do see them, you'll know for sure. They'll be pointing a rifle at you and probably firing."

Rachel sucked in a breath. "Why are you so calm? Doesn't that frighten you—the idea of being a target, or do you get used to it?"

"There's no point thinking about it, and there's no way to change it. You just deal with what is." Max had spent so much time with troops the last few years—with those who lived under the same cloud of violence and death as her—she'd forgotten how foreign her reality must seem to those who were strangers to war. She wondered, seeing the questions and confusion in Rachel's eyes, why she had looked forward to going home, where she'd be an outsider surrounded by people who had no concept of where she'd been or what she'd seen.

"The ultimate living in the now?" Rachel asked.

"You train for every eventuality, prepare for any contingency, until you know, down to your last cell, you're ready. Then you put it aside." Max shrugged. Fear could get you killed as quickly as arrogance. If she'd ever been philosophical, and she couldn't remember a time when she was, she'd long since lost any interest in trying to understand the why of the random happenings she saw around her every day—why one person took a round in the forehead, while another, standing inches away, went unscathed, as if there was some cosmic meaning to events. Maybe there was some great plan, maybe everyone's fate was preordained, but she couldn't see how that mattered. All that mattered was what she did in response. Was that living in the now or merely surviving?

Out here there wasn't much difference. She summed it up and hoped that would be the end of the conversation. Rachel Winslow couldn't possibly understand, and why should she? Even the suffering of the displaced civilians Rachel had come to help couldn't compare to the depraved cruelty of war, and Max had no desire to enlighten her. "The less you worry about what might happen, the better."

Rachel's brows furrowed. She clearly wasn't a woman who accepted anything at face value. "Is that scientific fact or personal opinion?"

"Experience."

"How long you been out here?"

"This time? A little over a year. The first time about the same."

"That sounds…hard."

"I joined the Navy. I knew what that meant."

"Did you," Rachel said softly. She cut her gaze to the camp and the jungle beyond. "How could you possibly? How could anyone?"

Max said nothing. She had no answer, and Rachel wasn't really talking to her. She was trying to make sense of a senseless situation. She'd learn not to soon enough.

Rachel turned back. "The helicopters—you're sure they're coming back?"

"Yes."

"Can you call them or something?" Her eyes brightened. "We have a satellite connection—maybe we can call headquarters in Mogadishu? If they know what happened—"

"They know," Max said. "The people who need to know already know, and they're not in Mog. They're at Lemonnier."

"Is that where you came from?"

"Yes." Max scanned the jungle, dense and green and impenetrable.

An ancient force onto itself, neither friend nor enemy. "The rebels were a lot closer than we expected. I'd rather not try radio contact now until we're sure they're not still out there. No point putting a big sign over our heads."

"How far are we from your base?"

"A few hours' flying time. They'll contact us if they can when they're back in range." Or they'd just materialize out of the dark, troops and birds dropping from the sky like something out of myth, or nightmare.

"When will they be back?"

Max debated how much to say. She needed to keep the civilians from panicking. Rachel and Amina had handled themselves better than most in the midst of the crisis, but the danger was far from over.

"Don't sugarcoat it," Rachel said briskly. "We have a right to know what we're facing."

"My guess is not before sundown, at the earliest. The birds are made for night maneuvers, and it'll take a while for command to sort out what happened here and why. This was supposed to be straightforward in and out." She didn't want to say it might not be sundown tonight. If a large rebel contingent with surface-to-air rockets or a stockpile of RPGs had located in the area, the birds might not be able to land. If an extraction team had to infiltrate on foot, it would take a day or two. At best.

Rachel grimaced. "Someone's intelligence was faulty."

"Maybe. Maybe not. The rebels could've hit here purely at random, and it was just a coincidence that we arrived at the same time."

"I don't know about you, but I find that coincidence a stretch." Rachel sighed, her exasperation clear. "I don't understand any of this. We've been here almost two months. They must have known we were no threat."

"They took a trouncing this morning," Max said. "Random attack or not, there's not a lot of reason for them to return. You said yourself you don't have much they might want except the medical supplies."

"Maybe that's reason enough," Rachel said, but she didn't look or sound convinced.

Max had an uneasy feeling Rachel might know something more about what had prompted the attack than she let on. Considering the mission objectives, she was almost certain Rachel knew they were coming that morning. The French medics had been ready to evacuate the patients before the birds had even gotten into range. "What else do you know about this morning?"

"What? Nothing—why should I?"

"You tell me. Someone in your life must be pretty important, because we were sent here specifically for you. You, most importantly."

"I don't know why," Rachel said, the heat rising in her cheeks. She didn't want to betray her father by revealing his call. She really didn't know why he'd insisted she leave, and she had no clue if the attack was related to her. All the same, her stomach roiled. Had her friends been killed because of her? Had the soldiers and sailors been shot because of her? She repeated softly, "I don't know."

"Who are you?"

"I'm Rachel Winslow." Rachel stared into the flinty blue eyes that examined her with stony calculation. Max de Milles didn't trust her. The realization hurt, though she couldn't say why. The woman was a stranger, hardened and cynical and cold. "You know that. You asked for me by name."

"That's because we were sent here to retrieve you. But I still don't know who you are that made that necessary."

"Does it matter? Am I any more important than the other eleven people who were here?" Rachel could hear how defensive she sounded, but she wasn't more important than her friends, her coworkers. She hadn't asked for special privileges. She certainly hadn't asked for people to put their lives in danger because of her. She wouldn't have this woman holding her responsible for something that had not been her choice.

"Someone thinks you're more important."

The way she said it made it sound as if Rachel felt the same way. Rachel's back stiffened. "Shouldn't we be concerned about what happens next and not spend time on fruitless questions? That sounds like something to suit your logical view of things."

The corner of Max's mouth twitched, and damn it if she didn't smile. Her remoteness faded for the briefest instant and she suddenly looked approachable. Human. And despite the dirt and sweat that caked her face, incredibly attractive. Rachel's heart skipped, a sensation she would not have believed if it hadn't happened again when a soft chuckle reverberated in Max's throat.

"Well, you're quick," Max said. "No, none of that matters all that much right now."

The tension in Rachel's shoulders lessened and a swift wave of relief passed through her, as if she'd been forgiven, which was ridiculous since she hadn't done anything wrong. Why she even cared what Max de Milles thought of her given the situation was equally absurd. Feeling foolish and uncharacteristically unsure, she bristled. "Well, now that we've established where we both stand, what's next?"

"We need to secure the camp in case our rebel friends come back."

"We can't possibly fight them. In case you hadn't noticed, we aren't exactly soldiers. Shouldn't we try to…I don't know, walk out of here on our own?"

"I'm assuming you know where you are," Max said, impressed with Rachel's spirit if not her stubbornness. Her reluctance to give up control could be a problem.

"Of course I know," Rachel said, her lustrous green eyes flashing. "I wasn't suggesting we walk the entire way, but we can hardly sit here in this tent waiting for someone to come back and shoot at us again."

"It's a couple hundred miles to Mog, and the jungle is peppered with mines. We'd never make it. Besides, when the birds come back for us, we need to be here." Max glanced back at Grif. He wasn't ambulatory and moving him at all might be dangerous. He wasn't going anywhere, and if he wasn't going anywhere, neither was she.

"There are villages not that far from here—that's where our supplies come through. They would help us."

Max shook her head. "You don't know that—and you can be sure the rebels know about the villages too. We don't want to stumble into a patrol out there, even if we could manage to find our way around the mines." *With an injured man and two women who have no combat skills.* Max shook her head. "We're staying."

Her dismissive tone sounded a lot like the one Rachel's father used with everyone, and her response was knee-jerk. "In case you hadn't noticed, we're not soldiers. We don't just mindlessly follow orders."

"Believe me, I'm aware," Max said. "But I plan on keeping you alive, so you'll just have to learn to take orders."

Rachel bit back another retort. She didn't even know why she was fighting what obviously made sense. She sighed. "You're right. I'm sorry."

Her apology caught Max by surprise. Stubborn and proud, but not so proud she couldn't admit being on the wrong side of an argument. "Forget it."

"I still don't see how you expect us to deal with another attack." Rachel scanned the jungle. She hadn't been more than a few feet beyond the camp perimeter since she'd arrived. "Shouldn't we hide or something?"

"I'm not planning a counteroffensive. If there's something here the rebels want, they'll be back after dark when they don't make easy targets. By then, we'll be in a bunker, better protected, and even a poor shot can hit something with an automatic weapon."

"A bunker." Rachel took in the tattered tents, the smoldering fires, and the pallets of food and other relief supplies they'd stockpiled for the Somali natives. This wasn't a military base. Was the woman crazy? "A bunker. I don't see a bunker."

"That's because we haven't dug it yet."

"Dug it." Rachel's head spun. Obviously Max felt no fear. Maybe she had stopped feeling anything at all. Rachel fought her instinct to object, to point out the insanity of the plan. Giving over control to a stranger would have been impossible even a day earlier, but now she had no choice. After all, as had been made perfectly clear, Max was the professional. "I'll do what you say…but I'm not a robot. I need to understand."

Max's gaze narrowed. "It's not enough to trust that I know what I'm doing?"

"Should it be?"

"We don't have time for a long engagement."

"Well, I'm not ready to elope," Rachel said flatly. "Tell me what you want me to do and why, and we'll get along." She paused. Had it always been this hard to let someone else help her? When had independence become a wall? No time to worry about that now. "I'm grateful that you're here—for all you've done. I know Amina and I probably wouldn't be alive if it wasn't for you and the others."

"I don't want your gratitude," Max said gruffly. Her mouth thinned. The smile was long gone. "That's not what I want."

Rachel wondered what she did want. If she even knew. "Well, *I* want you to know that you have it anyway."

"Let's give off worrying about who did or didn't do what. We've got other things to worry about."

"Is the past so easy to set aside for you?" Rachel mused aloud, wondering more about herself than Max. Maybe if she could let go and just be in the moment. She almost laughed—just not *these* moments.

"No." Max turned away. "Amina, will you take care of Grif? Check his vital signs every thirty minutes, let me know if you see anything that changes?"

"Yes." Amina had already pulled over another chair and was sitting by Grif's side.

"When the IV runs low, I'll show you how to change it."

"I can do that. I've assisted in the hospital here many times."

"Good, thank you."

"And me?" Rachel asked.

"We need someone to stand guard."

"Shouldn't that be you? You're the soldier—"

"Sailor."

Rachel frowned. "That doesn't seem right, out here in the middle of the jungle."

"Most Navy personnel spend very little time on a ship. Navy pilots, Navy medics, Navy SEALs—we're all over out here."

"All right. You're the *sailor*—shouldn't you be the one with the gun on guard duty?"

"I will be, later." Max blanked her expression. "But first I need to take care of the bodies. They're going to decompose rapidly in this heat, and we don't need them drawing predators into camp on top of everything else."

"Oh God," Rachel said softly, "how could I forget already? How are you going to bury them by yourself?"

"I'm not. I'm going to take them out and cover them enough to keep the predators away. We'll come back for the bodies later."

Rachel's chin came up. "I'll help you."

Tough woman. Max couldn't help but be a little impressed. "I appreciate the offer, but I'd rather not get shot while I'm working. I need you to watch my back."

Rachel studied her for a long moment. "All right. I can do that."

"Good," Max said abruptly, uncomfortable under Rachel's scrutiny, as if something she meant to keep hidden, something she no longer recognized, was suddenly exposed. She didn't like the feeling. Or worse, maybe she did. "Let's get started."

Chapter Eight

Max covered her nose and mouth with a strip of cloth she'd torn from one of the tattered tents. Breathing through the stiff fabric was like straining air through sand, but it cut down on the cloying odor of blood and death. She dragged the third body a dozen yards or so into the bush, checking every few feet to be sure she hadn't drawn the attention of the rebels, or a cat. She'd stationed Rachel at the edge of the jungle. If they were attacked, she could hold off the attackers long enough for Rachel to get back to the main tent, but once she was dead, there would be nothing to stand between the insurgents and the camp. If the rebels got past her, they might not fire on the tent, and Rachel and Amina would have a chance to survive. The rebels would execute Grif. Best-case scenario, the rebels would loot the camp and leave the women alive. Hoping they would also leave them unharmed was wishful thinking.

Max gritted her teeth and swiped sweat from her eyes. She wasn't going to waste time and energy she didn't have envisioning Amina and Rachel at the hands of men who thought nothing of taking what they wanted from any woman. She wouldn't let that happen. She wouldn't let Grif be shot while he lay helpless, or Amina and Rachel be taken as if they were spoils of war. Not while she breathed. She laid the bodies of the three men side by side in a patch of thick underbrush. She couldn't find any rocks, but the rounds the Black Hawks had poured into the jungle had cut down tree trunks like matchsticks. She dragged and rolled half a dozen logs over the bodies. It wasn't a proper burial, but it might protect their remains from being carried off and strewn about by predators. She'd make sure someone from Mog or the base came back for them as soon as they could.

Dripping sweat, light-headed from hunger and fatigue, she slashed at a tangle of vines with her knife to cover the burial mound. Behind her, branches rustled. She swung around in a crouch, making herself a smaller target, and swung her rifle onto her shoulder. Rachel stumbled to a halt, her lips parted on a gasp.

"Fuck!" Max's pulse hammered in her ears. "I told you to stay put!"

"I couldn't see you," Rachel whispered, "and you've been in here a long time. I thought—"

"I don't want you to think." Max lowered her rifle and retrieved her knife. Jamming the KA-BAR into the sheath on her thigh, she straightened, stepping between Rachel and the mound of log-covered bodies. "I need you to do what I say." She gripped Rachel's arm and propelled her toward camp. "What part of that don't you get?"

"The part where my brain suddenly stops functioning." Rachel jerked her arm loose. "And in case it hasn't occurred to you, if you go and get yourself killed, the rest of us don't have much chance of getting out of here."

Max swore under her breath. Images of bullets tearing into Rachel's unprotected body, of laughing men with their hands on her, of her victimized and broken made her head pound. Her vision wavered as she tried to rein in her fury. "This is the way it has to work—I make the rules. I give the orders. You don't argue, you don't question, you just do. And then maybe, just maybe, we'll all get out of here in one piece."

Rachel's fear and anger drained away as quickly as it had come, leaving her more tired than she'd ever been in her life. She couldn't imagine how Max was still functioning—still doing what had to be done. "You're right. I'm sorry. Again."

"Forget it. Again." Max held out her hand. "Do we have a deal?"

Rachel grasped Max's hand almost automatically, as if she weren't really aware of doing it. "I'll do my best. If you promise to stop pointing your gun at me."

Max smiled, caught off guard by the teasing note in Rachel's voice. They were nearly eye-to-eye. She was a shade over five-eleven and used to looking down at most women, but Rachel's eyes were on a level with hers, and this close she could pick out the tiny gold flecks dancing through the heather green. The hand that gripped hers was as strong as she would've expected from a woman like Rachel, but surprisingly softer than she anticipated. She hadn't touched any part of a woman in a long time and had forgotten what a contrast in strength and tenderness a woman's body could be. She glanced down at her own fingers curled around Rachel's. Her hands were covered in dirt and blood and, feeling oddly unworthy, she loosened her grip. Rachel's hand fell away at the same time as hers.

As she looked into Rachel's eyes, the silence in the clearing was as loud as gunfire. "Come on, I want to take a look at that cut."

Rachel swallowed, her gaze searching, as if she was trying to find some secret Max had hidden deep inside. "What cut?"

"The one on your cheek."

"I'm sure it's nothing," Rachel said.

Approaching midday, the clearing was an oven. Sweat tricked down the back of Max's neck. A film of moisture coated Rachel's upper lip, and Max had a sudden crazy urge to brush it away with her thumb. She clenched her fist. "It's not nothing. We're out in the middle of the jungle. If we don't get it cleaned up and it gets infected, you could be in trouble. Besides, this way the scarring will be less."

Rachel laughed, a choking sound devoid of humor. "A scar? From a tiny cut? And you really think I care?"

"Maybe not now. But when you're back in your normal life, you probably will."

"My normal life." Rachel said the words as if they were foreign to her. The intensity of her gaze heightened. "And what do you imagine that to be?"

Max had no idea. Rachel wasn't anything like the privileged, probably slightly pampered and entitled woman she'd imagined when she'd learned they were going on a mission to extract her. What she knew of her was born of death and horror, unimaginable to most people. But Rachel hadn't broken, not yet. She was fighting back. Hell, she was fighting Max when she had nowhere else to vent her anger. The answer to Rachel's question suddenly seemed important.

Staring around the stark empty encampment that had until then just been a battlefield in her mind, Max tried to imagine the place bustling with aid workers rendering emergency care and simple human kindness to people whose language they couldn't understand and whose lives and history must be foreign to their own. In order to do that in the midst of personal danger and unrelenting despair, they must have shared a common goal, a common passion. This had been a community, not just a group of strangers. "I'm sorry for your loss."

"What?" Rachel asked, sounding breathless, almost stunned.

"Your friends. Everything you had here. I'm sorry."

"I…thank you." Rachel's throat tightened, and to her horror, tears filled her eyes. After all the fear and terror she'd been battling to keep at bay, this simple bit of sympathy, of understanding, cut the legs out from under her. The horror of the morning rushed back to her. The gunfire, the hideous stench, the panic, the death. She closed her eyes, her head swimming. An arm came around her waist, and she was pulled close to a hard body.

"Easy," Max murmured. "Come on. It's a hundred and fifteen out here. You need something to drink. Some food."

Rachel opened her eyes, feeling foolish and weak. Max's face was an inch away, those impossibly blue eyes immeasurably kind. Her eyes were so fascinating, shifting from cold, hard calculation to unexpected compassion like the wind. Rachel's heart beat hard beneath her breast, and she flushed, embarrassed at what it revealed. She wanted to pretend she didn't need the comfort, but she did. Deep inside, in her primitive core where her instincts were to survive by any means possible, she was terrified, ready to claw and scratch and kill to stay alive. Terrified that the gunmen would return, terrified that she would be taken. Terrified of placing her trust in anyone, especially this woman whose embrace felt too natural, too welcome. Max de Milles might be a savior, but she was also a stranger, and anything Rachel was feeling right now was a product of the unreal world she'd been thrust into. Gratitude, comfort. That didn't frighten her. But the desire kindling in the pit of her stomach did.

The hand pressed in the center of her back was warm and firm. Max's chest armor, some kind of hard plastic shell, pressed against Rachel's breasts. She was exposed, vulnerable, and Max was like a mountain shielded in rock. Rachel thrust a hand between them, pressed her palm against the armor. Pushed away.

"I'm all right." *I don't need you to lean on.*

"Come on." A curtain dropped over Max's eyes, her hand fell

away, and she stepped back. "We're sitting ducks out here. And we've still got a lot of work yet to do today."

Rachel swallowed around the dust in her throat. "Yes. Right. What's next?"

"First the cut, then some food."

Max turned and walked away, leaving Rachel to follow. Rachel paced herself to Max's long strides, her heart still beating way too fast. The center of her back tingled where Max's hand had rested, and the heaviness in her pelvis throbbed. Her life was not her own, her fate was not her own, and now, even her body was betraying her. All she could do was pray this ended before she no longer recognized herself.

❖

Max pulled back the edge of the tent, ducked under the flap, and slipped into the semidarkness. She heard Rachel come in behind her, sensing her presence as if they were still touching. Still connected. Even as she knelt by Grif's side, she was aware of Rachel slumping down onto a cot that Amina must have brought out from the back. She needed to check Grif's vital signs, see if the bleeding had stopped, but she kept remembering the color fading from Rachel's face as she swayed outside in the heat, about to faint. Her instinct had been to pick her up into her arms, to keep her from falling. To keep her from harm. Nothing unusual about that. That was her job, to keep others from harm, to take care of them when they were injured. But she'd never experienced the wild sense of protectiveness she'd felt while holding Rachel.

Rachel's eyes sent so many messages—anger, defiance, grief, need—that called up feelings in her she couldn't afford to have out here if she wanted them all to survive. She'd wanted to keep standing there with Rachel, immersed in those shifting sensations, and that kind of distraction could be deadly. She didn't have time for tenderness, couldn't afford to be sidetracked by sympathy. Or the other tangle of emotions simmering in her belly. She kept her back to Rachel. Grif needed her now.

"How's he doing?" she asked Amina.

"His pulse is up a little bit," Amina said. "I found one of our first aid kits in the back and took his temperature. He has a fever."

Max's stomach clenched. Not good. Not a damn thing she could do about it. She checked her watch. Headed for twelve hundred hours. "In another two hours we'll dose him again with antibiotics. Have you had anything to eat?"

Amina shook her head, dark circles making her dark eyes appear larger, wounded.

"You think you can find something for us? Everyone needs to keep their strength up. And water?"

"We have food packs prepared to give to the displaced," Amina said. "They're stored on the supply platform out behind this tent. I'll get them."

"How far is it?"

"Just a few steps."

Max picked up her rifle. She couldn't let Amina walk around alone, even though she doubted a daylight attack. "I'll walk out with you."

"Thank you."

Once satisfied the field was clear, Max left Amina in charge of supplies and came back inside. She checked Grif's vitals, regulated the IV rate, and prepared another dose of antibiotics. After he was settled, she sorted through the supplies for what she needed to take care of Rachel and carried it to the cot where Rachel sat watching her with an unreadable expression.

"First I'm going to clean it out." Max squatted and soaked a gauze pad in saline. "It'll sting some."

"I can do it," Rachel said.

"It's easier if I do." Max dabbed the solution on the two-inch laceration below Rachel's right eye. "Besides, you might ease up if it starts to hurt."

Rachel half smiled. "And you won't mind hurting me?"

Max laughed softly. "Nope. I intend to be completely heartless."

Rachel shook her head slightly. "Somehow, I don't quite believe it."

"Maybe you should." Max stopped what she was doing. Rachel didn't know her, couldn't know her, and now was as good a time as any to interject a little perspective into their situation. "Don't mistake duty for anything else. I'm only doing my job."

"Yes. I got that part loud and clear." Rachel didn't argue the point. Max had a right to her boundaries. And if she chose to keep people at a distance, that was no one's business. Despite Max's insistence on appearing detached and aloof, however, her hands were gentle as she cupped Rachel's jaw in the palm of her hand and continued to clean the laceration. Rachel had nowhere to look except into Max's face as she worked, and she found herself visually tracing the tiny lines at the corners of her eyes. She suspected she'd developed the same lines after weeks of squinting into the unrelenting sun. Those little imperfections only added to the attractiveness of the picture. Max had a beautiful face. Strong and elegant with a square jaw and high straight nose. Looking into her eyes was like looking into the sea—deep and fathomless one minute, stormy and gray the next. Her black hair was thick and shaggy, and the untamed look made her appear carelessly handsome. Even the smudges of grease under her eyes and dust shadowing her jaw accentuated the rugged appeal.

"Where are you from?" Rachel asked, needing to distract herself from thinking about Max's face, or her hands, or the way Max had taken her into her arms as if she had every right to hold her.

"Djibouti."

"I meant—before."

For a second, Max looked confused, as if the question made no sense. Then a bit of color touched her pale cheeks. "Oh. New York City, I guess."

"Not sure?"

"Well, I'm not really from there, but that's where I live now. Where I work."

"Where did you grow up?"

"Buffalo," Max said shortly. The way she said it, her past didn't appear to be something she was interested in discussing.

"Big family? Only child?"

"Youngest of seven." A shadow passed through Max's eyes. "My father kept trying for a son. He never got one."

Something there, Rachel thought, and moved away from the pain she hadn't meant to stir up. "Married? Engaged?"

Max dropped the used gauze onto the small pile of litter by her side and opened the pack of Steri-Strips. "No and no."

"Never and never?"

"Not even close." Max tilted Rachel's face to the side. "Hold still."

Rachel waited while Max taped up her cheek. It seemed absurd, to be giving this tiny injury so much attention after all the horrible wounds she'd seen that morning. All the same, she was a little disappointed when Max finished. "Thank you."

"No problem." Max gathered up the debris. "Amina's finding us something to eat. Make sure you get something."

"You should too."

"Right. I will."

The walls Max so carefully maintained came down between them with a resounding thud, and Rachel wondered if her questions had been the cause. She'd barely broached the personal, but clearly Max's armor shielded more than just her body. She could respect that—she had plenty of her own walls, but the more she knew of Max de Milles, the more she wanted to.

CHAPTER NINE

Rachel sat next to Amina on the cot and opened the meal packet. She'd had MREs before—nutritionally balanced combinations of protein, carbohydrates, and fats in the form of familiar-looking foods that always tasted bland. The meal-ready-to-eat was designed to be eaten as-is or warmed with the self-contained cooking unit, but she doubted even heating the bits of chicken, beans, and rice would make it more palatable today. She had no appetite and was only eating because she knew she should. Beside her, Amina methodically did the same. Rachel squeezed her forearm. "How are you doing?"

"I don't know," Amina said softly. "Part of me wants to pretend it's all a dream, a very, very bad dream, but that seems disrespectful somehow."

"What do you mean?" Rachel broke open the Fig Newton cookie wrapper and nibbled on the corner. Sugar was a good energy source at least. "Disrespectful?"

"Of our friends who died here, and those who have been injured trying to help us." Amina's gaze drifted to Grif and Max, who leaned over him, checking him again, murmuring softly to him. He didn't appear to hear or to answer. "The least we can do is remember."

"Yes," Rachel said, although she wasn't worried about remembering. She was never going to forget, even though part of her desperately wanted to. "I'd like to think none of this is happening either but…I can't." She couldn't erase the images burned into her mind— Dacar, dead on the ground with part of his neck missing. Grif rushing to help her and then falling, a brilliant arc of warm red blood spurting from his leg. Grif, ignoring his own plight and telling her to leave him, to save herself. Max, facing her first with a gun, then with unexpected and immeasurable kindness in her eyes. The noise, the heat, the stench of cordite and blood. All of it was etched into her consciousness for all time. She shook her head. "I can't."

"Will the Americans be back?" Amina asked.

"Max said they will come." Rachel realized as she answered how completely she'd accepted Max's certainty. She never relied on anyone without question, not even her father, but she was trusting her very survival to Max.

"When?"

Rachel rolled down the foil and set the food aside. "Max says tonight after sundown. If they can."

"And what about al-Qaeda? Are they coming back too?"

"I don't know."

"What will we do if the enemy return?"

"We'll fight." Rachel hadn't really thought of the rebels as *her* enemy until now. She'd known of them well before she'd reached Somalia—of the threat they posed to the mission, of the barbaric acts they committed, of the terror they perpetrated on the Somali people whose land they overran, whose animals and food and crops they confiscated. She'd understood intellectually the rebels were a potential danger to her and the others, but *enemy* was not a word she would have used for anyone in her life. She counted only a few people in her life as friends—those with whom she shared her hopes and dreams and, rarely, her fears. Most, even the women she'd been intimate with, were more acquaintances whom she allowed only brief glimpses of her innermost self. She knew individuals she'd rather avoid, but no one she would have called an enemy until now. Here in this foreign land the compass of her life had been recalibrated, and everything took on a different meaning. She squeezed Amina's hand again. "They may not come back. Try not to worry."

"Impossible," Amina said, "but I am glad we are not alone here."

Rachel glanced at Max. She had no choice but to rely on Max's knowledge and skill, but she wasn't going to let Max carry all the burden of keeping them safe alone. She might not be a soldier, but she'd had plenty of practice caring for people in need. Grif needed care. She had no idea what Max needed, but she could still offer. She slid over next to Max. "Is there something that I can do for him? Or…you?"

Max set her stethoscope into her pack. "No. He's about the same. He just needs to be watched. Amina's doing a good job with that."

"Then you should eat something."

"I will, as soon as—"

"It's quiet right now. It might not be later," Rachel said. Max obviously considered herself indestructible, and ordinarily Rachel wouldn't have pushed her. Everyone was entitled to a little self-delusion if it harmed no one else, but they needed Max healthy if they were going to get out of this mess alive. "Follow your own orders."

Max sighed. "All right. You ought to try to get some sleep. We'll need to take turns tonight standing watch."

"What are you going to do now?"

"I'm going to collect all the weapons I can find, hit the hospital tent to stock up on medical supplies, and then I'm going to make us a safe place to spend the night."

"Then I'm going with you. Someone to watch your back, remember?"

"It's apparent that you never forget anything and I'm likely to find my words coming back at me." Max smiled. "I'll have to keep that in mind."

"You're right, but then, I doubt you ever say anything you don't mean, so there's no need to worry about it." Rachel smiled and handed her a MRE. "Eat first. Turnabout and all."

"Fair enough." Max pulled over a wooden crate, sat down, and shook out the plastic utensil that came in the package. She scooped up a forkful of beef and vegetables and pointed to the plastic bottles Amina had brought inside. "Drink another bottle of water to get hydrated if you're coming with me."

"I'm used to the heat," Rachel said, not wanting to be yet another thing Max had to worry about, but she downed another bottle of water all the same.

"Good." Max gave her a long look as she upended the foil pack and palmed the cookie that fell out. After disposing of the dessert in one bite, she emptied the big pack Grif had carried on his back and handed it to Amina. "Can you fill this with MREs and water?"

"Yes." Amina took the bag and pressed it to her chest. "Can you call your base? Is it safe to do that?"

"It's safe to send a short burst," Max said, "and I tried several times when I was…out in the jungle, but I'm getting nothing but static. Probably interference from the heavy tree cover and the distance we are from base. Radio silence doesn't mean they aren't planning to come for us. They'll get sat images and recon shots from drone flyovers. They'll use those to see what our friends out there are up to and figure out a way back."

"That's good then, right?" Rachel said. "If our people can see the rebels, they'll know if we're in for more trouble. They'll come sooner then, right?"

"If there are signs of heavy encampment nearby, they may need longer to coordinate the necessary personnel and air support, but they'll come." Max shifted some of the ammunition from Grif's pack to hers, shouldered her pack, and grabbed her rifle. "Until then, we get ready."

Rachel slipped her rifle over her shoulder with the naturalness she had once used to picked up a briefcase. How quickly she had come to accept the weapon and what it meant about her life. She caught up to Max, who was collecting the rifles and ammunition she had taken off the guards' bodies earlier. "What aren't you telling us?"

"You know what I know." Max motioned to the tent, and after they piled the weapons inside, they started for the medical tent.

"I'm not talking about what you know." Rachel strode beside Max, trying not to look at the forlorn belongings of her friends and teammates abandoned in the tattered tents along the way. Now she understood the shock and confusion she'd seen over and over again in the faces of the men, women, and children who had straggled into the camp, struggling to survive in a world turned upside down in an instant. "I'm talking about what you think. We're not children, and we're not afraid of the dark." She still was, so it seemed, but she wasn't going to let Max know that. She'd face those demons on her own when the time came.

The edge of Max's jaw tightened. "I know you're not children."

Rachel said softly, "Remember the part where you explain what's happening and I say *Yes, sir*?"

"Yes, *ma'am*."

"You don't look like a ma'am. And I can tell when you're trying to change the subject."

"If surveillance shows an al-Qaeda camp nearby, the birds will be at risk coming back in. If I were planning the op, I'd strike the rebel camp at the same time as I sent a team to rescue us to keep them busy. That kind of op takes coordination." She grimaced. "And it takes clearance from Washington. As soon as you throw politicians into the mix, everything slows down."

"So we might be here a while." Rachel knew her father would be doing everything he could to get her—all of them—out of here, but Max was right. Even with his influence, mounting any kind of offensive would require a lot of debate in Washington and beyond.

"A few days, possibly."

"What about Grif?"

"He'll make it," Max said flatly. "Wait here." She shouldered her rifle, pushed the flap aside on the medical tent, and ducked inside. "Clear."

Rachel followed her in. "The supply racks are in the back."

Max pointed to a canvas litter lying against the side of the tent. "We'll pile them on that."

Once they'd loaded the instruments and medicines Max wanted, they hefted the litter and carried it back. Amina sat by Grif on a pile of empty flour sacks, looking tired but calm. When she started to rise, Max shook her head.

"We've got this."

Rachel helped Max pile the medical supplies on a table and stowed the litter on the floor. "Next?"

"You sure you don't need a break?" Max asked as she started back outside.

Rachel wanted to curl up on the flimsy cot, close her eyes, and sleep for a year. She wanted to wake up and be in a hotel in Mogadishu, with a toilet that flushed and a shower that wasn't hanging from a tree and food that came on a plate. She wanted not to be afraid, not to see blood everywhere she looked, not to ache with loss. God help her, she wanted to go home. "I'm fine. Let's go."

Two hours later she was ready to admit defeat. She'd thought she'd gotten used to the heat. The temperature inside the tents, where she usually spent the day, was as high as or higher than outside, but the intensity of the direct sunlight elevated hot to a new level. Her skin felt as if it was on fire. Every breath scorched her throat. The surface of her eyes burned. Her shirt and pants were soaked with sweat, and rivulets of water ran down her face, over her neck, between her breasts. She wasn't sure she could stand another minute under the unrelenting rays. But Max wouldn't quit. How could she?

She concentrated on the rhythmic scrape of Max's shovel. Max had been at it for hours with only short breaks to drink water from the canteen clipped on her belt, steadily driving her short square spade into the ground, lifting a shovelful of dirt, flinging it over her shoulder in a red-brown arc. The hole was almost eight feet wide and more than half as deep by now. The dirt she'd heaved out of it was piled high around the edges, and the walls sloped inward. She understood Max intended for them to spend the night in that hole. She definitely knew she would not be sleeping.

"Won't we be trapped in there if they overrun the camp?" Rachel asked. Max undoubtedly knew what she was doing, but even conversation was better than thinking about the hell she'd been thrust into.

"If they overrun the camp, we'll be trapped no matter where we are." Max's shoulders and arms flexed as she dug the shovel into the soil again. "At least from in here a few of us can hold off five times our number in all directions. Even inexperienced shooters like the two of you. If we take enough of them out, they might think hard before sacrificing too many people to get to us."

"Do we have enough ammunition?"

Max wiped her forearm across her face and looked up. "We'll be all right."

"You should drink some more water."

"I'm out."

"Good thing I'm not." Rachel pulled another bottle from the pocket of her cargo pants, uncapped it, and handed it down to Max. Max had shed her armor and camo jacket and worked in just T-shirt and pants. Sweat plastered the tan T-shirt to her shoulders and chest. She was solidly built, the muscles in her torso sculpted beneath the tight cotton, her biceps and forearms etched with muscle. She wore no rings, only a large watch on her left wrist and dull silver dog tags on a chain around her neck. Her uniform pants, even with her heavy equipment belt laden down with ammunition, her sidearm, and other things Rachel couldn't identify, didn't quite obliterate the curve of her toned hips and thighs. Even dirty, sweat-soaked, and disheveled, Max was more attractive than any woman she'd ever met.

"You need to keep hydrated," Rachel said, her voice husky.

Max swallowed the warm water until the plastic bottle was empty, watching Rachel appraise her as she drank. She was used to being surrounded by troops, used to eating and sleeping in close quarters, used to semi-strangers seeing her in various stages of undress, but no one had ever looked at her the way Rachel did now, with appreciation and interest. Rachel's eyes tracked up her chest to her face and, when their eyes met, Rachel's cheeks flushed.

Max grinned, liking Rachel's consternation. She liked the way Rachel's mouth thinned a little too, as if she was irritated at being caught with her guard down. There wasn't much of anything to be happy about out here. Just being alive rated pretty high on the be-thankful list. The spark of playful pleasure Rachel set off in her when she least expected it was completely foreign. Even back in her other life, she hadn't enjoyed anything quite as much as the swift stirring in her belly ignited by Rachel's slow-lidded smile. She crushed the plastic bottle in her fist and stuffed it into an outside pocket of her pants. "Thanks for the water."

Rachel nodded, the tip of her tongue sweeping over her lips as if searching for words. "Anytime."

"Is there rice or flour on those pallets behind the tent?"

"Rice, I think," Rachel said. "Why?"

"Sandbags."

"Oh. I guess that means we have to carry them over here."

Max shook her head. Rachel was trying to be tough but her face was drawn and pale despite the sunburn coloring the stark arches of her cheekbones. She tossed the shovel up and out. "I'll take a look around. There must be something around here with wheels on it."

Rachel knelt by the edge of the pit and reached down to Max. "I'll come with you."

Max grasped her hand, dug her toes into the side of the pit, and with the other arm, levered herself out. She dusted herself off, shouldered her rifle, and scanned the jungle. Nothing out of the ordinary. The animals were quiet during the heat of the day. Even the birdsong had faded. "We've got a couple more hours till sundown. I can handle this. You go check on Amina."

Rachel hesitated. She dreaded the oncoming darkness. In the sunlight, she felt more in control, but in the dark, fears were so much harder to push aside, courage more elusive. She wondered if Max dreaded the dark, and somehow doubted it. Her focus was so singular, so intense, Rachel doubted Max really noticed much of a difference between day and night. She was not a woman who dealt in shades of gray. "I'm not letting you out of my sight. So stop trying to get rid of me."

"I could make it an order." Max pulled on her camo jacket. "You agreed to follow orders."

"Don't test me," Rachel muttered. "I know how to shoot this thing now."

Max laughed, a sound so alien in this place of death and horror, Rachel's heart lurched at the sound. That had to be the cause of the rush of blood through her veins. She turned away to break the spell, but she could still see the way Max's eyes gleamed with mischief and something a lot more intriguing.

CHAPTER TEN

Max dragged the small flatbed wagon across the camp for the fifth time. Her shoulders ached, the back of her neck was burned raw, and her skin itched everywhere from the sand embedded in her clothes, inside her socks, in her hair and ears. Her legs quivered, the muscles having turned to jelly in the soup of humid air, festering heat, and stress. Rachel waited for her beside the jerry-rigged sandbag barrier they'd built up around the foxhole out of fifty-pound bags of rice. Rachel hadn't complained, hadn't flagged, though every time she picked up one of the heavy bags of rice to pile it on top of the others, her arms visibly trembled. Max would have ordered her inside if she'd thought Rachel might go without a fight, but that was unlikely. And she had to admit, she needed her help. "This is the last of it."

"Can't say I'm sorry," Rachel muttered. "I never thought I could hate an inanimate object quite so much, but I'll never eat rice again."

Max laughed. The sound hurt her dry, sandy throat, but the little bit of humor helped ease the tension twisting her muscles into steel bands. "What do you do for showers around here?"

"We've got portable ones rigged up out behind the medical tent. Always guaranteed to be lukewarm." A shadow passed over Rachel's face. "There should be plenty of water stored up. Today would have been shower day."

Max didn't have to be a mind reader to know Rachel was thinking about those who hadn't gotten out. Somehow, giving Rachel some comfort, even a distraction, seemed as important as keeping her physically safe. Usually her job ended when the blood stopped flowing or the wounded were loaded onto transport for a trip to the base hospital.

She rarely had time or reason to worry about the toll this place took on the heart and mind, beyond a few minutes of battlefield comfort. Words they'd all repeated so many times she barely heard them any longer. *Don't worry, troop. Doesn't look too bad. Nothing keeps a Marine down long. You'll be fine.* Merciful lies, and she regretted none of them, but she wanted more than hollow reassurance for Rachel. She had none and felt lacking. "I'd say we've earned a shower."

Rachel's face brightened and some of the sadness left her eyes. "Can we? I mean"—a bit of color returned to her cheeks—"is it safe?"

"I'll stand guard for you if you stand guard for me." A fleeting image of Rachel under the water, sunlight bathing her and water streaming down the slope of her back and over the curve of her ass, popped into Max's head. Afraid for a second Rachel could read her mind, she said quickly, "I even promise not to peek."

Rachel gave her a look through narrowed lids. "Under other circumstances I might find that insulting."

The teasing lift of Rachel's smile caught Max off guard. Maybe Rachel *had* read her mind, but that didn't track. If they'd met anywhere else in the world, Rachel likely wouldn't give her a passing thought. Their lives were as different as the arid desert sands and the bright lights of Times Square. "Under other circumstances, you probably wouldn't care."

"Don't be so sure," Rachel said. "You don't seem to know—"

"Max!" Amina's scream cut through the air with the force of a gunshot. "Max!"

"Down!" Max pushed Rachel to the ground and crouched over her, her rifle on her shoulder. She panned the perimeter, expecting a surge of rebel forces or a barrage of gunfire. Nothing moved. She listened. Nothing. "Clear! Come on."

As soon as Max let her up, Rachel grabbed her rifle and they sprinted to the tent. Max burst inside, searching for enemy. Amina knelt by Grif, both hands pressed to his thigh. Scarlet streaked her arms.

"What happened?" Max dropped her rifle and squatted across from Amina.

"He woke up and started thrashing. The bleeding started so fast..." Amina's breath caught. "There's so much."

"Don't move." Max pulled her med kit closer and dug around for drugs and bandages. She was running low on both.

Grif jerked, nearly throwing Amina aside, and shouted, "Contact! We have enemy contact!"

"It's okay, Grif," Max said calmly. "I'm here. You're okay."

Grif pushed his big body up with surprising strength, bracing himself on his arms. He stared from one to the other, his eyes glazed with confusion. Sweat rolled down his face, rivers of tears coursing through the paint and grime. "They're shooting. Fuck. Shooting everywhere. Deuce!"

"I'm here. Keep your head down, buddy. You're okay." Max drew up an ampoule of Demerol, slid it into the IV, and pushed it home. "Everything's okay. I won't let anything happen to you."

For an instant, Grif's eyes cleared and he focused on Max. "Fuck, Deuce. I don't want to die out here."

"You're not going to."

"Tell Laurie I love her."

"Fuck, no." Max gripped his shoulders, her face close to his, and pushed him back down. She looked into his eyes as the Demerol started to take him away. "You'll have to do that yourself. I hate that kind of thing."

He grinned. "No wonder you never get any women."

"Yeah. Like you would know."

His lids fluttered closed and his body relaxed. Wiping sweat from her eyes, Max shifted down to where Amina held both hands on his thigh. Blood welled between her fingers and puddled on the floor. She'd run out of time. "Rachel, can you get that propane light from that table over there and figure out how to get it to work?"

Rachel crouched a few feet away, her pupils black and big as dimes. A pulse hammered in her throat. "Yes."

Her voice was firm.

"Good. Prop it on that chair."

For once, Rachel didn't have a single question. She bent over the lantern-shaped light, ignited the propane, and brought it back. "What are you going to do?"

Max nearly smiled at the question, welcoming the familiar in the midst of chaos. "I need to explore this wound and get the bleeding stopped. I need both of you to help me."

"In here?" Amina asked. "In the hospital ten—"

"Believe me, I'd like to have a nice clean OR table to put him on and a full set of shiny instruments, but we can't move him. Right now, getting the bleeding stopped is our number one priority."

"I'm sorry," Amina said.

"Don't be." Max knew she sounded gruff and didn't have time to worry about it. "You saved his life."

"What can we do?" Rachel said.

Max pulled off her jacket and gear and dropped it next to her rifle. "Find that big pack of medical instruments we brought over from the hospital. Open it up next to me."

While Rachel hunted for the instruments, Max tore open a foil container of Betadine, swabbed her forearms, and pulled on gloves from her kit. "Amina, get ready to take those scissors and cut the bandage free. Keep pressing down in the center of his thigh with your other hand. Rachel, put on a pair of gloves and open the gauze packs. I'll need you to keep the field clear."

"I…" Rachel glanced at Grif's face. "Will he know?"

"Not consciously, but he might react. If he does start moving around, I want you to kneel on his lower legs and keep them still."

"Okay," Rachel whispered.

"I need you to do exactly what I say when I tell you to do it."

"I will."

Max looked across at Amina. Her jaw was set, her mouth a thin tight line. "You ready?"

"Yes."

"You see those two small right-angle retractors that look like little scoops about two inches wide?"

"Yes."

"You're going to use them to hold the wound open so I can see inside." The less time she gave them to think about what they were about to do, the less likely they were to get nervous. "I'm going to take the bandages off, put the retractors into the wound, and you're going to hold them apart. You'll need to pull. You won't hurt him. We're going to save his life."

Amina swallowed visibly. "All right."

"Good. Now." Max removed the field bandage, and bright red arterial blood immediately welled up and spilled down Grif's thigh. Max slid the right-angle retractors into the center of the crater with their slim, eight-inch handles sticking out either side. "Amina, take these and pull. Rachel, keep the field as dry as you can. Just keep mopping it up."

"Yes," Rachel said, "I've got it."

Max grabbed a hemostat and a gauze pad and studied the depths of the wound. The round had passed through the thick inner thigh muscles, missing the bone. The femoral artery ran deep between the muscles, coursing from the groin down to the knee where it branched to supply the calf and foot. The deep femoral branch came off the main artery a few inches below the groin crease to supply all the big muscles of the thigh. That had to be what was bleeding. She just had to find the tear in the artery and fix it.

The key to finding a bleeder in the midst of a pool of blood and shredded muscle was to look—to see, to distinguish the border between the damaged and the undamaged. There, at the edge of destruction, the natural planes of the body remained, even in the worst trauma, pristine layers radiating out from the injury. Carefully she swabbed, ignoring the small bleeders that would eventually stop on their own. She identified the various muscles, tracing the course of the artery in her mind. It should be here, diving beneath the adductors toward the femur, but it wasn't. The round had probably taken out a segment of the vessel along with a sizeable chunk of muscle. She'd have to look higher to find the proximal end, the one leading from the main artery. If she could control that, the hemostatic gauze packs and pressure bandage would eventually take care of the rest of the bleeding until they could get him into the operating room and clean up the wound. She couldn't fix it if she couldn't see it.

"Amina, pull harder."

Amina sucked in a breath and did as Max asked. Grif groaned and his thigh tensed. The undamaged muscles flexed, blood squirted, and the field disappeared under a pool of red.

"Rachel," Max snapped, "keep him still."

Rachel straddled both of Grif's lower legs, a knee on either side of his calves, and held him down with her body. Leaning forward, she swabbed, her gloves drenched with blood.

Max put a finger deep into the wound, pulled back a ragged flap of muscle, and widened her field of vision, letting the filmy strands of fascia separating one band of muscle from the other guide her eyes along the native planes. A tan ring the width of a pencil pulsed in the depth of the wound like a tiny heart. "There you are."

Only five millimeters wide, the pliable artery jumped with every beat of Grif's heart, pumping out blood in a steady stream. Max slid the open jaws of the hemostat on either side of the severed vessel and clamped it closed. Immediately the bleeding slowed.

"Oh my God," Rachel murmured. "Is that it? Did you get it?"

"Almost." Max kept her gaze fixed on the end of the fragile vessel and supported the instrument in her palm. If Grif came to again and thrashed around, that artery would shred like wet Kleenex. "Just keep him still a minute longer."

"I will."

"Rachel, the blue foil pack. Pass it to me." Max opened the 4.0 nylon suture pack, gently rested the hemostat on Grif's thigh, and loaded the curved needle into the jaws of a blunt needle holder. Holding the hemostat steady again, she passed the suture through the vessel above the hemostat, brought the ends of the nylon around the instrument, and tied them down. When she eased off the stat, the stump of the severed artery filled with blood and throbbed as if it were alive and trying to escape. But the ligature held and the bleeding stopped.

"There you go, you bastard." Max took the first full breath she'd had in five minutes. She found another hemostatic bandage and packed it into the wound. After wrapping his thigh, she gave him another dose of antibiotics. She glanced from Rachel to Amina. They both looked a little dazed. "You did great. Both of you. Rachel, you can get off his legs now. He's out for a while."

Rachel stood and pulled at her blood-caked gloves. "It's so hot in here. Isn't it? I—don't feel…"

Max grabbed her as she started to sway. "Easy. You're okay. Just a little too much sun."

"I'm fine," Rachel muttered, leaning against Max's side. "I'm not usually—"

"This isn't usual. Come on. Lie down over here." Max kept her arm around Rachel's waist and guided her to the cot. "That's it. Close your eyes."

Rachel stared up at her. "I don't believe you did that. It was… amazing."

Max smiled. "Thanks, but not really. It's what I do."

"All the time?"

"Yes."

"That's horrible."

"I know. It is." Max pulled an IV bag from the supplies she'd pilfered earlier. "You're dehydrated. I'm going to give you some fluid. You'll feel better when you wake up."

"I don't want to sleep."

Max understood. Most of the time, neither did she. "Then you don't have to. But you do have to stay here until the IV runs in. Deal?"

Rachel frowned. "I don't think I like your deals. I think they're rigged somehow."

"Well, until you figure out how, just go along with it." Max slipped in an IV and hooked up the fluid. When she finished taping the line down, Rachel was asleep.

"You should rest too," Amina said from beside Max.

"I will." Max looked from Rachel to Grif. "When we get out of here, I'll have a big meal, a bigger glass of whiskey, and I'll sleep for a week."

Amina smiled. "I never thought I'd say this, but that sounds really good."

CHAPTER ELEVEN

Rachel jerked awake, surrounded by the rattle and roar of gunfire and helicopter rotors, the taste of sand in her mouth, the stench of cordite, the sweet cloying odor of fresh blood. Terror so deep she couldn't think enveloped her. Above her the sun shuddered behind thick clouds of dust. Pain and fear dimmed her vision. She grabbed a breath and gripped the sides of the cot with both hands. The room spun and more memories assaulted her. Grif's anguished cries of pain, Dacar's blank accusing eyes, Max's lethal gaze above the barrel of an assault rifle. Max. Another breath forced down her tight throat. Max's hand on her back, steady and sure, the tenderness in her eyes she tried to hide, the certainty and gentleness of her hands as she tended to Grif's damaged body.

Rachel centered herself. She was in the tent. She was alive. The erratic pounding of her heart settled into a steady cadence. Her right forearm ached and she held up her hand. Clear tubing ran to a plastic catheter taped above her wrist. An IV bag sat next to her, clipped to the back of one of the wooden chairs. She swallowed. Her throat was dry, her eyes ached. Nausea was a constant companion.

But she was alive. "Max?"

"You're awake," Amina said. "How do you feel?"

Rachel turned her head and looked at Amina as she had so many times in their tent—in the early morning before rising and the last thing at night before going to sleep, when they'd whisper a few minutes about things beyond the heat and oppression of this tortured land. Amina would speak longingly of family and friends, of hopes and dreams, and Rachel would listen. She had little that was personal to share and tried not to dwell on what that said about her life. If Amina noticed her silence, she never let on. Her lovely dark eyes, then as now, had always been warm and calming and accepting.

Tonight, Amina stretched out on a cot across from her, lying on her side, her head propped on her elbow, just as she always did. Strands of her ebony hair had escaped the tie at her nape and curled loosely around her shoulders. Rachel couldn't remember ever seeing Amina with a single hair out of place, but nothing was as it had been, and so many things she'd once worried about didn't seem to matter now. What mattered was food and water and keeping each other safe. What mattered was Grif, lying on a makeshift litter in the space between them. He appeared to be sleeping. She hoped so.

"I'm fine," Rachel said.

"Really?"

Rachel laughed wryly. "No, actually I feel terrible. My head feels like the inside of a snare drum. But I'm all right, considering. How are you?"

"I'm all right too, I guess." Amina glanced at Grif. "I'm so sad about Dacar and the others. So sad and so angry."

"Yes. Me too." The anger, Rachel realized, was much sharper than the sadness—a knife blade slashing through her, dulling the crushing pain of loss. She wouldn't forget the dead, nor fail to mourn them, but she'd keep her anger for the strength she found in it. Amina was no stranger to loss. Both her father and older brother had been killed in some kind of clan conflict when she was just a young girl. Perhaps she'd replaced pain with empathy, channeling her grief into the aid program and a passion for justice. Rachel didn't think she'd be able to find any empathy for those who killed for power and lust and greed. No, she'd keep her anger and, for the time being, her rifle. She scanned the tent and her stomach tensed.

"Where's Max?" Rachel asked.

"She said something about reconnaissance. She went out twenty minutes ago."

"Alone?" Rachel grimaced. "Of course, alone. There's no one else here. How long have I been sleeping?"

"Not long. An hour, perhaps."

Rachel sat up on the side of the cot, and the throbbing in her head disappeared in a rush of adrenaline. "She shouldn't be out there without backup. Why didn't she wait for me?"

"She's a soldier," Amina said softly.

"She's a doctor."

"And you're already seriously dehydrated. It's still a hundred degrees out there."

"I'm going after her." Rachel loosened the tape on her wrist, closed the port on the IV, and pulled the needle from her arm.

Amina rose, opened a paper pack of gauze, and taped a folded square over the IV site on Rachel's wrist. "I don't think you should. We are not soldiers."

"I think we are now." Rachel hugged Amina quickly and let her go. "Look after Grif. I won't leave the camp, but I can't sit in here waiting."

"It will be night soon. It will at least get cooler."

"I'm not worried about the temperature." Rachel didn't want to say what they were both thinking. When night fell, they might be rescued. Or the rebels might return. She didn't know, and there were no answers. All her life, she'd sought answers—why her father cared more about power and prestige than happiness, why she never met a woman who would risk social status for love, why no matter how much she achieved, she still felt restless and dissatisfied. Suddenly the questions seemed self-indulgent and the answers didn't matter any longer. What mattered was what she could do in the moment. What mattered was now. She shook her head as she took her assault rifle and stepped out into the camp. Max was turning her into a soldier after all. As she searched the camp and couldn't find her, the tension in her middle swelled. Shaking off a wave of fear at the thought of Max in danger, she wondered what else Max was doing to her.

❖

Max stopped in the first clearing she could find where she could actually see the sky through the dense canopy. The sun was an angry red eye in the west, and she estimated another hour before dark. She tried her sat com again.

"Foxtrot Charlie, this is Fox MD2, requesting immediate extraction. Over."

Like all the other times she'd tried from closer to camp, she got only static in response. She repeated the message and waited.

...D2...repeat...

Max gripped the radio, her pulse jumping. "Foxtrot Charlie, this is Fox MD2, requesting immediate extraction. Over."

...status...

"Four to transport. We have wounded. Over."

Static.

Max squeezed the radio, wanted to scream at it. Steadily, clearly, she said, "Foxtrot Charlie, come in. Over."

Nothing but dead air.

Max waited another ten minutes, repeating her message, and got no further response. She checked her compass and set a course back to camp, her fatigue and hunger and worry fading a bit. That fragment of contact, the sound of a friendly voice from home, was almost as heartening as the drone of rotors drawing near. The troops in Djibouti, her family far more than the mother and father with too many children and not enough means or interest to care for them, knew she was out here, and help would come. She'd never doubted it, but the insidious feeling of being isolated and abandoned lurked inside her, emerging when she was at her weakest. Not knowing when or if another attack was coming had gnawed at her all day. She'd told Rachel it didn't matter what was coming—all that mattered was to be prepared and face it head-on. She wasn't worried for herself. She would never feel the round that took her out, but she had two civilians and a seriously wounded sailor on her hands and at least a few more hours to wait until the birds returned. If there was a race between the Black Hawks and the rebels to get to them, she put her money on the Black Hawks.

The attack that morning had been a disorganized raid by a few rebels who'd likely stumbled on the camp by accident. The small scout force might have attacked without knowing the identity of the Red Cross contingent. She doubted the insurgents would have cared about the neutrality of the aid workers even if they had known, considering they assaulted the locals whenever the villagers or herders came close to rebel territory. The main rebel force was probably still miles away. The rebel survivors would have wounded, and by the time they reached their base, even if another attack was planned, it would take time to organize the forces and return. A return raid might not even be a priority—unless they had a specific target. Just like she'd had. Rachel.

Two Black Hawks had been sent to extract Rachel specifically. Rachel had avoided talking about herself, but someone with power had arranged something like that. If she'd been the focus of the attack that morning too, the rebels were likely to return for another try. Max blew out air. Thinking about Rachel in the hands of the rebels short-circuited her reason. She needed to concentrate on what she knew and what she could do. She'd heard from base. Help would be on the way, and until it arrived, she had to be ready to fight again. She started back for camp, glad to be bringing good news to Rachel. To Rachel and Amina and Grif.

The footpath was hardly recognizable at first, barely wide enough for a hyena let alone a human, and she'd stepped onto it before she'd realized it. The trail ran parallel to the camp, about fifty yards into the jungle, and was only one of hundreds crisscrossing the area, traveled by hunters, herders, and nomadic tribes—and, in the last few months, by rebel forces using the jungle as a sanctuary from aerial and ground attack. This was probably the route the rebels who'd raided the camp that morning had taken. From the looks of the trail, it wasn't a major access route. Nothing suggested mechanized transport or even a large volume of foot traffic.

Stomach crawling with dread, she stood absolutely still and looked for signs the ground around her had been disturbed. Intelligence gathered from the Somalis indicated the land all along the jungle trails was mined. If she lost a foot or leg out here, she'd die of exposure, animal attack, or infection if she didn't bleed to death first. Amina and Rachel would probably survive without her until help arrived as long as the rebels didn't attack again. They were both tough and resourceful, but Grif was already critical. He could go south at any second, and without a medic he'd never make it.

She backed away slowly, carefully retracing her steps along the route she'd taken from camp. She could just make out the first break in the canopy indicating the edge of camp when branches swayed directly in front of her where no breeze could penetrate. She ducked behind a tree trunk and aimed where she'd sensed movement. Five minutes. Nothing. She crept closer, mouth dry and heart hammering. Had the rebels circled behind her? Were they already in the camp? Had she been wrong about everything? Had the rebel forces been closer than she calculated? Had they returned before dark? Were Rachel and Amina and Grif already dead?

She halted just at the edge of the jungle and scanned the camp. All quiet. Keeping low, she ran to the side of one of the smaller tents, using it for cover. Stones crunched behind her and she spun around. Rachel knelt by an adjacent tent, her assault rifle angled across her chest. She glared at Max.

"I could've shot you, you know," Rachel said.

Rachel's bravado was so genuine, Max's anxiety evaporated on a swell of relief. She grinned. "Getting pretty cocky, aren't you?"

"I didn't say it would only take one bullet." Rachel straightened, her narrowed eyes still flashing. "Are you all right?"

Max shrugged, annoyance resurfacing now that she knew Rachel was safe. "Of course I'm all right. What the hell are you doing out here?"

"I was about to ask you the same thing." Jaw tight, Rachel stalked toward her. "What are you doing, going off by yourself into the jungle?"

Max felt her eyebrows climb. "I thought it might be a good idea to make sure our perimeter was reasonably secure."

"And what would you have done if you'd wandered into the middle of a bunch of rebels? Fought them all by yourself?"

"I would've hightailed it back here. What was your plan if a dozen of them stormed into camp while you were out here playing patrol?"

"What you taught me. Point and shoot. A lot."

Max smothered another grin. Rachel had done just what she would have done. Grabbed a weapon and gone out to check. All the same, she was prepared to die. Maybe Rachel was too, but she wasn't going to let that happen. The thought of Rachel being hurt roughened her voice. "What are you doing out of bed?"

"I'm not a patient," Rachel snapped. "And you're not Rambo. Stop taking chances."

"I'm sorry if I worried you."

Rachel's teeth ached from clenching her jaws. The woman was infuriating. Did she really think she was invincible, or did she just not care if some sociopath shot her or, worse, dragged her off to torture her first? Just about every scenario she could imagine had passed through her mind while she waited for some sign of Max. Only Max's warning earlier not to stray into the jungle because of mines had kept her inside the camp. That and she hadn't wanted to leave Amina alone. When Max had slipped out of the jungle, she'd wanted to shout with relief and run to her. Now she just wanted to throttle her. What if she'd never come back? What if she never saw her again? The sinking feeling in her stomach was far worse than the fear she'd felt at the idea of the rebels returning. She had a rifle—she could fight. The one thing she could not fight was death. Max took too many chances, and that scared her in a way she'd never been afraid before. "You didn't *worry* me. You just pissed me off."

"Well, that's nothing unusual." Max glanced up at the sky as if searching for something. When she looked back at Rachel, the startling blue of her eyes pulled Rachel in, and for just an instant, the war and death and fear disappeared.

"Did you find anything out there?" Rachel asked, determined to break the spell. Max de Milles might be an attractive woman—okay, an amazingly attractive woman—but she also had a God complex that was likely to get her killed. And she was controlling and authoritarian and just plain frustrating on every level. So forgetting about her incredible blue eyes and gorgeous grin was a very good idea.

Max hesitated. "A trail runs pretty near the camp. I think that's the way the rebels came in this morning. No sign of them now."

Rachel sighed, relief tinged with annoyance. "Damn it, Max. You might have run into them."

"I also got through to the base."

"Oh my God! Why didn't you say something!"

Max laughed. "I would have, but you weren't finished dressing me down."

Rachel gripped Max's arm. "Are they coming?"

"I told you they were," Max said. "The transmission was broken up, but they know we're here. They'll come."

Rachel's joy dampened, and she glanced toward the tent. "No word when?"

"No. Are Amina and Grif okay?"

"Yes. Amina says his vital signs are stable. He was still asleep when I came outside."

"How about you? How are you feeling?"

"Hungry, but the thought of another packet of preserved chicken doesn't really appeal." Rachel realized she still held Max's arm and let go. "And I'm still pissed off at you."

"Uh-huh. We've got a little light left and the area is clear. Will it help if I stand guard while you take a shower?"

Rachel studied her. "I'm not sure two minutes under a trickle of lukewarm water is going to be enough to drown my annoyance."

"It's a start."

Chapter Twelve

Rachel stepped into the three-by-three-foot square plywood enclosure and tilted her head back. A nozzle hung from a pole above her face and warm spray drenched her like gentle rain. The makeshift stall was open to the sky, and if she didn't think about Max standing guard with an assault rifle, didn't picture all that had happened, she could almost believe when she stepped out into the encampment, her friends would be gathered around the fires preparing for supper. Maribel would be recounting some story of Paris, her mellifluous French-accented voice floating above the low bass background rumble of Dacar and his men, while the conversation of Amina and the others filled in the melody, and the jungle night sounds provided a chorus. Pumping a handful of liquid soap into her palm and spreading it over her skin, she could almost believe life as she knew it would continue—night would fall after a long hard day, bringing the peace and satisfaction of a job worth doing. She might even imagine a shower such as this one, and indulge in the fantasy of the sensuous flow of hands skimming over her body. Fantasy, she admitted, rather than a pleasant memory, the fiction a reminder that she'd rarely been touched with love. Lust and desire, yes. Love and passion, not that she'd ever recalled. Not that she'd ever missed until the specter of death haunted her every moment.

She tilted her face to the blood-red sky again. Sunset would soon give way to the dark. Water sluiced through her hair and down her body, bravely etching inroads into the dust caking her skin. She'd left the wooden half-door open, needing an escape route if the enemy suddenly appeared. Through partially closed lids, she saw Max standing with her legs widespread, her rifle canted across her chest, her back to the shower. She'd seen the body beneath the armor that afternoon as Max dug the foxhole, and now she pictured the stretch of her thin cotton T-shirt across her sculpted shoulders, the tapering of her muscular back to her waist, and the faint flare of her hips. Beneath the uniform, Max was sensuous as well as strong.

"How much longer?" Rachel asked, rinsing away the last bit of suds.

Max turned and their eyes met. Rachel stilled, her hands cupping her breasts, water streaming down her torso, over her belly, and between her thighs with the sensuous glide of a lover's skin on hers. Max's gaze moved lower, then slowly rose and returned to hers.

"Two minutes," Max said, her voice rough enough to be angry, but her eyes weren't angry. Her eyes were flame. "I want you and Amina secure before sundown."

Rachel let her hands fall to her sides, unembarrassed by her exposure. Max had seen her naked in far more important ways than this. Max had seen her terror and grief and anger, all the things she usually kept hidden behind a façade of control and unconcern. "Yes, all right. Is there time for Amina?"

"If she hurries."

"I'll get her." Rachel twisted the clamp on the water line closed and shook out her dusty clothes. Max's back was turned again, and as she dressed, she tried not to think about the way her nipples had tightened under Max's perusal or the twisting in the pit of her stomach or the tingling between her thighs that pulsed even now. She'd been looked at by women before, by women she'd taken to her bed and by those she hadn't. She'd seen appreciation, seen longing, sometimes even envy. She'd thought she'd seen desire, thought she'd seen hunger, but she'd been wrong. She knew what hunger looked like now, and she doubted anything less would ever stir her again. She drew a ragged breath. "What about you?"

Max turned around again, the blue of her eyes as black as the ocean beneath a storm-tossed sky. "Amina first. I'll be fine."

"Thank you." Rachel fumbled the buttons closed on her once-white shirt, stiff and yellowed with ingrained dust.

"Gather up the weapons and pack any loose ammo in one of the backpacks."

"I will." Rachel strode toward their makeshift base without

looking back. She didn't need to ask why. When night came, they'd have to be ready for anything.

Max watched her go. The water had turned her auburn hair nearly black, and the dark strands curled around her neck and face with careless abandon. Her face showed signs of a light burn from all the hours in the sun, but the skin on her chest and abdomen was smooth and creamy. An image of her oval breasts and light tan nipples rose in Max's mind. She should've looked away, but she couldn't. She'd been in the desert for months, and for years before that, she'd existed in the desert of her life—working, spending nights alone, letting her achievements fill her needs. She hadn't touched a woman in almost two years, and she'd barely been present for that. After an OR party she hadn't been able to avoid, she'd passed a few hazy hours of mutual desperation with a nurse who'd been flirting with her for half a year. Never mind that the nurse was married with two children, except, as the nurse was quick to point out, she and her husband were in the midst of a trial separation, so technically the sex wasn't cheating. Max hadn't asked for details. She'd had one too many drinks to hear the inevitable tale of disinterest, distance, and disillusion, and the nurse was not so drunk she couldn't be responsible for policing her own marriage. There'd never been a repeat, although the nurse had indicated she would be more than willing.

Max could barely remember now what the woman looked like, if her breasts had been large or small, her stomach toned or full, her hips narrow or wide. She couldn't recall the texture of her skin or the scent of her hair. Just a glimpse of Rachel had awakened all her senses, as indelibly as if they'd touched. Her fingers tingled with the glide of silky skin beneath her hands, her breath hitched at the firm press of a nipple against her tongue, her skin heated with the slickness of desire spreading over her thigh. She should have looked away, but she didn't want to. Her body came alive when she looked at Rachel, and the sensation was so foreign and so exhilarating, she couldn't let it go. Not yet.

The tent flap parted and Amina hurried toward her, a bundle of clothing in her arms. "Thank you so much. It's so hot inside."

Max did a quick scan of their surroundings. Nothing moved. Everything was quiet. "All right. Go ahead."

"How long?"

Behind Max the water came on and she checked her watch. "Two minutes."

"Two whole minutes! Oh, it's so wonderful."

After all Rachel and Amina had been through, a few minutes under a stream of tepid water seemed little enough reward. Max was used to going days without a shower, eating and sleeping in the dirt. The first thing she did when she got back to her CLU was take a long hot shower, hoping the steaming water would wash away the blood and mute the screams. It never did. Maybe Amina and Rachel would be luckier. She hoped so.

The water stopped, the wooden door squeaked opened and thudded shut. Amina's breath was soft and regular as she moved about. Max was careful not to turn until Amina stepped up beside her, fully dressed. "All set?"

"Yes. I want to thank you—"

"No," Max said. "You don't need to. You've looked after Grif alone in that sweatbox all day. I owe you the thanks."

Amina flushed. "Come back now. You need some rest and food."

"You go ahead. I want to look around."

"Don't stay out too long or Rachel will insist on joining you again."

Max grunted. "And I suppose telling her to stay inside wouldn't do any good."

Amina smiled. "I don't think so."

"Come on. Let me walk you back." Max escorted Amina to the tent and broke off to circle the perimeter one more time. The sun was down and the light was fading. Time to move the civilians to the bunker. By morning, this would be over.

❖

The bunker Max had constructed was barely large enough for Rachel and Amina to stand or sit side by side after they piled the extra weapons, ammunition, food, and water at one end. The sky overhead, clear enough for a million stars to shine through the wisps of clouds, helped make the tight space seem less confining. Max had left gaps at irregular intervals in the rice-bag barrier to allow anyone inside to get a 360-degree view of the camp.

Rachel stood, body pressed against the dirt wall, still warm from the day, and peered out. Shadows played with her perception in the moonlight. The flutter of a tent flap became a man slipping closer, the flicker of starlight off hard-packed sand the glint of a gun barrel. For a moment she was five again, huddled in bed with knees drawn up and arms wrapped around her legs to make herself small, staring into the dark corners of her room where monsters lurked. She'd stopped calling out for her parents to come. They'd told her she was imagining the long fingers and looming forms that glided across the ceiling above her bed.

Close your eyes and go to sleep, Rachel, her mother had said, *there's nothing there.* But she'd known better.

She didn't sleep with the light on anymore, but she still distrusted what she couldn't see. She wouldn't be sleeping tonight, wouldn't have slept if a platoon of soldiers stood between her and the jungle. As the dark closed in around her, she would watch for the enemy to slip out of the jungle and creep across the open yard. Max wouldn't be sleeping, but she couldn't trust everything to her. She did trust her, totally. Trusted her to stand for her and Amina and Grif, to stand between them and danger, but trusting her to do it all alone wasn't fair. Then again, none of this was fair. Or rational. Everything about this place was totally insane. If she thought too long about the complete madness of being in the middle of a jungle waiting for someone to shoot at her, to kill her, she would lose her tenuous hold on her own reason.

"I swear to God you'll be sorry," she muttered to the monsters in the dark and gripped the rifle by her side.

"What is it?" Amina asked.

Rachel drew in a breath. "Nothing, sorry. Just venting."

"Don't be sorry," Amina said. "It is better to shout than cry."

"You're right." Rachel looked out through her portal again. A shadow coalesced into a figure. Her breath stopped and her mind went blank.

"American friendly," Max's voice whispered.

"God," Rachel gasped.

Max leaned over the barrier and handed her a stack of blankets. "On the off chance there's explosions out here, cover up with these."

"Thanks." Rachel didn't even question the why of it—she was numb to the possibility of one more form of horror. She passed them to Amina and made room for Max to climb in, but Max turned away. "Where are you going?"

"I can't leave Grif alone, and I'll have a better chance of cutting off an attack from out here."

Rachel understood the bunker now. Max wanted her and Amina out of the line of fire. She'd never planned to join them. *What if there's too many? What if they*— "Max, what if they come in force?"

"You know what to do."

"I'll help you move Grif. He'll be safer in here."

Max shook her head. "I just checked him. His pressure is low, his heart rate is up. If he bleeds again I'll lose him."

"Then I'm coming with you." Rachel pushed her feet into the toeholds Max had dug into the side of the bunker and reached up onto the wall to pull herself out.

"No, you're not." Max loomed over her, blocking her way. "You'll be safer where you are. Out here, I can't protect you."

"I can help."

Max squatted and faced her over the barrier. "Listen to me. This isn't your war. You're just caught up in the middle of it. You're not a soldier. You've done great today, but this is my job. I won't have you hurt."

Rachel swallowed. Moonlight wreathed Max's head. The camouflage paint had worn off, and the smudges of dirt disappeared into the velvet sheen of darkness. Her face was as smooth as carved marble. She was very beautiful. "I will be very unhappy if you go and get yourself killed. So be careful not to."

Max smiled. "I'll consider that an order."

"See that you do."

"Don't worry. Chances are good we'll have a quiet night."

Rachel wanted to grab Max and pull her to safety, but she could no more do that than she could close her eyes against the monsters. Instead, she reached over the barrier and touched her fingertips to the strong line of Max's jaw. "Keep your head down, Deuce."

"Roger that." Max pressed her cheek into Rachel's palm for the briefest of breaths. "See you soon."

And then she was gone, a shadow merging into the other shifting shadows. Rachel leaned hard against the wall, bracing herself on folded arms to steady her shaking legs.

"She came here for you, didn't she?" Amina murmured.

"Yes."

"We're fortunate, then."

"Yes, we are." Rachel stared hard, searching for Max, and couldn't find her.

CHAPTER THIRTEEN

Max flipped down her night-vision goggles, and the world morphed from black to shades of green. The jungle, lush and thick in daylight, flattened into a monochromatic wall several stories tall. Scanning slowly, she let her brain decipher the layers of overlapping images, much as she did when she looked into a wound and found the natural planes buried in debris. Order out of chaos. She steadied her breathing, centered her consciousness, let the night come close. There a flash of moonlight gleamed off a pair of close-set eyes peering from beneath the brush at the edge of the clearing. Hyena, maybe. Branches flickered lazily in an insolent breeze that did nothing but move the still-hot air over her sweat-slicked skin. In another few hours the temperature might drop enough to dry her sweat to a dusty, itchy film, but as with the gnats that clouded around her face and crawled along her lashes and into her ears, the constant physical discomfort had become the norm. Turning in slow increments, she checked for a branch that moved out of sync with its neighbors, the darting shadow of a predator startled from its hiding place, the coalescence of random forms into a recognizable human shape. She listened for the silence that signaled the ultimate predator was on the prowl, heard only the chittering of insects, the distant roar of a cat, the wild bark of a hyena.

Satisfied they were alone, she glanced back to check the bunker, not trusting Rachel to stay put as she'd asked. An undercurrent of respect cut through her annoyance. Rachel was as stubborn as she was courageous, which was considerable. That she didn't fully comprehend the danger didn't lessen her bravery. If she was captured, as an American—almost certainly one of some kind of notoriety—at best she'd be held for ransom and not killed, but even captivity would not protect her from brutality. She'd very likely become the property of the rebel commander, and abusing and humiliating women was often a show of power. With luck he wouldn't share her with his top lieutenants, but sometimes passing around a woman was another way of declaring dominance. No matter the outcome, death or debasement, she would be scarred forever.

Max's jaw throbbed as she gritted her teeth. Rachel and Amina shouldn't need to know those things, shouldn't need to think about them, and she didn't fault Rachel for her reckless fearlessness. But tonight, she needed her to be just a little afraid. Fear bred caution and was nothing to be ashamed of. She was always a little bit afraid, somewhere in the deep recesses of her soul, but she had long ago learned that fear could be turned into a weapon. For her, fear of remaining forever a shadow, invisible to those who should have noticed, had become the driving force to forge a life where she could feel worthwhile, even if she never wholly escaped the shadows. She slipped inside the tent where Grif lay on the litter alone. Here was her worth. A life to protect. She knelt by his side, flipped up her goggles, and focused the lowest beam of the flashlight clipped to her belt onto his leg.

The dark irregular island in the center of his bandage had not expanded. The bleeding had stopped. She lifted his hand to check his pulse.

"What the fuck are you doing, Deuce?" Grif rasped in the dark. "Making a pass?"

She grinned, the sound of his voice easing the band of tension circling her chest just a little. "Dream on, buddy."

"Been dreaming, I think," he muttered. "Weird shit. What—"

"Shut up a minute." Max slid her fingers onto his radial pulse and counted silently to herself as she followed the sweep hand on her tactical watch. Still tachy, but regular. She placed his hand gently back on his belly and shifted a little higher so she could look down into his face. In the dark, she could barely see his eyes, but they were open and fixed on her. "You're looking better. How do you feel?"

"Like fucking road kill. Where are we?"

"At the aid camp. You remember the mission?"

"Yeah. Clusterfuck." He licked his lips. "Fuck, I'm thirsty."

"Here." She unhooked her canteen, supported his head, and helped him drink.

When he finished, he sank back, breathing heavily. "What about extraction?"

"Timing unknown." Max didn't need to sugarcoat anything for him, wouldn't want him to spare her the truth if things were reversed. "The coms are spotty, but they know we're here."

"Casualties?"

"Three of the Somali security guards are dead. Most of the others were evacuated." She opened a pack of cookies, held one to his mouth. "Here. You can use the fuel. We took a couple of hits before the birds could get out of here."

He grimaced. "Fuck. I remember heading for the bird with—" He tried to sit up.

"Whoa. You're not going anywhere. You had a pretty big bleeder in your thigh and I don't want it opening up again."

"What about the objective? Winslow?"

Max jolted, confused by a millisecond of disconnect. *The objective. Winslow.* Rachel had stopped being the objective, the goal of a mission, without her realizing it. The hours they'd worked together, clashing wills and revealing long-held secrets, felt like weeks, time compressed by shared horror and danger and moments of naked clarity. "Rachel. She's still here with Amina, another civilian. I've got them in a bunker in the center of the camp."

His face clouded. "You expecting company?"

"Maybe. No sign of any forces nearby, as far as I was able to check, but best to be prepared." She shrugged. "I figured they'd be better protected and better able to defend themselves if they were dug in."

"So what are you doing in here instead of out there with them?"

She grinned. She'd missed him—missed his counsel and the understanding that required no words. He knew, without her needing to say, what they faced. His courage fed hers, and she hoped she gave a little of that back to him. "I can't get you down into the bunker without moving your leg more than I want to. You lost a lot of blood but things are stable now."

"That must be why I feel about as strong as a gnat." He raised his head and looked around. "Supply tent?"

"More or less."

"They'll check it."

"Yep." If they got by her, but he didn't say it. Didn't need to. "That's why I'm about to drag your sorry ass into the back where you won't be lit up like a neon sign that says shoot me."

He nodded. "Give me a gun and as much ammo as you can spare."

"Without saying." She crab-walked around to the head of the litter, gripped the wooden poles that supported the canvas bed, and slowly pulled him backward across the dirt floor into the far reaches of the tent, to where anyone casually checking from the doorway might miss him. She knelt beside him again, took his automatic from her belt along with an ammo clip, and put it all next to his right hand. "You probably won't need to use this, but it's got a full clip and there's a spare there."

"What are you gonna do?"

"Hunker down outside and shoot any fuckers that get close."

He laughed. "You should've been a SEAL, Deuce."

"Wrong equipment."

"Yeah," he grunted. "I'm pretty fond of mine, but maybe it's overrated sometimes."

"Different strokes. Besides, I'd rather patch holes than make 'em, but you do what you have to, right?"

"True." His mouth twisted and he exhaled sharply. "Listen, if things go sideways, tell Laurie it was quick. I don't want her picturing all kinds of shit."

"We'll be okay." She squeezed his arm. "I'll be back soon."

"Keep your head down, Deuce."

Max smiled, remembering Rachel's fierce whisper. "Planning on it."

She left him because she had no choice, just as she had left Rachel and Amina. She'd rather be beside them, her body a shield, but she couldn't protect them all. She picked a position on the far side of the camp where she had a clear view of the spot where the rebels had emerged from the jungle earlier. Chances were if they came back, they'd return the same way. She crouched and watched and waited, listening for a change in the night sounds with half a mind, the other half-tuned for a burst of static on the radio that would tell her help was on the way. When the first explosive rumble shook the air, close enough for her to feel the vibrations through her knees where she knelt on the ground, her pulse leapt. Adrenaline surged, the call to action overpowering fear. Finally, it had begun.

❖

Thunder broke the silence with a crash that shook Rachel to the core. Stunned, heart frozen in her chest, she stared above the canopy as fireworks lit up the sky. Breathtaking tails of brilliant red and orange slashed heavenward. Sunbursts of bright yellow umbrellas floated across the inky backdrop, a staccato light show that would have been beautiful if it hadn't been so terrifying. Rachel pulled her dazzled gaze away from the sky and stared through the gap in the barrier toward the jungle, waiting for the phantom forms, nightmare images dragged from her subconscious, to take shape and race toward her. She steadied the rifle on top of the mound of rice bags, her finger trembling on the trigger. Where was Max? Her mind screamed for her to press the trigger, to fire into the shadows, to shoot at every flickering finger of darkness that reached toward her.

"Max, damn it," she whispered. "Where are you?"

"Are they coming?" Amina said, crowding close to Rachel in the small space.

"I don't know. Do you see anything?"

"No, but I think I'm too frightened to see."

Rachel was more worried her own fear would make her see things that weren't there. Reminding herself she'd taught herself never to trust what she couldn't see clearly, she forced herself to breathe, just breathe, and concentrated on the dark, sorting shadows into recognizable shapes. There a tree, over there a log, there a trick of light turning a tatter of canvas into a skulking man. "Max is out there somewhere. We don't shoot unless she does. Wait for Max."

"Yes." Amina's voice was steadier. "Max will come."

"She will." Rachel was absurdly pleased that her voice did not tremble. "Remember. Don't shoot until she gets here."

"How long do we wait? If…"

Rachel swallowed. She didn't know. Couldn't think beyond Max returning. Couldn't let herself picture anything else. "We'll know when. Keep watch while I check behind us."

"All right."

Rachel half turned to scan around the camp the way Max had taught her. Only the shadows looked back. "I don't see——"

Amina screamed. A shape catapulted over the rice bags and into the foxhole. Rachel's heart rocketed into her throat and she raised the rifle.

"Friendly." Max crouched beside them. Her face was partially obscured by the protruding night goggles. Her body was nearly shapeless in the half dark beneath layers of armor and camo. She could have been anyone, except for the distinctive line of her jaw and the slight squareness of her chin and the incongruous fullness of lips far too sensuous for her usual stern expression.

Rachel had never seen a more beautiful sight. "Are you trying to get me to shoot you?"

"Not just yet." Max pivoted to watch the sky. "Looks like ground-to-air rockets. That's tracer fire—machine guns shooting back."

"What's happening?" Amina asked.

"Rebel ground forces firing at inbound birds, I'd say. About three clicks away from here."

Rachel looped her arm around Amina's waist, as much for her own comfort as Amina's. "Are the rebels coming, then?"

"Maybe," Max said. "Maybe not. Maybe we were just the bait all along. I think they want the Black Hawks."

"Why?" Rachel glanced back and forth between Max and the jungle, half expecting someone else to drop down beside them, this time an enemy with a rifle or a knife.

"Intelligence, the weapons, maybe just the bragging rights." Max shook her head. "Who knows how they think? Any kind of victory, even if it's fabricated, probably helps them recruit more followers."

"It's crazy," Rachel murmured.

"Yeah, it is." Max gripped Rachel's arm. "I'm going back out. Don't fire unless you hear shooting first. Then if anyone approaches and it's not me, fire at anything that moves."

"Stay here." Rachel heard the tremor in her voice this time and didn't care. She wasn't afraid to be left alone—she was afraid for Max to be alone out there in the dark. "Please."

Max's fingers tightened on her arm. "We've got a better chance if I go. I'll be back."

"Do you keep your promises?"

"Yes."

"Then promise."

Max hesitated, moonlight glinting in her eyes. "I'll do my best. I promise."

"Your best better be damn—"

Max jerked her rifle to her shoulder. "Get *down*."

Rachel ducked and pushed Amina behind her. Keeping her head below the top of the barrier, she crowded next to Max and squinted into the dark. Another explosion lit up the camp and she saw them. Shadows within shadows, creeping out from the jungle. Animals? Humans? Her imagination?

"Max?" She held her breath, afraid the pounding of her heart would give their position away. Beside her, Max was as still as stone. For an instant, Rachel imagined taking shelter against her, leaning on her strength. She knew she could and Max would not think less of her, but she would think less of herself. Tugging her lower lip between her teeth, she forced herself to see the nightmares in the night.

Chapter Fourteen

Max steadied her rifle and focused through her night-vision goggles on the spot where she'd detected movement. If she hadn't spent her share of time on night maneuvers, she never would have recognized the faint blur in her vision for what it was—the fleeting break in the tree line made by four men ghosting into camp. Four men inside their perimeter, circling around to converge on the center from four directions. Four against three, and Amina and Rachel were completely untrained. Their best hope was to even the odds.

"Rachel," she whispered, "move around behind me and watch our rear. Keep your head down."

"Right." Rachel shifted as carefully as she could, certain that every crunch of stone beneath her boots, loud as a cannon shot, was audible for miles. She might as well shout, *Over here!* And what would she do if she saw someone?

Shoot? Yes. No. Could she? Until this moment, the idea of actually killing another human being had never been real. Earlier, when she'd been infuriated at the senseless slaughter of her friends and alternately terrified and outraged that the rebels might return to wreak more violence, she'd wanted to strike back as viciously as she'd been attacked, or thought she'd wanted to. She'd wanted to lash out to ease her pain, but now, peering into the dark with her finger on the trigger of a weapon that only a day before she would never have considered even picking up, she wondered if she could take a life. And if she could, what did it say about who she'd become?

Amina crouched beside her, and Rachel knew in that instant she would pull the trigger if it meant protecting herself and her friend. She would have to worry about the consequences later. Max was only a few feet away, but she dared not look over her shoulder, dared not look away from whatever lurked in the dark. Just knowing Max was behind her, protecting her, made her feel safe in a situation where safety was impossible, and she held on to that feeling while she searched for danger. Her eyes felt dry and tight, and she realized she wasn't blinking for fear that one millisecond of inattention would cost her everything. How did anyone survive this madness day after day? And at what cost?

She couldn't see anything out there except the soft flutter of tent flaps. That was all it was, right? That faint shimmer in the hazy moonlight slivering across the bare ground like shards of glass scattered by a giant hand. If someone was coming, she couldn't see them.

"Max," she whispered, "I can't see anything. What—"

"I've lost them too," Max said.

"Are you sure they're out there?"

"My gut says yes, but whoever they are, they're good." Max swore under her breath, the vehemence surprising Rachel. "They might be searching the tents. Grif is alone. I'm going out."

Panic surged. "No. If they're here—"

Max edged next to her and unexpectedly clasped the back of her neck, her grip warm and strong and welcome.

"You'll be all right," Max murmured, her mouth close to Rachel's ear. "You can do this."

"I can't," Rachel whispered urgently. "Not without you. I won't know when…I'm not sure if—"

Max's fingers tightened on her nape, gentle and firm. Max's breath seemed to slip beneath Rachel's skin and soothe the sharp edges of her terror. "Yes, you can. I'll be back. Remember?"

Amina pressed close to Rachel's side. "Trust her…and yourself."

"I…" Rachel gathered herself, tamped down the fear that clogged her throat. She never wanted Max to move her hand. She didn't want to let the nightmares back in. "All right. Go. Go see to Grif." She reached for Amina's hand. Amina was steady and her certainty helped bolster Rachel's resolve. "We're good."

"That's my girl," Max murmured.

For the first time in her life, Rachel didn't mind being called a girl. She didn't need to argue that she was a woman. Everything about the way Max spoke to her, touched her, said she already knew.

"Be careful." Rachel wouldn't beg Max to come back quickly. Max would do what she needed to do, and so would she.

"You too."

And then Max levered herself up, rolled over the bags, and was gone. Rachel tried to follow her movement across the ground and thought she saw her flickering in and out of the shadows, but she couldn't be sure. All the shadows looked the same. She wet her dry lips. "Amina, can you watch out the other side."

"Yes. We'll be all right," Amina whispered.

Rachel watched and waited. In the distance, closer now than before, the pop of rifle fire, the sharp crack of explosives, and the constant barrage of things bursting in the sky continued. She had the absurd thought that she'd never be able to look at a light show again, never be able to hear thunder without experiencing an instant of terror. No matter what happened out here tonight, she was already changed forever.

Max raced for the cover of the nearest tent, expecting a round to take her down at any second. Whoever was out there surely had night goggles and saw her as she had seen them, and they were better than she was. She might have a rifle, but she was no tactical sailor. She could shoot as well as most on the firing range, but she was a surgeon first. Necessity made her a warrior, and she'd fight as long as she could to protect Grif and Rachel and Amina, but she was outnumbered and out of her element.

And *what-if*-ing wasn't going to do her a damn bit of good. She had a plan and she wasn't going to come up with a better one now. First step was to make sure Grif hadn't fallen asleep or passed out from the pain—if he was awake, he could defend himself, even with one leg out of commission, better than Rachel and Amina. Once she knew he was secure, she could decide whether to head for the jungle in the hope of drawing the intruders away, stand out in the open and fight, or take a defensive position in the foxhole with Rachel and Amina. She checked the immediate area, saw no one, and sprinted across the twenty yards between her and the admin tent. Halfway there something hard and huge hit her in the midsection, her feet left the ground, and she flew a good ten feet and landed on her back with her rifle under her. The air whooshed out of her lungs when she hit, and a heavy body landed on top of her, making it impossible for her to drag in air. Gagging, gasping for breath with muscles that wouldn't work, she fumbled for her sidearm. A formless face, masked by night-vision goggles and opaque camouflage paint, hovered over hers. The glint of steel flashed as a knife blade touched her throat.

A deep male voice rumbled, "Hernandez, SEAL Team Four. Who are you?"

"De Milles…" Max's ribcage heaved as air rushed back in and she bit back a moan. Cracked rib or two. "Navy Medical Corps."

He eased to the side and the crushing weight lessened. "Good to see you, de Milles."

He grabbed her jacket, hoisted her up, and dragged her across the open ground to the cover of the nearest tent. "Sorry about the tackle. Had to be sure you weren't some *muj* in a confiscated uniform. Where are the others?"

Max had only a second to savor the relief. They were still in the middle of a firefight and a long way from safe. "One wounded in the big tent on the left. Two civilians in a foxhole in the center of the camp."

"One of the civilians name of Winslow?"

"That's right," Max said. "What's the situation?"

"The birds can't make it here—too much ground activity. We have to walk out a ways." He murmured into his com link, instructing someone to get Grif.

"How close are the rebels?"

He shrugged. "If they give up on trying to take out a bird, they could be here in twenty minutes. Best guess—we'll have a forty-minute head start."

"Listen," Max said, "I want to get back to the civilians. Get them ready to move out."

"Water and ammo. We're traveling light and fast."

"Roger that."

She crawled on hands and knees back to the foxhole, whispered, "It's Max," and rolled over and in.

"What's happening?" Rachel asked.

"Four SEALs are here to get us out," Max said. "We're leaving."

"Where are the helicopters?" Amina asked.

"They can't get here. We're walking out." Max kept her tone upbeat. A forty-minute head start might be enough for trained navy SEALs, but they'd be walking out with two civilians and a wounded man on a litter. If the rebels moved on the camp soon and picked up their trail, the rebels would catch up to them before they'd gotten a mile. "You up for that?"

Rachel gave a short laugh. "I'll walk from here to Mogadishu if I have to. What should we do?"

"Grab a light pack from the pile of gear and fill it with water and some MREs." Max stuffed her pockets and pack with ammo.

"How far will we have to go?" Amina asked.

"I don't know—far enough away so the birds can get to us." Max climbed back out, reached down, and helped first Amina, then Rachel out of the foxhole. "Stay close to me."

She led them quickly to the point where the SEALs had emerged from the jungle. Two men in combat gear seemed to materialize out of the air.

"We're Jones and Adeen, your escorts this evening," one of them said with a wide grin and a Texas twang. "Are you ladies up for a stroll?"

"Can't wait," Rachel said.

Hernandez and the last SEAL, a tall thin African American, jogged up with Grif on a litter between them. Hernandez said, "Let's rock and roll."

The SEALs sandwiched Rachel and Amina between the first two men and the litter bearers. Max slid in beside Rachel. "How are you doing?"

"Happy to be moving. I just wish it wasn't so dark."

Max rested a hand on her lower back. "Don't try to see—just follow the man in front of you. Your feet will know what to do. After a while, your eyes will adjust and it will get easier."

"I can't imagine anything ever being easier."

"I'm sorry," Max murmured, wishing she could rewind the clock to the moments before Grif was shot and Rachel and Amina still had a chance to get out. Wishing she could undo the horror and fear that followed.

"You have nothing to be sorry for," Rachel said softly. "Without you we might have tried to make it out on our own—and who knows where we'd be now. I know you kept me sane."

She shivered and Max instinctively slid her arm around her and pulled her close. "You were amazing. Just hang on a little while longer."

"No choice." Rachel sighed. "Do you need to check on Grif?"

"Yes, for a minute."

"Go. I'm okay now. Just a momentary pity party."

"You're entitled." Max didn't want to let her go but Grif needed her. "I'll be right back."

Rachel's smile was visible even in the murky light. "So you keep saying."

Max grinned. "Limited repertoire."

"I don't believe that."

"Ask Grif sometime—he'll tell you."

"I just might."

Still smiling, Max slipped back to the side of the litter. Grif's face was tight with pain. "Doing okay?"

"Better than I was." Grif grunted. "Fucking leg hurts like a mother."

"I'd rather hold off on the pain meds unless it gets really bad."

"Yeah. I don't want to be knocked out if things get hot either." Grif coughed and took a minute to catch his breath. "How are the women doing?"

"They're tough," Max said with a rush of pride. "Smart and resourceful too. They'll make it."

"You done good, Deuce."

"You just hang in there." She squeezed his shoulder. "I won't be far away."

He nodded and closed his eyes. Max worked her way back up to Rachel. "Everything okay?"

"I don't think I've ever been happier in my life." Rachel's voice was tinged with bitterness. "And isn't that a sorry statement."

Max rubbed Rachel's shoulder. "You've just been through a hell most people can't even imagine. The shock is setting in. Once you get out of here and get some rest, life will make sense again."

Rachel's fingers touched hers, warm and soft. For a heartbeat, the jungle, the battle, the insanity of life in the balance disappeared. Max shuddered, glad for the cover of darkness to hide the wanting she couldn't control.

"Will it?" Rachel said. "Once you've seen this madness, can you ever go back?"

Max didn't answer. Her truth was not one she would wish on anyone, especially not Rachel.

Chapter Fifteen

Rachel would never be frightened by shadows again, not after discovering what true darkness was really like. Time in this disorienting blackness lost all meaning. Once they'd left the encampment, the canopy completely blocked out the sky for long moments that might've been hours or minutes or days. When even the shadows died and she stared open-eyed into utter blackness, she stumbled along blind, following the soldier in front of her by instinct and senses she'd never known she had. Maybe she was drawn to his body heat, like some ancient creature pulled to the surface of the ocean by the primal call of the sun. Maybe she crept along in his wake out of a primitive drive for self-preservation while he became a human shield, pushing aside the clawing branches and vines that grasped at her from either side.

Her heart raced wildly and panic bubbled in her throat. She couldn't relax enough to capture a full breath, afraid the instant her hypervigilance ebbed, she'd be attacked. She doubted she'd ever relax again.

Amina was nearby, being guided by another one of these phantom rescuers whose faces Rachel had never seen and on whom she relied completely. Every now and then she caught Amina's scent, still as sweet and light and undaunted as Amina's spirit. She clung to that elusive reminder of the life she'd known before the nightmare until the pungent jungle smells finally pressed in from every side and obliterated it.

Isolated in the dark, her only touchstone was a faint pressure in the center of her back from Max's fingers. The entire endless time they'd been walking—stumbling, in her case—Max was always there, just beside her, never letting her get lost. Every now and then, like a gift made all the more precious by its sudden appearance when she'd given up hoping for it, a bit of moonlight filtered through the trees. When her eyes grasped it in a desperate attempt to right a world gone mad, she'd catch the outline of a helmet and a darker shape against the other shapeless forms. Max.

Some of the choking heaviness in her chest lightened, and she centered herself in the light press of Max's fingers, a reminder, silent and strong and unwavering, that she was not alone in this terrible madness. She reached into the dark and found Max's arm. Gripped it.

"You're doing great," Max whispered.

Rachel choked back a disbelieving laugh at the bald-faced lie. How did Max know what she needed when she'd refused to admit needing anything even to herself? Could Max feel her panic—read her mind? Or had she always been so transparent and just been fooling only herself all these years? Max was so very good at seeing what she'd always managed to keep from others. She'd always worked so hard to maintain the façade of courage and control, from pretending she wasn't terrified to go to bed as a child to convincing everyone, including herself, she didn't need anything more than a meaningful career and casual, convenient physical relationships to be happy.

Maintaining any kind of façade out here was impossible. They were all naked, reduced to their most basic needs and desires and fears. From the moment Max had stepped out of the dark and looked into her eyes, she'd seen beneath her mask.

"Thanks for lying," Rachel said, finally free to let the mask drop away. "I'm scared witless."

"Nothing to be ashamed of." The fingers against her back became a palm, pressing a little more firmly, gliding down and up. A comforting caress. No, not a caress. Max, doing what she did so very well. Taking care of people.

"I'm sorry," Rachel whispered, feeling selfish for wanting the comfort, for asking more of Max when Max had already done so much. She should be stronger than this. Just like the child whose parents left her in the dark to face her fears, she had to be stronger if she wanted to be loved. God, what was next—begging Max not to leave her again? Max was just being Max and reading anything else into her actions was a mistake. She released Max's arm. "I'm fine. You don't need to—"

"Maybe *I* need to." Max's voice was rough, urgent. "Maybe I want to."

Rachel shivered. *I want to...* what? *Help you? Protect you? Touch you?* She didn't need that. Didn't want that. Did she?

"Hold up," a low male voice ordered.

Rachel stopped on command, feeling like a soldier of sorts.

The SEAL leader said, "Over this ridge there's a nomad camp. All indications are it's deserted. There's room enough for the bird to set down. Two minutes. We'll make a run for it."

Max said, "Roger that."

Two minutes. Two minutes and it would all be over. A million thoughts crowded into Rachel's head. Was this it? Was she about to die? Had anything she'd ever done really mattered? She'd arrived in this place so far from home filled with purpose and passion, determined to make a difference in a way that really counted, not, as her father wished, in the marble halls of government where greed and personal appetite distorted the higher purpose of the office, but here on the front lines where people put their beliefs into action. She'd chosen a life completely the opposite of everything she'd grown up with to prove she was capable of banishing the monsters all on her own. To prove to her parents?—to herself?—that she was not afraid. She'd committed her time and energy, and sacrificed her comfort and her personal life, in pursuit of her goals. She hadn't anticipated she'd have to risk even more—that she'd have to put her life, not just her ideology, on the line in the most fundamental of ways. Max had shown her what true bravery was. She had become part of a new team, a new cadre determined to survive, and she would give her life for any one of them—for Max, for Amina, for Grif, for these nameless, faceless men who had risked their lives for hers.

In her last remaining moments, she turned quickly to Max. Maybe it was a trick of her imagination, maybe somewhere high above a leaf fluttered, allowing moonlight to slip through the canopy, but Max's face was clearly visible in the darkness. So much she wanted to say and no words that could ever say enough. "Thank you. For everything."

Max paused for a long time. Her eyes glinted, intense and penetrating. "You're welcome."

Rachel smiled. Max understood.

"Get ready," the SEAL in front of her said.

Rachel couldn't imagine running through this inky soup, but she would if it meant getting out of here. If they told her to fly, she'd figure out a way to do it.

"I'm going back with Grif," Max said.

Rachel gripped her arm. "Just make sure you get on the helicopter. Please."

"I'll be there." Max's hand glided over her back before her fingers skimmed down Rachel's arm to her hand. Max squeezed her fingers. "Stick with Hernandez, no matter what."

"But—"

"Don't look back. Just go."

Hernandez gripped her upper arm firmly. "Let's go."

Rachel was tugged forward and Max disappeared. Her feet caught up with her body, pedaling forward faster and faster, and then she was running, crashing through underbrush, gasping for breath, her arms in front of her face to ward off the branches slapping at her. Closer and closer she raced toward the angry buzz of thousands of bees—a rogue hive that turned out to be helicopter rotors whirring madly. Mercifully, the jungle finally released its stranglehold and she burst into a clearing, the moonlight so intense she blinked furiously to clear the tears welling in her eyes. There in the center of a clearing ringed with decaying huts and tiny overgrown plots marked out by low stone walls sat a helicopter. Just ahead of her Amina give a sharp cry of joy and lurched forward to keep up with the SEAL whose arm encircled her waist. Rachel slowed and jerked around, searching the towering wall of vegetation behind her. Where were the others? Where was Max?

Gunfire erupted. Lightning streaked from the helicopters and the air resounded with automatic weapons fire. Rachel cried out.

"Come on!" Hernandez jerked her toward the Black Hawk, and her feet nearly left the ground.

"What about the others?" she shouted.

"Just keep moving. And keep your head down!"

"We can't just leave them." Her words were lost in the vortex of swirling sand and pulsating air.

Up ahead, someone inside the helicopter reached down and lifted Amina up as if she were a child. When Rachel was a few feet away, hands grasped her by the waist and arms and she was airborne, her feet flying from the ground and landing on the metal floor of the helicopter with a bone-jarring thud. Once she regained her balance, she stared at the figures crowded into a small space almost as claustrophobic as the foxhole had been.

"Are you injured?" A female voice, the face partially obscured by a helmet. Kind brown eyes. Not indigo, not Max.

"I..." Rachel spun toward the open door. The ground below was swallowed in the night.

A hand on her arm. Her face was clearer now. Young, intense. "I'm Corpsman Delgado. Are you injured?"

"No," Rachel shouted above the din, straining to see through the murk and dust. "I'm...fine."

"Good. Over here."

Delgado led her to a place against the side of the helicopter's belly and she slid down, her legs turned to jelly. Someone placed a blanket over her. Amina crowded close and gripped her hand.

"We made it," Amina said, tears streaking her cheeks and triumph shining in her eyes. "It's all over."

Rachel eased her arm around Amina's waist and leaned into her. "Yes. It's all over."

She hoped Amina believed the lie. A series of pings rattled against the metal shell and someone shouted, "We're taking fire."

The Black Hawk vibrated as the motor revved. Delgado hooked a safety strap to a line above their heads, her body swaying as the helicopter rocked from side to side. They were taking off.

"No," Rachel cried, throwing the blanket aside. "Max!" She tried to get to her knees and nearly fell.

"Stay down," a soldier yelled and blocked her way.

"Where are the others?" Where was Max? Max would never have left her. She couldn't leave her. With a scream trapped in her throat, she braced herself on her arms and started to crawl across the floor toward the open door.

The soldier held her back. "Here they come."

A SEAL vaulted out of the blackness into the helicopter, knelt at the edge of the opening, and leaned out. The end of the litter appeared and he grabbed it. Another SEAL piled in and did the same. The litter and Grif were hoisted aboard. The Black Hawk rose. Rachel stared at the opening, an opaque black abyss, and waited, time suspended. Minutes became hours became a lifetime, and her heart stuttered to a standstill.

An arm, two, reached out of the dark and the SEALs each gripped a wrist. They pulled and Max's body flew inside. She landed on her back and lay still.

Rachel waited, frozen. Max turned, met her eyes, and grinned.

"About time," Rachel mouthed as her heart started beating again.

"Told you I'd be right behind you," Max yelled.

"Yes, you did," Rachel murmured.

Max pushed herself up and bent over Grif. Rachel slumped back beside Amina. The Black Hawk ascended into the night. She didn't know where she was going, and it didn't seem to matter. She had no idea what she would do when she arrived. She wasn't even sure she knew who she would be when she did.

Chapter Sixteen

The helicopter climbed straight up, and the ping of bullets against the metal body faded. Making a wide arc, it banked sharply, turned 180 degrees, and picked up speed. Wind rushed through the cabin and Rachel pulled the blanket tighter. SEALs with machine guns leaned out either side of the helicopter. Delgado knelt with Max over Grif's litter, switching IV bags and pushing drugs into the line. The dark beyond the dim cabin lights was impenetrable. Rachel couldn't see where the helicopter was headed, not that she really cared as long as it was far away from the Juba jungle. All that really mattered was that Max was safely aboard. They were all safe now—they had to be. She couldn't even let herself think they wouldn't reach their destination after all of this. There must be some fairness in life. An image of the starving Somalis straggling into the aid camp flashed into her mind, and she knew fairness had nothing to do with it. Men perpetrated great crimes and great acts of selfless bravery, and sometimes the reasons for both were incomprehensible. She'd been lucky Max and Grif had reached her. Maybe life was far more random than she'd ever wanted to believe.

She couldn't tell time in the dark, the engine roar made conversation impossible, and before long she dozed. She snapped awake, adrenaline pouring through her, when the helicopter angled, nose down, and dropped. Now she caught glimpses of light through the portals, pockets of illumination in the inky night that grew brighter with each passing second. She had once thought there was nothing more beautiful than the Manhattan skyline at night, but she knew better now. Wherever they were headed, those scattered constellations of flickering lights were without a doubt the most glorious sight she'd ever witnessed.

"Amina, look!" Rachel grasped Amina's arm and pointed. "We're almost—"

"Hey!" Delgado shouted.

Rachel looked over as Max slumped forward. Delgado grabbed her around the waist and lowered her to the floor. Rachel's heart plummeted.

"What is it? What happened?" she shouted, but no one answered. No one even heard her.

Delgado opened Max's jacket, looked inside, and began cutting away parts of the sleeves. She tore the wrapper off one of the bandages Rachel had seen Max use time and time again on Grif's leg and pressed it to Max's right upper arm. Max was hurt.

Rachel pushed aside the blanket, ducked the restraining arm of the soldier kneeling close by, and scrambled forward a few feet next to Delgado. Max lay motionless, her eyes closed. Max was never still, never unaware. Rachel wanted to shake her and tell her to wake up and explain what the hell she was doing.

Rachel tugged Delgado's shoulder. "What's wrong with her?"

Delgado spared her a brief glance and then went back to what she was doing. "…a round…arm. Lost a…blood…idn't bother…tell anybo…"

The words were muffled but Rachel heard them clearly enough. Max had been shot. The words marched across her brain like cues on a teleprompter, but she was having trouble making sense of it all. Max couldn't be shot. Max was a doctor, and she was out there to take care of everyone. She wasn't supposed to get hurt. She wasn't supposed to—

This was wrong. So wrong.

"Max?" Rachel gripped Max's leg just above her knee. Max's fatigues were stiff with dirt and other things, but Rachel didn't care. She needed to touch her. "*Max.*"

Max's eyes fluttered open and roved blankly until they settled on Rachel's face.

"Hey," she said, her expression hazy.

"Hey, yourself," Rachel said, anxiety and fear sharpening her tone.

Max's grin widened. "Uh-oh. Pissed again. How come?"

The ball of panic crushing the air from Rachel's lungs started to melt. She reached across Max's body and found her hand. The fingers that twined through hers were too cold, but still strong. Still Max. "I thought we talked about this. You weren't supposed to get hurt."

"Didn't, much." Max turned her head, frowned at Delgado. "What did you give me?"

Delgado grinned. "Just a little something to keep you down. I know you. You'd be trying to get up before we had a chance to take care of you or driving me bat-shit telling me what to do."

Max's brows came down even harder. "Damn it. S'nothing. I ought to know—"

"Don't be such a hard-ass." Rachel said sharply. "Let someone take care of you."

Max squinted at Rachel. "You want a shot?"

Delgado's shoulders shook, but she didn't say a word.

"You're an idiot." Rachel shook her head. Under less terrifying circumstances this playful side of Max would be intriguing. As it was, all she cared about was Max, awake and talking. She was as dizzy as if she'd just downed a bottle of champagne. "And did I mention hardheaded?"

Max's smile flashed. "Bet you like it just the same."

"Ask me some other time and I'll tell you what I like." Rachel stroked the top of Max's hand with her thumb. "Crazy hero is not top of my list."

Max started to say something, but her eyes clouded and lost focus.

"Max?" Rachel turned to Delgado. "Is she all right?"

"Drugs kicking in. You need to go back and sit down." Delgado wrapped Max's arm with a bandage and injected medication into the IV line taped above the hand Rachel held. "We'll be home in just a couple minutes."

Home. Maybe for them. For her, another stop in a strange land. She stayed until Max's lids slipped closed before returning to her spot next to Amina.

"What happened? Is she all right?" Amina asked.

"I think so. God, she was shot and didn't tell anyone. Why is she so damn stubborn?"

Amina laughed. "You ought to be able to answer that. The two of you are very much alike."

"We most certainly are not." Rachel glowered. "Max is…well, she takes altogether too much upon herself."

"I think you have some experience with that."

"Not like Max," Rachel said softly, watching Delgado and one of the SEALs move Max's lax body onto a litter. "She's many things that I'll never be."

❖

The helicopter touched down with a jolt, and the roar of the engines died away to a soft whine. The SEALs surrounded Rachel and Amina and hustled them out onto the landing field. Rows of long, low one-story rectangular buildings bordered an expanse of bare land where dozens of helicopters, armored vehicles, and other machines were lined up waiting to march into battle. After weeks in the jungle, the tarmac beneath her feet was as foreign as the bright halogen lights that captured them in a cone of illumination so glaring her eyes watered. Shielding her eyes, her first instinct was to escape into the shadows where she'd be less visible. Where she could see who was coming before they saw her.

She turned back to the helicopter, searching for Max. A half dozen military personnel converged on the open bay of the helicopter and lifted out the two litters bearing Grif and Max and carried them off in another direction. She started after them. Two steps later a hand on her arm stopped her.

Rachel whirled back. A woman about her age, a few inches shorter in blue BDUs and her hair tucked up in a tidy blond bun at the back of her neck, smiled at her. Marine insignia flashed on her collar.

"Ms. Winslow, I'm Major Barbara Newton," the blonde said. "If you'll come with me, please."

"Where are they taking Max—Commander de Milles?"

"The wounded will be transported to the base hospital. Don't worry, they'll be fine."

"How do you know that? You don't even know what's wrong with them."

"If you'll come with me, please." Her calm smile never changed. She had to be press corps or public relations. "I'm sure both of you would like a shower and something hot to eat."

"I'd like to go to the hospital," Rachel said. She'd had plenty of dealings with the PR people who managed her father's career—his life, really, public and private. She knew not to yield. "I want to see the officers who rescued us."

"Let's get you settled first."

Amina took Rachel's arm, pulled her aside, and murmured, "You probably won't be able to see Max for a while anyhow. If you do what she wants now, you might get away sooner." She raised her voice. "You'll feel better if you have something to eat."

Rachel wondered if the Marine major really thought a hot shower and meal were all that was necessary to erase everything that had happened. Amina was right, though, and clearly a better natural politician than her. She wasn't going to escape until she at least seemed to be cooperating for a while, and in the meantime, she'd get the information she needed to find Max. She smiled at Newton. "Of course, yes, thank you. I'm sorry, things have just been...hectic."

"I know, but it's over now."

It's over. Rachel couldn't help but think how glibly the phrase was applied and how little it pertained. Another lie she wondered if anyone really believed.

"Thanks," she whispered to Amina and, still holding Amina's arm, followed Newton's brisk strides toward a waiting Humvee. Once she and Amina settled in the backseat and Newton got in front, the vehicle left the airfield and drove into a large complex lit by more halogen lights on poles spaced at intervals along streets laid out in rigid grids and lined by dozens upon dozens of the tan metal containers. What she wouldn't have given for a few of those back at the camp. She stared out the thick, pitted window to avoid thinking about the failed mission and the lost lives.

Military personnel and civilian workers moved about on foot or by transport even though it was the middle of the night. Vehicles passed them, helicopters arrived and departed. After fifteen minutes and several turns, the Humvee stopped in front of another building similar to the ones they'd passed, only much larger. Major Newton turned to face them. "This is the base HQ. We'll get you settled in your temporary quarters, and once you're squared away, I'll take you to meet the base commander."

Rachel stared at her. She'd been around politicians all her life, and Major Newton was another one who just happened to be wearing a uniform. What she'd really meant was they'd debrief. Of course someone would want a recounting of their experiences in the jungle. Probably quite a few people, and it wouldn't be quick.

"I want to see Commander de Milles first."

"We will certainly arrange a visit as soon as possible. Come on, let me take you inside and show you your quarters."

Newton headed toward the building, leaving Rachel and Amina no choice but to go along. Inside, a hall ran down the center with doors spaced at regular intervals on each side. Newton turned down another corridor and eventually stopped before a closed door with no markings. She opened it, held it ajar, and said to Amina, "Ms. Roos, you'll be in here. I think you'll find whatever you need in the way of clothes and other necessities on the bed and in the bathroom."

Amina glanced at Rachel.

"I won't go anywhere," Rachel said.

Amina nodded. "I'll see you in a little while, then."

Major Newton led Rachel down the hall past several more closed doors and opened one. "Here you are. I'll be by in half an hour and we'll get you both fed."

"I need a phone to make an international call. Can you—"

"Yes, we'll take care of that." Newton smiled. "I'll see you in a few moments."

Rachel stepped into the room and Newton closed the door behind her. A dull overhead light revealed the plain furnishings: a single bed, a metal dresser and desk, an open-faced closet slightly deeper than a bookcase with hangers and shelves. She almost laughed. Too bad she hadn't brought a suitcase. On the bed were a pair of fatigue pants and a shirt without insignia, obviously military issue. A pair of dark leather combat boots stood at attention next to the bed. She lifted the tan shirt and examined it. Cut for a woman and close to her size. The pants, plain desert brown, looked to be her size as well. She wondered just how much they knew about her. The idea was disconcerting, although she shouldn't be surprised. Of course there was a record of the Red Cross delegation and details of everyone in it. And the military just loved keeping files.

She disliked being caught up in the huge military machine, but the sooner she went along with this part of the plan, the sooner she'd get to see Max. And she would dearly love a shower. A meal might not be bad either. She stepped through a narrow door into an adjoining bathroom, a small tight space ingeniously designed to provide everything that was needed in a compact area. She stripped off her clothes and, not knowing what else to do with them, stuffed them into a trash can by the small sink. She turned on the water and steam filled the tiny bathroom. Naked, she stepped under the spray and started to shake. Her legs buckled, suddenly too weak to support her, and she slid down until she was sitting on the cool metal floor, her knees drawn up and her head back against the stall. Water pulsed over her face and body and ran into the drain beneath her.

Out of nowhere sobs shook her chest. Her mind went mercifully blank. She let the water wash away her tears until strength returned to her limbs, and she pushed herself upright. Mechanically she washed her hair, soaped her body, rinsed, and shut off the water. She wrapped a towel around her chest and found a toothbrush and toothpaste neatly stowed on a shelf above the commode. She brushed her teeth, dried her hair, and dressed in the fatigues that had been left for her. Clean socks and the new pair of boots completed the outfit. Slowly she sat on the side of the bed, flashes of the last day playing through her mind in fast-forward like a movie reel spinning too fast. Rotor wash kicking up clouds of sand. Gunshots and screams, terror and triumph. Through it all, Max was there. Max was hurt, and Rachel didn't even know how badly. She didn't know where Max was. She only knew she wasn't there and everything inside her insisted that she should be.

A knock came on the door. "Ms. Winslow, it's Major Newton. May I come in?"

Rachel glanced around the room she'd be happy never to see again. The space was too small and, as Newton had just proved, she couldn't see who might be coming. Quickly she rose and opened the door. "I'd like to see—"

"Come with me, please. As soon as you've met with the base commander, I'll get you information on Commander de Milles."

"And a phone."

Commander Newton smiled. "Of course. Whatever you need."

Rachel sincerely doubted that, but she had no choice but to fall in step.

CHAPTER SEVENTEEN

Yellow haze in the east. Dawn. Not much longer now. If they were coming, it would be soon. Morning twilight—when shadows hid the truth. There. A momentary flash of movement in the bush. A stealthy predator—cat, wild boar, man. The soft clink of metal sliding on metal. A round chambering, a scope adjusting. Straining to hear. The heavy air muffling sound, distorting direction. Searching, scanning, in front and behind. Tree trunks one upon the other, impenetrable, shielding the enemy. A scream, a shot. Pain. Adrenaline surging. *Rachel.*

Max's eyes flew open and she blinked against the searing sun.

"Rachel?" Gasping, chest tight, Max jerked, grabbed for a weapon. Pain lasered down her arm. Where was Rachel? Not the sun, a light. Where?

A shadow loomed over her. A deep voice said, "Easy there, Commander."

Max squinted and a face came into view. Clean-shaven, ruddy complexion, not the leathery tan of someone who spent days under the sun. Sandy hair, sharp blue eyes, cold and appraising. Tan desert camos. No insignia. No name.

"Where's Rachel?" Max's voice cracked and she swallowed against the dryness. "Where's Grif?"

"Being taken care of," he said smoothly. He was perched on some kind of stool next to her cot. He looked comfortable, as if he knew her and was just paying a friendly visit.

She'd never seen him before. She turned her head and checked out her surroundings. Her right arm was propped on a pillow by her side. A bandage circled her upper arm. She remembered running in the dark, her hand on Grif's shoulder, steadying him on the litter. Rachel up ahead, shielded by the SEAL, almost safe. A punch to the arm, the round hitting her, taking her down. An instant of pain, sharp and bright, a surge of adrenaline. Lurching to her feet, the pain blunted by the need to get Rachel and Grif and Amina to safety. Running, breaking free of the grasping jungle, the Black Hawk just ahead, skids lifting into the air. Rachel being pulled aboard, safe. Raising Grif's litter up into the belly of the bird. The Black Hawk rising—two, three, four feet. Last one on the ground—reaching up, wondering if anyone would see her.

They'd been there, the hands of her comrades, grasping hers, yanking her aboard. They'd seen her, knew her. The pain disappeared beneath the relief of seeing everyone safe. Rachel, Grif, Amina, the SEALs, all accounted for. She'd lain on her back, catching her breath, and found Rachel's gaze reaching out to her across the space between them. Bright and intense, even in the gloom, a connection as unexpected as it was welcome, like another hand reaching for hers in the dark. She'd held on to that gaze for as long as she could, savoring the sense of not being alone.

Max studied the man who studied her. She was alone now. Hers was the only cot in a ten-by-ten cubicle. An IV bag hung above her left side and a line ran into her arm. She was in a recovery room at the base hospital. Where was everyone else—the medics, the other patients? Where was Rachel?

"Where are the others?"

He smiled, but there was no friendliness in his expression. His eyes remained glacial. "Everyone's fine."

"I want a report on Grif. Where's the medic?"

"How did he come to get wounded?"

"Don't you know?" Max frowned. "Who are you?"

"How large is the rebel force out there?"

"How would I know?"

"How many were you in contact with?"

Max hesitated, trying to read what he wasn't saying. She hadn't slept in two nights, was half-drugged from whatever meds she'd been given, and was mentally exhausted. But she wasn't so out of it she couldn't tell this guy was interrogating her. "I saw three, maybe four, as we landed."

"What about later?"

"We never had contact later."

"Who ordered the abduction of Rachel Winslow?"

Max stared at him. He wasn't military, he was something a lot more dangerous. NSA. DOD. CIA. Whoever he was, he wasn't a friend. And he was interested in Rachel. She studied him the way she studied a target through her scope—coldly, dispassionately. He had just become the enemy. "Who said there was an abduction attempt?"

"The attack on the camp yesterday morning was fortuitous, don't you think?" He folded his hands over one knee, his tone casual, conversational, as if they were chatting over drinks at the officers' club.

"Bad timing," Max said. "It happens out here."

"Yes, bad timing, especially considering that the plans to evacuate were specifically focused on her."

"I wondered about that," Max said. "Why her?"

"Do you believe in luck?"

"No."

He shook his head. "Just before we arrived, the camp was attacked. If we hadn't had good tailwinds, we would have been fifteen minutes later, and she'd have been gone. That was lucky, don't you think?"

"We?" Max laughed. "Sorry, I didn't notice your ass on the line out there. What desk were you riding while the RPGs were exploding everywhere?"

"Bad luck for the rebels, maybe—they almost pulled it off. Almost as if they knew about our plans."

"You've got to be kidding. You think one of us tipped off the rebels about the mission?"

He smiled, waggled one hand. "I don't know. What do you think?"

"I think you're looking for someone to blame for a mission that went south and almost lost you a highly valuable asset."

The ice in his eyes turned stony. The rest of his face never changed. How'd they all do that, these intelligence guys—gender not an exception—eradicate any sign of emotion? Maybe the agencies preselected for sociopaths, or maybe they trained them to distrust everyone and care about only their own agendas. She'd never really given it much thought, never had to. But she'd seen enough of the spooks to be able to recognize them. They all had the same flat, dead look in their eyes, even when they were smiling.

"You're looking in the wrong place if you're looking at any of us," Max said.

"Really. Well, I'm all ears. Where would you be looking?"

"Well, that's your job, isn't it?"

"Yours is battlefield medicine, but somehow you ended up being the only one remaining behind. Who did you talk to while you were out there?"

"No one."

"What did you find in the jungle?"

"Nothing."

"Who is coming for Rachel Winslow?"

Is not *was*. Max's jaw clenched. Physical combat wasn't her thing. She could use a weapon when she needed to, but she was trained to shoot in self-defense. She could defend herself hand-to-hand if she had to, but she didn't settle her grievances with her fists. But she wanted her hands on his throat every time he mentioned Rachel's name. "You tell me."

"We'll chat again when you're feeling a little stronger. Maybe your memory will improve." He smiled the same way someone might before they slid a knife between your ribs. Rising, he adjusted his trousers, brushed the wrinkles from the thighs as if they offended him, and walked out the door.

Max bet everything in his closet was pressed and hanging in exactly the same direction, sorted by color and type. Guys like him never quit—and she needed to figure out what exactly he was after. She stared at the ceiling, replaying the conversation. Somebody's feet were to the fire, and they were looking to pass the blame onto someone else. Rachel was connected, that much had always been clear. And now someone was needed to take the blame for the fact that she'd almost been captured or killed. Had no-name secret agent implied Rachel might still be in danger? Max's head pounded. She couldn't believe anyone really thought one of their team had tipped off the rebels. Everyone knew military installations—hell, all government organizations, period— were as leaky as an old roof in a hurricane. Spies, sympathizers, and counterintelligence agents were everywhere, including inside the base. Plenty of locals came and went, supplying and preparing food, stocking the PX, and selling odd goods at the bazaars that sprang up at dawn and disappeared at dusk. All kinds of information was bought and sold every minute. Electronic communications were just as insecure. Maybe the rebels hit the camp purely by chance, or maybe they'd gotten wind of the Black Hawk extraction somehow and the attack was intentional. Either way, what mattered was that Rachel was safe. For now.

The pain in her arm ratcheted up a notch and she bit back the moan. Rachel was probably on a transport back to the States already. She'd never see her again, but at least she knew Rachel was out of the line of fire. The new ache in her belly had nothing to do with her GSW. Rachel was under her skin, and she wondered how long and how many drinks it would take before she got her out.

No better time to start than now. She lifted her left arm to her face and pulled off the tape securing the IV with her teeth. One quick jerk and the plastic catheter slipped out. Slowly, she sat up and waited for her head to stop spinning. When she was sure she wouldn't topple over, she stood up and searched for her clothes.

❖

Major Barbara Newton led Rachel and Amina to a small cafeteria where workers were busy setting out rows of big stainless steel pans filled with eggs, bacon, sausage, toast, even pancakes on a long steam table. The air was damp and hot and smelled of grease and coffee. Picnic-style tables set end to end divided up the rest of the room. They were mostly empty. A big clock on the wall read three thirty.

"Please," Major Newton said, "help yourselves. It's a little early for breakfast but hopefully this will do."

Amina said, "Thank you."

Rachel's stomach lurched at the thought of food, but if she wanted to escape Newton's surveillance and find out exactly why she hadn't yet been able to contact her father or Max, she'd have to play along. While she had nothing specific to complain about in the treatment, she was being handled. And she hated being handled.

"Yes, thank you." Rachel followed Amina to the hot trays and put a scoop of scrambled eggs and several slices of toast on her plate. Coffee, blessed coffee was what she really needed, and she filled a large paper container with what smelled like fresh brew. She followed Amina to a table and sat down across from her. Newton took a cup of coffee and joined them.

"I take it you had no warning the attack was coming," Newton said.

Amina glanced at Rachel. Something in her eyes said she found all of this very odd too. Rachel took a bite of toast and took her time chewing. "No. We haven't had any trouble until now."

"The rebels never made contact previously?"

"Not that we were aware of," Rachel said, "but then they could easily have come into camp under the guise of being Somali locals and we never would've known."

"I suppose that's true. You never noticed your security people with any...suspicious individuals?"

Rachel stared at her. "No. Why do you ask?"

Newton smiled in her friendly fashion and went back to her coffee.

"May I call my family soon?" Amina asked.

"Of course," Newton said. "They're probably completely unaware of the attack and aren't worried, but I'm sure they'll be very happy to hear from you."

"Yes," Amina said, "but the supervisors in Mogadishu will wonder if they can't make contact soon, and news travels quickly."

"It does, yes," Newton said softly.

Amina's color heightened as she held Newton's gaze.

Rachel asked, "What about Dacar's family and the others? Who will—"

"We'll contact your agency in the morning and coordinate that. The families will be advised as soon as possible."

Amina pushed her plate. "Good. Thank you."

"Of course." Newton stood. "If you're ready, we'll see about those phone calls."

Newton led them back to the hall where another female in uniform waited.

"Ms. Roos, Lieutenant Carmichael will take you to the communications room," Newton said to Amina. "You can call your family from there."

"Thank you." Amina glanced at Rachel. "I'll see you soon?"

Rachel nodded, wanting to get Amina far away from whatever Newton intended for her. "Yes."

The lieutenant led Amina away, and Rachel folded her arms. "What's going on?"

"Captain Pettit is waiting to meet you. Right this way."

Rachel had come to expect nothing from Newton. Maybe she'd learn more from Pettit. "Fine."

Newton led her through another series of hallways to a door bearing a plain brass placard announcing Captain Edward Pettit, Base CO. Newton held the door open, and as Rachel walked in a big man with cocoa complexion, short-clipped salt-and-pepper hair, and immaculate desert BDUs rose from behind a desk covered with stacks of papers and folders.

"I have Ms. Winslow to see Captain Pettit, Chief."

"Yes, ma'am. Right this way."

Newton didn't follow as the chief petty officer escorted Rachel to another door on the far side of the small anteroom. He rapped and pushed the door open for her. "Ma'am."

Rachel walked through and the door closed behind her. This room had windows looking out onto a parade ground where armored vehicles and personnel moved about. The man behind the broad metal desk was tall and thin and looked to be in his late fifties. His skin was tanned as if he spent a fair amount of time outside. His sandy hair was regulation short and he wore the same desert BDUs as most of the other personnel.

Rachel focused on the other man in the room—the one who sat beside the desk with his hands clasping his crossed knee. He was not wearing a uniform, although his desert camos resembled those of most of the people Rachel had passed. The first thing she noticed about him was his cool blue eyes. Max's eyes, as deep blue as a night sky, carried heat Rachel could feel from yards away. This man's gaze left frost on her skin.

The man behind the desk stood. "Ms. Winslow. Please, have a seat."

Chapter Eighteen

Rachel held out her hand to Captain Pettit. "Captain, I want to thank you and your troops for everything you did for us. I hope any injuries sustained are not too severe and everyone recovers quickly."

"No thanks are necessary, Ms. Winslow. We're out here to protect our citizens and allies." His handshake was firm, but not overbearing, his palm rough and dry as befit a man who did more than sit behind a desk. His eyes, a light shade of green, held hers for a moment with genuine warmth. "I trust you've had everything you need here."

"Major Newton has been very accommodating." Rachel glanced at the man sitting next to the captain's desk. He was watching her but made no move to introduce himself. His gaze, unlike Pettit's, was chilly and remote, rather like a glacier viewed from a distance. Flat, hard, and cold. She wasn't intimidated by men who attempted to intimidate her. She'd spent her life around powerful men and women who were experts at the game of silent intimidation, subtle innuendo, and verbal jousting. She smiled. "I'm sorry. I'm Rachel Winslow."

He rose, slowly and surprisingly gracefully for a man who must have topped six-four. His frame was remarkable in its absolute symmetry and proportion, almost as if he'd been fashioned from an anatomical drawing—shoulders just the right width to balance his tapering torso and narrow but not too narrow hips. Thighs that were neither too bulky nor too thin. His uniform, for that's what it was despite the absence of identifying patches or insignia, fit him so impeccably she suspected it was tailored for him. Who tailored BDUs? What kind of man needed that kind of control over every small detail?

Rachel held out her hand. *Your move.*

The handshake felt more like a test than a greeting. His grip was just a little firmer than polite, in case she'd missed his position of power, and he held her hand just a little longer than might have been socially acceptable. The signals were subtle, so if she didn't know better she might have thought she imagined his show of dominance. She wasn't imagining his thumb briefly sweeping over her knuckles in what under other circumstances might have been a caress. She kept her eyes on his until he loosened his grip, and then she withdrew her hand.

"Michael Carmody," he said as if that was all that was necessary.

No rank. No affiliation. Intelligence. Considering where they were, most likely CIA. She turned back to the captain, dismissing Carmody, knowing he wouldn't like that. Good. She didn't like being a pawn in anyone's game, and she was feeling that way more and more every moment.

"There is one thing," Rachel said. "I haven't had a chance to find a phone. I'd like to check with the rest of our delegation. Are they here?"

"The medical team has been transported to the French embassy," Pettit said. "We're awaiting instructions from the other embassies as to the plans for the rest of the aid team."

"Everyone is well?" She decided not to inquire about Max and Grif until she got some idea of what these men—no, not these men—what Michael Carmody was after.

"Yes," Pettit said. "A few minor injuries, nothing serious."

"Thank goodness." The murder of the security guards was horrible enough. Rachel was just grateful it hadn't been worse. "I'm sure you're very busy, but if you could arrange for me to have access to a phone?"

"Of course," Captain Pettit said. "If—"

"That will have to wait for just a bit longer," Michael Carmody said, interrupting the captain without the slightest hint of apology. "Have a seat, Ms. Winslow. I'm sure you must be tired."

Was he really expecting her to admit to any kind of weakness as he moved his chess pieces onto the field of battle? She could refuse, but that would gain her nothing. Of course she was tired. When the last molecules of adrenaline burned away, she'd probably collapse. A physical standoff was out of the question, and she'd learned from watching those in power that the appearance of cooperation often gave one the advantage in the long game. She sat in the only unoccupied seat in the room, a plain armless wooden chair that faced the captain's desk. Crossing her legs, she sat back. "I'm sure at some point I'll feel like sleeping for a day, but thank you, I'm fine."

"Perhaps," Carmody said in a slow, nearly hypnotic drawl, "you could tell us what happened at the aid camp."

A distinct look of displeasure crossed Captain Pettit's face and was quickly smothered. His distaste for whatever was going on reaffirmed Rachel's assessment that Carmody was the one behind this not-so-subtle grilling masquerading as a debriefing session. She angled her body slightly so she faced Carmody. "I would have thought you already knew that."

"It's always nice to have a firsthand account," he said with a thin smile.

"I'm afraid mine might be a bit jumbled. A great deal was happening all at once, and I'll readily admit, I was too frightened at first to pay much attention to the details." She'd been too damn busy running for her life. "If you gave me some idea what you were interested in?"

"One never knows what's important, does one?"

She could really come to dislike this man quite a bit, with his superior attitude and faintly sexual appraisal. "Oh, I don't know. Sometimes I think one does."

His eyes grew even colder if that was possible. "What time did the attacks start?"

Rachel folded her hands in her lap to hide the involuntary trembling. She didn't want him to know that thinking about what happened stirred a cascade of adrenaline-fueled fear. Of course, if he was who she thought he was, he would already know that. "I can't tell you precisely, but near dawn."

"After dawn or before?"

Dawn. The thunder of explosions catapulting her from sleep into awareness. Her heart racing, her limbs frozen in the first seconds of instinctual panic. Opening her eyes in the dark, breathless with the instant rush of night terror, cornered and helpless in the face of whatever monster was coming for her. She clenched her hands and her nails bit into her palms. She wished she couldn't remember but knew she'd never be able to forget. "If it matters, I think just before."

"And no one in the camp appeared to have any concerns that something was about to happen?"

"Not that I was made aware."

"No increased security? No precautionary measures?"

"As I said, I am unaware of what anyone in the camp might or might not have known."

"And what about you, Ms. Winslow?" Carmody asked. "Were you aware that an attack was imminent?"

She didn't know whose side this man was on and she wasn't about to provide him with ammunition. She didn't want to lie, either. She'd heard of too many people strangled in their own webs of deception. If she only had some idea what he wanted. Who he wanted—Dacar, Max, her father? Her? Had her father breached security by contacting her the night before? But that made no sense—everyone involved here at *Camp Lemonnier* knew of it—the security level couldn't have been that high. And why *not* inform her? She would have known when the Black Hawks arrived less than ten hours after her father's call. "I had no idea the attack was coming. If I had, I assure you I would not have gone blithely to sleep and waited for it."

"How long have you and your team been out there?"

Another matter of record. Nevertheless, telling him what he already knew cost her nothing. "A little over two months."

"And you've had no trouble from rebels?"

"No, none."

"And what about your supply lines. How often do you see Americans?"

Rachel frowned. "I'm sorry, I don't understand. We don't see who delivers the supplies—as least, I don't. The closest road, if you can call it that, ends in the nearest occupied village about twenty miles away. Some of our people make the trip by UTV and pick up our supplies at that point. The bulk of our camp—tents, foodstuffs, medicine, and equipment—was airlifted and set up before I arrived."

"You've never accompanied anyone from your camp to this village?"

"No. It's usually an all-day trip and I have other duties."

"And you've never seen any Americans accompanying anyone at the camp?"

"No."

"What about Somali locals? Anyone strike you as unusual or a frequent visitor?"

"Unusual? I don't think one ever gets used to starving men, women, and children, but no—nothing stands out that I recall."

"How about men with rifles?"

Rachel smiled. "That has become a little more usual."

"How much contact did you have with the rebels between the attack and the time of your rescue?"

Rachel stiffened. "None, thankfully."

"You never saw anyone near the camp?"

She was staring through the tent flap again into the blinding sun, holding an unfamiliar weapon while a man who tried to save her life writhed in pain behind her. The jungle closed in around her, filled with ominous shadows. She saw monsters everywhere. "No, no one."

"How about Commander de Milles? How often did she go out to meet someone?"

Ice cascaded along Rachel's nerve endings. The jungle receded, the heavy air lifted, and she could breathe again. Think again. The enemy was no longer faceless. She was looking at him. "Never."

A carefully arched brow, one she swore had been waxed to a perfect line, twitched upward. "Never? She never left the camp?"

"That's not what you asked me. Yes, she checked to see that we were not in immediate danger from rebels close to the camp."

"And how do you know she didn't meet anyone?"

"I never heard gunfire, and if she had run into rebels, there would have been."

"Well, that assumes she ran into an enemy."

"And," Rachel said, wishing she had that rifle back again, "I know because I followed her."

Captain Pettit coughed softly.

Carmody stared at her, a flat appraising gaze that looked a lot like the way a snake regarded a mouse right before it struck. "You followed her into the jungle. Where you could have run into landmines or rebel forces?"

"I'm afraid I wasn't thinking about that at the time. But yes, I followed her."

"That was very brave of you."

"What exactly do you think happened out there, Agent Carmody?" Rachel said, tired of his games.

"I think you're very lucky to be alive," he said softly.

"I wouldn't be if it weren't for Commander de Milles and the others." She shifted her attention from Carmody and faced Pettit. "I'd like to use the phone now, and I'd like to see Commander de Milles and Lieutenant Griffin. I owe them my life and I'd like to thank them personally."

"I'll see that you're given privacy for your call," Captain Pettit said.

Rachel rose, pleased that her legs were not shaking. "Thank you."

Pettit reached for a phone on his desk. "Chief, could you please take Ms. Winslow to the com room." Pettit hung up and addressed Rachel. "When you're finished, someone will escort you to the hospital."

"Thank you once again, Captain, for all you and your troops have done for me and my team." Rachel let her gaze pass over Carmody, who stared back, before walking to the door.

The chief petty officer led her through another series of hallways into a large room where half a dozen people sat in front of computer terminals, large maps, and monitors showing aerial views of what looked like miles of uninhabited jungle and desert. The detail of objects on the ground was startling—she could practically count the branches on some of the trees. She'd been out there somewhere just hours before. She wondered if the people in this room had been able to see her.

"This way, ma'am." The chief took her to a small room separated from the larger one by a plain wooden door in a windowless wall. The room held a desk, shelves with stacks of papers and field manuals, and a landline.

"You can call direct on that, ma'am."

"Thank you, Chief. And how might I get to the hospital?"

"I'll arrange for a driver to wait out front, ma'am."

"Thank you. I appreciate it."

"Yes, ma'am."

He left, shutting the door behind him, and Rachel slumped onto the metal chair behind the desk. She stared at the phone and wondered how secure it might be. Strange, she felt less safe here surrounded by those she was supposed to trust to keep her safe than she had in the jungle with only Max between her and all the demons that surrounded them. Max. Now Max might be in danger, maybe Grif too. A wave of hot fury washed through her. She reached for the phone and dialed her father's direct number. He always had his calls forwarded to his cell no matter where he might be. She needed information, and he was never out of the loop. She couldn't fight an enemy she couldn't recognize, and it was her turn to stand between Max and whatever lurked in the shadows.

Chapter Nineteen

How's Grif?" Max asked as Tim McCullough, the corpsman on duty who'd walked in while she was hunting for her clothes, taped a square of gauze over her IV site.

"They just finished working on him a couple minutes ago." The red-haired, blue-eyed, fresh-faced twenty-year-old looked like he belonged on the porch of a fraternity house somewhere, drinking beer and bothering girls, not out here putting together the maimed and the mutilated. His eyes when they met hers were the age of someone who'd already seen too much and knew there was worse to come. "You ought to stay here for a couple more doses of IV antibiotics."

"Just give me the pills." She could tell when she moved her arm the wound was just soft tissue. Painful but not a long-term problem. She wanted out of the hospital so she could find Rachel, or at least find someone who would know if she was safe somewhere, and she wanted out from under prying eyes and questions. Her nameless friend from the morning would be back, and before she answered any more questions, she wanted to talk to the other team members and find out what the hell was going on. She couldn't do any of that lying on her back with an IV line running into her arm. "And tell the AOD I'll take full responsibility."

McCullough barked out a laugh. "Fuck that. If I say you're good to go, he won't argue. If I was you, I'd want out of here too. Just take the fucking pills."

"Thanks. I will." Her stomach tightened. She didn't remember the last half of the flight back, but she remembered taking fire. "Did they bring any of the civilians in here?"

"No. You and Grif were the only casualties from that run. He's still in recovery from the leg wash out. Probably won't be awake for a while."

Max exhaled slowly. "How are the guys from earlier?"

"Everything was pretty minor—Burns will be heading home for shoulder reconstruction. The others will recoup here for a few days and be back on active in a week or so."

"Good." She was just as glad Grif wouldn't be talking for a while. Maybe by the time he came around, whoever had sent her visitor would have gotten what they wanted and called off their dogs. "What was the name of the guy who was in here earlier?"

McCullough shook his head. "He didn't say."

"Who brought him?"

Another head shake. "He just walked in. Had a vehicle out front and a base pass from the CO. Said he wanted to talk to you in private."

"Did he say anything about Grif?"

"Wanted a sit rep. We gave it to him. Same I just gave you."

"Okay. Do me a favor, if he comes back to see Grif, call me."

"I don't think you want to get in the middle of that."

Max smiled. "Yeah, but I do. Where's Grif now?"

"I'll check."

Max pulled on the clean BDUs McCullough had left on the bed and had just managed to get the fly buttoned when he returned.

"Grif's pretty zoned. Like I said, he won't know you were there."

"Yeah," Max said, "he will."

McCullough shrugged. "Come on."

Grif looked disconcertingly vulnerable with the tubes and lines attaching him to monitors and IVs. She gripped his hand and leaned close. "Hey, Grif, it's Deuce. You're back at base, in the hospital. You're doing fine." She wondered when he'd be transported to one of the regional hospitals. A wave of loneliness caught her by surprise. Rachel was already gone, and soon Grif would be too. She cleared her throat. "Oh, and your equipment all checks out. Laurie will be happy about that. Just make sure you get your ass out of bed and get through rehab quick so you can get home where you belong." She released his hand and straightened. "See you, buddy."

She walked out just as the sun came up. She'd been right the night before. By dawn, it was all over.

❖

"Dad, it's me."

"I was informed you were all right."

Rachel almost laughed. She supposed she was all right, by all ordinary criteria. Physically, she was bruised and scraped and scratched and sore, but nothing that wouldn't mend with some sleep, good food, and a week or so of anti-inflammatories. Somewhere inside, though, she was bleeding. That would mend too, but she wondered about the scars. When she looked in Max's eyes, she realized the shadows she saw were really scars. "I am. I'm fine. Thank you."

"We've been in touch with the embassy. Arrangements are being made for your transport stateside. I imagine we can get you headed home in the next twenty-four hours." He paused and when Rachel didn't reply went on with the merest hint of irritation. "Is there something else you need?"

"What? No. I don't need anything." Home. She immediately thought of her tent and Amina sleeping across from her. Wasn't home simply the place where you felt most yourself? She tried to imagine herself in her condo in Manhattan, making fundraising calls and organizing meetings with donors, or at a political gathering disguised as a dinner party at her parents' mansion in Falls Creek, accompanied by a beautiful woman with all the right breeding and all the right credentials who was looking for just the right wife. Those places seemed more like a foreign country to her than the stark, arid plains and dense, overpowering jungles of Somalia ever had. The people here—Amina, Grif, Max—knew her better than anyone from her past. "Dad. I'm not leaving right away."

"What? You can't be thinking about returning to the aid camp. From the reports, it's been pretty much demolished and that whole area is a rebel stronghold."

"No, I'm not thinking about going back," she said, and the words hurt. She'd accomplished something there, touched lives, made a difference. Now it was all lost. But that didn't mean her conviction had been shattered. If anything, her desire to bring resources to those who had none was even stronger. "I want to meet with the organization directors in Mogadishu, and I need to see that the other members of the team are all taken care of."

"Rachel," he said in that flat voice he used when he'd made a decision and didn't see any point in further discussion, "there are certain circumstances of which you're unaware—"

"I think I know what some of those circumstances are," she said, thinking of Carmody's interrogation. She suspected some kind of interagency power struggle was going on, and she'd ended up in the middle of it either by virtue of being in the wrong place at the wrong time, or because she was her father's daughter. "I'd be happy if you filled me in so I'm not guessing."

"I'm afraid that's something I can't go into right now. Suffice it to say your continued presence in the area is not a good idea."

"Unless I'm given a credible reason to leave that doesn't have to do with some kind of political agenda, I'm staying."

"I really don't think it's wise for you to linger. That entire region is not nearly as stable as you might think."

She did laugh then, a hollow sound that almost hurt. "Dad. I think I know that better than most. I just saw three of my friends murdered yesterday morning."

"I'm…sorry you had to witness that. Obviously the plan to get you out was not as well-executed as it should have been. Believe me, we're looking into that."

"Dad, do you know someone by the name of Carmody?"

"Should I?"

"I think so." She doubted Carmody was her father's man—he'd never have interrogated her the way he did. So if he wasn't on her father's side, maybe he was against him. She'd probably already said too much on a line she couldn't trust was secure. "He's been around."

"Has he." Her father's voice had grown cold, and she could see the diamond edge to his eyes as he considered all the ramifications of a stranger probing into an operation involving not only his daughter, but security at the major US base in the region.

"I spoke with him briefly earlier."

"Interesting. And perhaps another reason for you to reconsider your stay."

"I appreciate your concern, but I'll be fine. Could you put in a word for me with Captain Pettit for transport and that sort of thing?"

"That's already taken care of, but if you insist on staying, I'll assign security to you. They can drive you and see to anything else you might need. Someone will be there before the end of the day."

"That's not necessary—"

"Rachel, there are times when I know better than you."

"Are there any times when you don't?"

He sighed. "I'd hoped this trip and a firsthand look at the realities of these situations would temper your enthusiasm, if not your stubborn streak. I can see that it hasn't."

"No," she said softly, thinking of the hours in the foxhole, peering into the dark—looking where she once would rather have looked away. She'd been changed, but not in the way he'd hoped. "I need to stay."

"Then I'm afraid you don't have any choice. If you're staying, you'll have protection. Otherwise, you'll be on a plane this afternoon."

He knew she'd accept. They'd played this game all her life. She had no choice and he knew it. She didn't know the area, she didn't have any personal resources readily available, and she couldn't disregard safety issues. She wasn't foolhardy about her own well-being, and she wouldn't put her father and others in political jeopardy by making herself a target, even though she seriously doubted she was in danger. The best she could do was accept his compromise. All things considered, he was giving in without as much of a fight as she might have expected. "All right."

He paused. "I'll be in touch."

"I love you. Say hi to Mother for me. Tell her I love her."

"Yes. Well. See that you take care of yourself."

"I will," she whispered.

The line went dead and she slowly set down the receiver.

Her vision blurred. She was so very tired. All the false energy, and probably false courage, the adrenaline had provided had burned away now that she was safe. Safe was relative, she supposed, but at least no one was likely to shoot her here. The idea of curling up under the covers and closing her eyes was incredibly appealing, except she feared when she closed her eyes she'd be back in that hot humid tent, listening for the sounds of someone coming to kill her. She straightened and rubbed her tired eyes. Her weary, bruised, and battered mind could form only one thought. She wanted to see Max. With the world coming apart around her, Max was the only island of sanity.

Chapter Twenty

A re you sure about this, ma'am?" the driver asked.

Rachel stared at the sand-colored metal box and tried to imagine living inside it. She guessed it to be about twenty feet long—it would fit inside her family's garage with room to spare for a few of their five cars. Two wooden steps without a railing led up to a single door with a shaded Plexiglas window. At about the midpoint of the long side, another window was filled by the rear end of an air-conditioning unit extending out several inches. The roof was flat. It looked like every other metal box in row after row of metal boxes lined up along dirt lanes just wide enough for two Humvees to pass in opposite directions. The stenciled black letters *C-19* were the only things distinguishing it from the others. She swallowed. "Yes."

"Would you like me to wait?"

She studied her surroundings through the front and back windows of the Humvee. She could maneuver the streets of an unfamiliar city with an unerring sixth sense of direction, but left alone in this repetitive maze she might just wander forever. "Where are we, exactly?"

"At the northeast corner of CLUville—that's what we call this part of the base."

"And where would headquarters be?"

He pointed forward. "About twenty, twenty-five minutes in that direction if you're a brisk walker and don't mind the heat."

"I'll be fine. There's no need for you to wait."

He squinted past her at the living unit. "Yes, ma'am."

He sounded about as uncertain as she felt and his indecision was enough to spur her out of the vehicle. She needed to do this. "Thank you again for the ride."

"Yes, ma'am."

She took a few steps away and paused, waiting for him to drive away. He hesitated, nodded to her, and finally left. Turning, she climbed the two stairs and rapped on the door. Nothing happened.

She didn't really want to call attention to herself since technically she wasn't supposed to be wandering around the base. When she looked behind her, she was alone. She knocked again. "Max? Max, it's Rachel."

Please, be here. I don't know where else to look.

The sun beat down on the back of her neck, heating her already too-sensitive skin. She'd managed over two months in-country without getting a bad burn, but one day standing guard while Max dug the foxhole had put an end to all her care. The sunburn was a not-so-welcome reminder of where she'd been at this time the day before. She'd have to think about it sometime, just not right now. Right now she'd like very much to forget.

"Max, please. If you're there—"

The door inched open and she stepped down to the bottom step to make room for it to swing by her. Max stood in the doorway in olive-green boxers and a matching T-shirt. A clean white bandage circled her right upper arm. Her hair was damp and wavier than Rachael expected, clinging to her neck in lazy curls that made her look sexy and unexpectedly carefree. Her long, lean legs were tanned, another surprise. Her feet were bare. A darker green oval between her small breasts indicated a spot she'd missed drying after her shower or maybe a trickle of sweat that had collected in the shallow valley in the center of her chest. Rachel had to drag her gaze away from that spot and the image of the soft curves of flesh on either side. When she looked up, Max's eyes sparked with a quick glimmer of heat and something darker. Something hungry.

"I thought you'd left," Max said.

"I didn't." Rachel's heart pounded wildly. "I thought you were in the hospital."

"I was. How did you find me?"

"I badgered the medic to tell me where you probably were."

Max smiled wryly. "Did you see Grif?"

"I asked—he was still asleep."

"Yeah." Max sighed and ran a hand through her hair, ruffling it further. "You okay?"

"Not so much, really." Rachel had never found asking for anything easy, but any pretense of being fine after all that had happened was wasted on Max. She had to know better. "Can I come in?"

Rachel's vulnerability caught Max by surprise and her first impulse was to pull Rachel inside and keep her safe. But they weren't outside the wire now and things were a lot more complicated. Rachel had faint circles below her eyes and a weariness in their depths Max recognized and wished she didn't. Her face was pale, except for streaks of sunburn over the arch of her cheekbones and down her neck. Her auburn hair shimmered with gold highlights, bits of sunlight trapped in the thick strands that made Max want to bury her fingers there to warm them. The khaki fatigues fit her surprisingly well, almost naturally, and when she squinted against the sun, tiny lines radiated out from the corners of her eyes. She was more beautiful even than Max remembered.

"I can't vouch for my housekeeping."

Rachel shaded her eyes. "Is it any cooler in there than it is out here?"

"Maybe ten degrees."

"Sounds like heaven."

Max stepped back and Rachel climbed into her CLU. Other than Grif stopping by now and then for a quick drink after a duty shift, she'd never had a visitor. She saw it as Rachel must see it—stark and impersonal and empty. A lot like her inside.

"This is my bunk down here." She led the way past CC's neatly made rack with the shelf above that held family photos and mementos from home to her own bare cubicle. She didn't have any photos on the wall or other items from another life lying around. She smoothed the wrinkled blanket on the bed and kicked a pair of fatigue pants into the corner. An open bottle of whiskey sat on the floor, and since there wasn't much to do about that, she just left it there. She pointed to the single chair heaped with clothes. "Sorry. Not much in the way of accommodations."

"This is fine." Rachel stopped her in the midst of moving the pile.

"Really. Any place that isn't crawling with bugs where I'm not likely to be shot at works just fine for me. Do you mind if I just sit on your bed?"

"No," Max said, trying to figure out where she should go when Rachel sat on one end of her bed. Finally she just sat down beside her.

"How is your arm?" Rachel asked.

"Fine."

"I was surprised they let you out so soon."

Max grinned the grin Rachel recognized, just a little cocky and just a little bad. Rachel laughed and the bubble of happiness eased some of the ache in her chest. "Ah, I see now. They didn't *let* you do anything. You strong-armed—"

"Come on, it's not quite that bad," Max said. "We have kind of a treat 'em and street 'em attitude around here. Nobody wants to be laid up in a hospital tent, and unless an injury is so severe it's going to require prolonged recovery and rehab, everybody is just as happy getting back to duty."

Back to duty, as if the danger and risk were just a normal part of life out here. For Max, the day before had probably been close to routine. What for Rachel would be a lifelong horrific memory was only one of hundreds of horrors that Max had seen. She touched Max's arm. "When will you fly again?"

"Maybe never, this time around. I'm due to ship back to the States in a few days, at least I was. I'm not so sure right now."

"Why?" Rachel asked.

Max hesitated, and that was unlike her. Rachel had never known her to be anything but straightforward. She took a wild guess. "This have anything to do with someone named Carmody?"

Max's eyes narrowed. "Does he happen to be early forties, square top, cold eyes, definitely unfriendly?"

"You forgot the snake in the grass part."

"Yeah, that's him. He bother you?" Max's tone was dark and tinged with belligerence.

"Bother me." Rachel smiled. For a moment, Max reminded her of a high school girlfriend wanting to protect her from the unwanted advances of the boys on the football team. A silly thought, but the idea pleased her. "Yes, I think you could definitely say that. Did he bother you too?"

As if reading her mind, Max laughed and the darkness left her eyes. "Quite a bit."

Rachel sighed. She wished Carmody was as harmless as an adolescent boy with too much testosterone and an overinflated ego. Carmody wasn't a nuisance, he was dangerous. "What do you think's going on?"

"I don't know. He didn't give much away." Max took her hand. "It shouldn't matter too much to you, though. You're a civilian, and I imagine you'll be heading home pretty soon."

"No, not right away." Rachel slid her fingers between Max's, the connection so natural she almost didn't realize she'd done it. "I want to go to our headquarters in Mogadishu. I need to follow up with the team to make sure everyone's all right."

Max frowned. "You know, it's possible that raid yesterday was aimed at you. Mog is still a pretty rough place. Maybe you should rethink that trip."

"I can't imagine why I would have been a target. I've been out there for weeks, and no one paid me the slightest attention."

"You don't know that. And these groups are unpredictable—you never know what they have planned."

"I won't take chances," Rachel said, appreciating Max's concern. Max, unlike her father, hadn't told her what to do, even though she could see Max was worried. "I promise."

"A lot of people seem to be interested in you." Max rested their joined hands on her bare knee. "Who are you, Rachel?"

Rachel met Max's steady gaze. Her eyes were so blue, so easy to fall into. Rachel caught her breath. Who was she? That was the question, wasn't it? To her father she was a stubborn, problematic daughter who wouldn't embrace the party line. To her mother she was the disappointing daughter who rejected her mother's values and refused to follow in her footsteps. To the women who purported to desire her, she was either a trophy or a stepping stone. Only out here had she'd ever felt like herself. Only Max had ever seen her. "You know who I am, don't you, Max?"

"Well, I know certain things," Max said, feeling the weight of every word. Knowing somehow what she said mattered more than anything she'd ever said to anyone. The intensity in Rachel's gaze was almost a plea. "I know you're not afraid to face danger. I know you're stubborn and independent. I know you're loyal to your friends and committed to your mission. And I know—" Max paused, searching for the lines she shouldn't cross. She was tired but she'd only had one drink before she'd decided she'd rather think about Rachel than forget her, and she knew what she was saying. What she wanted to say. "I know you're really beautiful. I especially like the way the green of your eyes changes when you're angry or when you're—" She stopped. Maybe that line wasn't hers to draw.

"Or what?" Rachel asked. "When I'm what, Max?"

The whir of the air-conditioning unit sounded like the rasp of insects in the underbrush. The CLU was dim, the air heavy, like twilight in the jungle. They might have been a hundred miles away from civilization, just the two of them, alone, in a timeless, ageless world.

Rachel's lips parted and she moistened them with the tip of her tongue. Her gaze held Max's and her fingers lightly brushed the bare skin of Max's thigh. "Max? Are they changing color now?"

"Yes."

"And you know why, don't you," Rachel whispered.

Max swallowed. Her skin flamed where Rachel's fingers rested and heat scorched along her spine and simmered in the pit of her stomach. Her fingertips, her lips, her nipples tingled. She was breathing too fast. Overdrive. Overload.

"I need to kiss you."

Rachel's lips lifted at the corners and the forest green of her eyes glinted with gold warmer than sunlight. "Do you?"

Max leaned closer until her mouth was only millimeters from Rachel's. "So bad, or else…"

"Or…?"

"Certain parts of me might burst into flames."

Rachel's fingertips slid beneath the lower edge of Max's boxers. Her palm pressed into Max's thigh. Her chest brushed Max's bare upper arm. Her lips skimmed over Max's jaw. "You're not supposed to incinerate until *after* you kiss me."

"Kissing you won't burn me up." Max's chest felt as if a grenade was about to go off inside. "I think…" She gasped. She was so hot everywhere. So hot, so parched, as scorched as the land that had seared her soul. Rachel's lips were so cool against her skin. "I think kissing you will be like falling into cool clear water."

"Find out," Rachel murmured.

Max groaned softly and covered Rachel's mouth with hers. Rachel leaned into her and their lips reformed against one another, reshaping, fitting together, exchanging softness for softness. The tip of Rachel's tongue skated over the surface of Max's lower lip and was gone too soon. Max slid her palm around the back of Rachel's neck and held her still, changing the angle of her kiss, tugging Rachel's lower lip between hers, savoring the silky fullness between her teeth.

Rachel moaned softly and pressed closer until Max fell back on one elbow and pulled Rachel down with her. Rachel sprawled across her chest, both of them with their feet still on the floor, hands and mouths grasping and seeking. Rachel half crawled on top of her and Max groaned.

Rachel gasped and tried to sit up. "Oh God, your arm. I forgot about your arm!"

"My arm's perfect." Max pulled Rachel's mouth back to hers. She'd been right. Kissing Rachel was like sliding naked into a crystal-clear mountain lake, brisk and refreshing and incredibly exciting. Every cell vibrated with energy, her nerve endings tingled. She felt clean and alive in places she hadn't realized had been numb and lifeless. She wanted to be naked. She wanted Rachel on top of her, under her, sliding over her like water cascading down a mountainside. She wanted to drown in her.

Rachel pushed up Max's T-shirt and stroked her stomach, making Max's hips jerk and her clitoris tense beneath the thin cotton of her boxers. Rachel took her time exploring Max's body, slowly edging the T-shirt up to the undersides of her breasts, stroking her fingers up and down the center of her belly. Max struggled to stay still, to let her look and touch, to expose what she kept hidden. When Rachel's thumb brushed under the cotton and over her breast, she shuddered.

"Rachel, I can't—"

"God, you have a beautiful body." Rachel's gaze was locked on Max's body, her expression fierce. When she looked up, the hunger in her eyes stole Max's breath. "I can't believe how amazing you are. I want to see you naked."

"Rachel…"

"I know." Rachel's eyes burned into hers. "It's crazy. I know. I don't do this sort of thing—no, that's a lie, I do, I have. But never like this. God, Max. I've never wanted to touch anyone so much."

"It's—"

Rachel pressed her fingers to Max's mouth. "I don't care what it is. I don't care if it's the aftermath of stress or the reaffirmation of life or laughing in the face of evil. I don't care about any of that. I think you're gorgeous and sexy and strong. I don't think I've ever been so excited in my life. Don't stop kissing me."

"I won't." Max couldn't stop. If she pushed Rachel away, the last struggling remnant of her soul would wither and she would be nothing but a shell. She dragged Rachel all the way onto the bed until they faced each other on the rough military-issue blanket, heart to heart, body to body. She kissed her. "I won't stop until you tell me to."

Chapter Twenty-one

Rachel couldn't bear to lose touch with Max's lips. Max's mouth was as captivating as her eyes—intense and commanding and exquisitely gentle. She felt as if she'd never been kissed before. She hadn't. Not like this. Not when the merest brush of flesh on flesh drove a spike of pleasure into her depths, sharp and bright and brilliant. She traced the sweep of Max's cheekbones with her fingertips and wove her fingers through her hair. Max was the heat she hadn't known she wanted—the flame that pushed back the dark. She arched against her, craving the pressure of Max's body against her breasts, her belly, her thighs. Max was strong, all hard muscle and bone, and breathtakingly tender, her hands and mouth gliding over Rachel's face in soft benediction. Max and only Max had ever wanted to see her, know her, touch her. Closer. More. Her clothes were in the way. Max's clothes were in the way. She wanted to climb inside her. She wanted Max inside her. She couldn't get her breath.

"You feel right." Max stroked Rachel's throat and slid one hand lower, lightly skimming over Rachel's breasts to her waist. "Holding you feels right."

"Yes. No. Not enough," Rachel gasped. "I want your hands on me everywhere. God, I'm losing my mind."

Max opened the first button on Rachel's shirt and slipped her hand inside. "Maybe you are. But if you are, so am I."

Rachel grinned. "Good. Because I don't want to be crazy without you."

Max laughed and nipped at Rachel's chin. She kissed her throat and teased her fingertips beneath the cotton stretched tight across

Rachel's breasts, circling closer to Rachel's nipple with each stroke. "We might want to slow down just a little, though."

"Why? I can't think of a single reason." Rachel pulled Max on top of her and arched when Max's thigh came to rest between hers. She covered the hand Max had slipped under her plain dark military-issue bra and pressed Max's fingers into her breast. The pressure made her want to come and for a second her mind blanked. She groaned and her vision swam. She was too close, too soon. "I can't think at all."

Max braced herself on her good arm and looked down into Rachel's eyes. "All those things you said earlier. About stress and laughing at death and all that. I don't want you to regret—"

"Do you always worry so much when you go to bed with a woman?"

"No, but this isn't like that."

Rachel stroked Max's face. "I know. I don't know what it is, exactly. But I know it's like nothing else."

"I feel like I've never touched a woman before," Max whispered.

Rachel jolted, her clitoris swelling so fast she nearly came. "And you think I could stop now?" She yanked Max's mouth back to hers.

Max's kiss was like her—strong and gentle, slow and deep, a kiss that touched her in places where nothing ever had. Rachel pushed both hands under Max's T-shirt and caressed her back, smoothing her palms over the columns of muscle and bone and smooth skin. Even with her eyes closed, she could see Max with every stroke. Sensation was everywhere—immeasurable pleasure, wonder, and fearsome awe. She kissed Max's throat, tasted her—clean and vital. "What is it? This power you have over me?"

Max shook her head. "No. Not me." She rested her forehead on Rachel's. "It's you. I can feel you inside me, filling up all the empty places. I don't want to stop."

"Then don't." Rachel wrapped her calf over Max's leg. Max's eyes were so deep and so dark Rachel should have been afraid of getting lost in them, but she wasn't. This was a darkness that thrilled her. "I've never been more sure of anything in my life. Make love to me, Max."

Max opened the rest of the buttons on Rachel's shirt, parted the fabric, and rubbed her cheek over the valley between her breasts. Rachel's nipples tightened beneath the material that restrained her breasts. Her breasts ached and she clasped Max's head, guiding her to the spot where her nipple peaked. "Please."

Max cupped her breast, long fingers closing around her sensitized flesh, squeezing, spearing the pleasure into her core. Rachel moaned. Never like this. Never. Max's teeth closed around her nipple, tugging it through the fabric. Lights burst behind Rachel's closed lids. Her heart pounded. Her breath fled. She stiffened, gasped. Panic raced through her. Explosions, screams in the dark.

"Oh my God!" Rachel jerked away.

"Rachel?" Max raised her head. "What just happened?"

"I'm sorry. I'm sorry." Rachel clung to Max and buried her face in the curve of her neck. "That was—God. For a second, I was back there. The explosions, the blood, the…dead. I'm sorry."

"Hey, what are you apologizing for?" Max held her tightly and rolled onto her side, keeping Rachel close against her. She kissed her temple and wrapped one leg over Rachel's hips to pull her into the cradle of her body. "I see them too sometimes. Most times."

Rachel shuddered. "How do you make it stop?"

"You don't. At least I haven't." Max ran her hands up and down Rachel's back, stroking and stroking, not knowing what else to do. "Sometimes I drink. Well, a lot of times I drink."

Rachel raised her head. "Does it help?"

Max grimaced. "No. But it's better than walking outside the wire and waiting for an RPG to fall on my head."

Rachel pushed herself up and ran her hands through her hair. "Have you tried that too?"

Max hesitated. They'd already gone so far past anything she'd ever shared with anyone, physically and in every other way. But this— this was her secret torment. Her secret shame. Hers was a false bravery, born not of valor but out of a need to prove her own worth. She couldn't even honor their sacrifice with true courage. If Rachel knew she was no warrior but a reluctant participant haunted by nightmares and regret, what would she think? And if she didn't tell her, everything between them would be a lie. "A few times, yeah. Tempting fate, maybe. I don't know, maybe I thought I didn't deserve to still be around when so many weren't."

"Oh, Max." Rachel sighed and stroked her face. "I'm so sorry."

"Listen, I'm okay. At least no worse than anyone else. And you—you have nothing to be ashamed about." Max sat up and clasped Rachel's hand. "What happened out there, you weren't ready for that. No one ever is, but at least we're military. We train for it, we know it might be coming, we have more time to prepare. Now you're exhausted, stressed, and in mourning for those you lost. I'd be surprised if you *weren't* having flashbacks." She squeezed Rachel's fingers. "When you're home, if it keeps up, you can talk to someone. Okay?"

"Is that the doctor saying *Do as I say* or do you actually take your own advice?"

Max glanced at the half-empty bottle on the floor. "Not all the time."

"Well," Rachel said, her voice sounding a little stronger, "I will take your advice when I get home. For now, I wouldn't mind a little of your remedy."

Max laughed and reached for the bottle. She uncapped it and handed it to Rachel. "Sorry I don't have any—"

Rachel took the bottle, swallowed a healthy amount, and coughed violently, tears forming in her eyes. "Yep, just as vile as I remember." She handed it back to Max. "Thanks. I think."

Max set the bottle down and slipped an arm around Rachel's shoulders. "Better?"

Rachel caressed Max's thigh and rested her palm on the inside of her bare leg. A faint scar ran across the muscle, doing nothing to mar the beauty. "You've been taking care of me for the last two days. I appreciate it."

"I don't want your gratitude." Max cupped her face. "I'd like to kiss you again."

"Yes," Rachel whispered, "I'd like that very much."

Max's kiss was a slow, lingering kiss that feathered along the torn and tattered edges of Rachel's soul, soothing her, comforting her, kindling the fire again. Rachel gripped Max's shoulders and kissed her harder, delving deeper, pressing her breasts to Max's, sliding a leg over Max's hips until she straddled her in the middle of Max's bed. "I want you."

Max cupped Rachel's ass and pulled her tight against her hard abdomen. Rachel rolled her hips and felt her control fray. When she would have pulled back with anyone else, she thrust harder, willing her body to explode. Max pushed both hands under her shirt and clasped her breasts, and Rachel threw back her head and laughed. "You do things to me with all my clothes on I've never felt naked."

Max kissed between her breasts. "I'd just as soon have you naked."

"God, yes." Rachel stripped off her shirt, pulled off her bra, and threw them onto the floor behind them. She pressed her breasts to Max's face. "Put your mouth on me."

Max lifted Rachel's breasts in her hands and sucked her nipple into her mouth. Rachel's clitoris pulsed and she rocked harder against Max's belly. "Like that. Just. Like. That."

"You like that," Max said, her voice low and self-satisfied.

"Oh yes."

Max's fingers closed over her other nipple, squeezing one as her mouth tugged the other.

Light exploded behind Rachel's eyelids, bright bursts of white and red and yellow, and she wasn't afraid. The dark gave way to light and pleasure rolled through her. "Max. *Max…*"

Max gripped Rachel's hips and pulled her tighter against her body, her mouth and fingers working in time to Rachel's thrusts. Rachel clenched her fists in Max's hair and watched Max make her explode. "Oh my God."

Max pressed her cheek to Rachel's breast and held her close until her shudders stopped. When Rachel collapsed, she kissed her. "You're so beautiful I think my heart stopped."

Rachel couldn't move. She was completely demolished. "My God. I've never…I didn't…I have never come like that in my life."

Max laughed. "I said you were amazing."

"I think you did all the work," Rachel said, her words lazy and slow.

"Believe me, that wasn't work."

Rachel licked a drop of sweat from Max's throat. She tasted salty and powerful. She wanted her again. She was losing her sanity here. "All the same, you have no idea what you do to me."

Max kissed her. "I think I might a little. Because you…you make me feel like a god."

Rachel braced her hands on Max's shoulders and pushed herself up until they were eye to eye. "I might've called you God there a time or two—okay, maybe ten—but don't let it go to your head."

Max nipped at Rachel's chin and kissed her again. "You can't put the genie back in the bottle."

"Oh, I don't want to put it back." Rachel kissed her hard. She was half-naked, totally exposed in every way, and incredibly alive. Max had been the first to see her as she was, the first to touch her where it mattered. The last thing she wanted was to undo any of it. Desire rose again, hot and hard and fast. "I want to do it again. I want you."

"Let's start with the getting you naked part." Max reached for the button on Rachel's pants.

"Not just yet." Rachel shifted onto her knees and pushed Max back onto the bed. She grabbed the bottom of Max's T-shirt and shoved it up over her breasts. She wore nothing under the shirt. Her breasts were small and firm with perfectly centered pale pink nipples. Rachel's throat went dry and she tugged at the shirt while she stared. "Off."

Max grabbed the bottom and had it halfway off when a sharp rap on the metal frame ricocheted through the space. Max froze.

A deep male voice called, "Commander de Milles. Open up, please."

Max half sat up. "Rachel, stay back here."

"Why? Who is it?" Rachel whispered.

Max gripped her around the waist and moved her aside as if she weighed nothing. "Get dressed."

Suddenly chilled, Rachel fumbled for the bra and shirt as Max yanked on a pair of pants and shoved her feet barefoot into her boots. Max glanced down, saw that Rachel was dressed, and said, "Just stay here. You'll be fine."

"Max—"

Max strode through the CLU and pushed open the door, holding it at arm's length. Rachel followed and looked over her shoulder. Two bulky men in blue camo BDUs stood at the foot of the steps with their arms folded across their chests. Both wore caps pulled down so low their eyes were barely visible. Neither smiled.

"If you'll come with us, Commander," one of them said.

Nothing in their expressions indicated they even saw Rachel.

Max didn't move. "Ms. Winslow will need transportation to her quarters."

"We'll arrange for that, Commander."

Max turned to Rachel. "Wait here. Someone will come to take you back."

"What's going on? Who are they?"

"I have to go." Max smiled, her smile crooked and weary. "Go home, Rachel—get out of this place."

Another Humvee pulled up behind the one idling in front of Max's CLU. A man and a woman got out, both dressed in desert khakis. Both were white, trim and tanned, in their early thirties. Both looked a lot like Carmody. The woman, a brunette with a perfect face that registered absolutely nothing, walked up beside the uniformed men. "Ms. Winslow. We'll take you back to your quarters."

Rachel gripped the back of Max's T-shirt, as if she could keep her there, away from these strangers. Keep her safe. "Thank you, but I'm fine. I'm going with Commander de Milles."

Max reached behind her back and gently eased Rachel's fingers free. "You're not part of this, Rachel. Go home."

"But—"

Max strode down onto the hard dry ground and said to the two men, "Let's get out of here."

Rachel watched them pile into the Humvee and drive away. Max never looked back.

Chapter Twenty-two

The Humvee disappeared around the corner, and Rachel was left standing on the steps of Max's CLU in the hot, bright sun. A burst of annoyance helped push aside the wave of sadness left in Max's wake. Max saw her as she wanted—needed—to be seen, but she still had more to learn if she believed for a second Rachel would leave her now. Squinting into the glare, she looked down at the two people regarding her impassively. "Who are you?"

The woman held out her hand. "Abigail Kennedy."

Her accent said New England, her carriage and demeanor said privilege. She was in her early thirties, with medium-length, sun-streaked brown hair, professionally cut into a casual, layered, easy-to-care-for style that would look good out in the desert or at a cocktail party. Clear, straightforward blue-eyed gaze. Perfect heart-shaped face, nicely proportioned straight nose, full-lipped smile. Very pretty and trying to play it down with the absence of any makeup, no jewelry of any kind, and the same neutral-colored shirt and pants everyone wore in one form or another. Her attempt to blend in couldn't quite hide her breeding or her background. Rachel had seen a thousand like her growing up in DC, at prep school, then college, and later at diplomatic events she'd been obligated to attend with her parents. Women like her generally wanted to be in charge, but they'd never go outside the wire, as Max would say. They'd order someone else to do that. Under other circumstances she might not have judged her quite so harshly, but right now she wasn't given to being nice.

Kennedy still held out her hand and Rachel shook it briefly. Cool and confident, just like Abigail Kennedy.

Rachel looked at the man who stood a pace behind Kennedy. Another perfect specimen. Six feet or a tad taller, with a rangy build and the requisite broad shoulders. Dark hair, long enough on top to be stylish but not too long, neatly trimmed around his ears and the back of his neck. A long thin face, dark brown eyes to go with the hair. Eyes some women might call soulful. Just a little stubble on his nicely formed jaw. Five o'clock shadow at what…ten in the morning? She wondered if that was a studied effect. She held his gaze.

"Adam Smith, Ms. Winslow." He held out his hand. "We're from your father."

"That was fast."

"Fortunately, we were…at the embassy."

That didn't tell her anything, and she doubted Kennedy and Smith would elaborate. All manner of people were stationed at foreign embassies, especially in areas of active military engagement: diplomats, Foreign Service attaches, journalists, and agents from all branches of intelligence. Her two new bodyguards could be anyone. They probably weren't any happier with their babysitting assignment than she was to have them. She sighed. "What's going on?"

Both shook their head. Kennedy spoke first. "We're just here to accompany you until you leave for the States. Accommodations have been arranged for you near the embassy. We'll drive you back to your quarters here so you can pick up your things."

Rachel snorted. "I'm afraid what you see is what there is. I didn't exactly have time to pack a bag, and I don't need to retrieve my military issue toothbrush."

Abigail colored. "Yes, sorry about that. We'll see that whatever you need is provided." She stepped back and gestured to the Humvee. "If you'd like to go now."

"What I'd like is a ride to the base hospital. There's someone I need to see."

Neither of them moved.

"You are here to accompany me, isn't that right? Well," Rachel said, striding down the stairs, "I'm going to the hospital. If you'd like to tag along, fine."

She started walking back in the direction she'd come from that morning. She'd paid attention to the route from the hospital to Max's, and she thought she could get reasonably close. If she got lost, anyone she passed would be able to direct her. She'd be more than happy to do without her escort. Kennedy and Smith might be exactly who they said they were—two people who had been handy to be reassigned to a protective detail for a few days. But she didn't trust them. Right now, she didn't trust anyone except Max, Grif, and Amina.

Sweat broke out everywhere after a few steps. The temperature was already close to a hundred, and breakfast was a long time ago. So was sleep. She hadn't thought about either one when she'd been with Max. Those moments inside the CLU were as far away from the heat and desolation of this place as the stars were from earth. Max and the way Max made her feel—alive and free and more connected than she'd ever been—were all that mattered. She would have been happy to stay there for the rest of her life. She would be happy to be anywhere with Max for the rest of her life. Rachel's legs trembled, and the trembling had nothing to do with the heat or hunger or fatigue. Max. All the many fascinating sides of Max flashed through her mind—Max with a warrior's strength and sense of purpose, her eyes gleaming with determination; Max with a surgeon's skill and supple hands, defeating death; Max, comforting her with tenderness and understanding. Max was like no one she had ever known and she wasn't letting her go.

The Humvee pulled up alongside her. Kennedy spoke from the passenger side. "Please get in, Ms. Winslow. We'll be happy to drive you."

"Thank you." Rachel climbed into the back. She needed to conserve her strength. It might be a long time before she slept again. The ten-minute drive passed in silence, and she tried not to let her thoughts wander to what might be happening to Max. Every time she did, fear reared up from the recesses of her mind and her heart raced and her stomach turned over. Max was in trouble, and while Max might have tried to convince her she was no part of whatever was happening, she knew better. She'd been part of it from the beginning. If she hadn't been out there in the jungle, those Black Hawks wouldn't have been either. Maybe even the rebels wouldn't have been there. Max and Grif certainly wouldn't have ended up fighting to keep them all alive, and probably Max would not be caught up in the middle of whatever political game was being played out right now. But whatever had brought them all together, she'd always been part of it.

And what was happening now was no different than what had

happened out in the jungle. She and Max, possibly Grif, and maybe even Amina were under attack. The enemy wore a different uniform and was coming in the daylight and not the dark, but they were no less dangerous. She wasn't leaving Max or Grif or Amina. She didn't have a rifle, but she had other weapons.

The Humvee pulled up in front of the hospital and she climbed out. The front doors of the vehicle opened, and Kennedy put one long, slim leg down on the ground.

Rachel blocked her exit. "There's no need for you to come in. I'm sure this thing has air-conditioning. I won't be long."

Kennedy looked over her shoulder at Smith, who shrugged. Finally Kennedy pulled her leg back into the vehicle and closed her door. Rachel retraced her route through the hospital to the office where she'd inquired earlier about Max and Grif. The same ensign, a fresh-faced redhead with honest-to-God freckles who'd helped her then, was still on duty. He pushed some papers aside and grinned up at her when she approached his desk. "Ms. Winslow, you're back."

She smiled and read his name tag. "Good memory, Ensign Feeny. Is Lieutenant Griffin awake yet? I'd really like to see him."

"Let me check for you. He sure is popular."

Rachel kept her smile in place. "Is that right?"

"Yep. I've had half a dozen calls about him already this morning."

"Well, you must have a line wanting to visit, then."

Feeny shook his head. "Not yet. I'm supposed to call HQ when he wakes up." He shrugged sheepishly and gestured to the piles of forms on his desk. "I'm a little behind."

"I know how that is. If you could point me to him, I'll get out of your way."

"Oh no, ma'am, I'm happy for the company."

"Thanks," she said, impatience bubbling in her throat. HQ wanted a call. Captain Pettit might just want a status report on one of his wounded. All sorts of people would need to be notified, including family. All of that could be nothing out of the ordinary, but she didn't think so. She could still see Carmody sitting by Pettit's desk, looking smug and predatory.

Feeny rose. "Come on. He's in a regular berth now."

He walked her down a series of hallways with curtained cubicles on either side. She caught glimpses as she passed of beds, some of them empty, others occupied with men and women sleeping or reading or staring into space. The place was clean and brightly lit and smelled of the things hospitals usually did—food, antiseptic, pain.

Feeny pushed aside a curtain and motioned her into a space with two beds, two matching metal tables side by side between them, and a window above. The tan walls were bare and bleak. One bed was empty. Grif slept in the other. A stand on wheels stood at the end of his bed with a pitcher of water and a medical chart.

"Thank you," Rachel said quietly. Feeny nodded and left. She moved a metal chair from the corner next to Grif's bed and sat down. He was a big man, but he'd seemed so much bigger out there in the jungle, even injured. Maybe it was because his combat gear was gone, or maybe the sterile, artificial purity of the white sheet covering him diminished him somehow, but he seemed smaller, frailer. She missed the streaks of camouflage below his eyes. She even missed the smudges of dirt. He and Max had both looked so foreign and frightening in those first few chaotic seconds. She saw Max as she'd first encountered her—pointing a rifle at her, a fierce expression beneath the war paint and the grime. She thought of Max as she'd been just an hour before, fresh from the shower, her skin smooth as satin, the sharp planes of her face unmasked. The armor had been gone but her strength had remained. Tears filled her eyes and she impatiently brushed them away. Max was a warrior. She would be all right, but she wasn't going to fight this fight alone.

Rachel clasped Grif's hand where it lay on the bed and squeezed his fingers. "Hi, Grif. You probably don't remember me. I'm Rachel."

Grif's hand twitched and he opened his eyes. "Laurie?"

"No, Grif, it's Rachel Winslow. You're in the hospital. You're hurt, but you're doing better now."

Slowly he turned his head, blinked, and frowned. "You're not my wife."

"No, I'm not. I'm Rachel. We spent some time together out in the jungle."

"I remember." He frowned. "Were you sitting on me?"

She laughed softly, the memory of Max operating in the midst of all that insanity filling her with a rush of triumph. They'd survived. All of them, together. "I was."

"Thought so. Where's Max?"

"She's here. She's okay."

He sighed. "Good."

"Something's going on, Grif," Rachel said. "They're asking a lot of questions about what happened out there. Has anyone been here?"

"No. At least, not that I remember." He blinked several times and when he focused on her again, his gaze was sharper. "Where's Max?"

"I don't know. Two men took Max away. I'm a little worried."

"Two men—did they have patches, badges? Like Masters at Arms? Military police?"

Rachel tried to picture the blue uniforms, the name tags and patches. "I think maybe, yes."

"That's not normal." He raised his head, surveyed his body. Tubes ran out from beneath the sheets in several places and two IV bags hung from a metal pole anchored to the opposite side. "I'm not going anywhere for a while. Fuck."

"You need to concentrate on getting better. Max would say the same thing."

"Yeah, but she's a hard-ass and never thinks she needs any help."

Rachel smiled. So Grif saw beneath the camouflage too. "Tell me what to do. How would I find out what's going on?"

"I don't know if you can. If there's some kind of investigation, they're gonna keep it quiet. If you poke around, they'll just stonewall."

"Okay. A frontal attack is out. I guess I'll have to find a way in they won't be able to shut down."

"Good plan." He grinned. "Where's the other woman? The one who was with me all the time."

"Amina. She's here too. She's all right."

"Tell her I said thank you. She's very brave."

Rachel swallowed hard. "She is. You all are."

Grif's eyes closed. "Don't leave Max all alone."

"I won't. I promise." Rachel stood. "Go to sleep, Grif. I'll tell Max you said to keep her head down."

He opened his eyes. "Could you call my wife? I don't want the only message she gets about this to come through channels."

"Of course. I'd be honored. Tell me your number. Laurie, right?"

"Yeah." He recited a number.

"Is there anything special you want me to tell her?"

"Tell her I'm fine and everything works."

Rachel laughed. "I'm sure she'll be very glad to hear that."

She left him, knowing he'd protect Max when they came to question him. Outside, she climbed back into the Humvee and said, "I'd like to go to headquarters now."

"Certainly," Kennedy said. Apparently, Smith didn't speak.

Rachel closed her eyes and let the cool air from the AC revitalize her. Penetrating the wall of silence was going to be impossible on her own. She didn't know anyone at the military base who would talk to her. Her father might be able to help, but involving him might not be a good idea, not when she didn't know the reasons for the investigation or who was behind it. Besides, she hated calling on him to solve her problems. Fatigue settled over her and she shook it off. She still had work to do.

"Ms. Winslow," Kennedy said.

Rachel jerked upright. God, she'd fallen asleep. She looked outside. The Humvee idled in front of HQ. "I don't know how long I'll be."

"We'll wait."

Rachel climbed out and went inside. She found Pettit's office after a few wrong turns, knocked on the door, and the same chief petty officer opened it.

"Ma'am? May I help you?"

"I'd like to see Captain Pettit, please."

He studied her a second before holding the door open. "If you'd wait a moment, ma'am." He walked to the inner door, knocked, and disappeared. A minute later he returned and escorted her into Pettit's office.

The captain rose from behind his desk. "Ms. Winslow. How may I help you?"

"I'd like to see Commander de Milles."

"The commander is in a meeting right now."

"A meeting." Rachel fought to keep her expression neutral. She thought about her father's eternal calm even when she knew he was seething and injected some of that icy control into her voice. "A meeting that required two military police to escort her?"

The captain's shoulders stiffened. "I'm afraid I can't discuss this with you."

"Captain, I would be dead. Lieutenant Griffin would be dead. Amina Roos would be dead, and probably others, if it weren't for Commander de Milles. Whatever happened out there, accident or planned, was none of her doing."

"As I said, I'm not at liberty to discuss—"

"I thought it customary that a commanding officer supported his troops. Not turned them over to outside agencies to be interrogated."

A muscle bunched along his jaw. "Certain evidence has come to light. The commander's being questioned, as are several other members of the mission, as part of routine follow-up. That's all I can tell you."

Certain evidence. Well, that told her something beyond routine was going on, and Pettit probably had no control over it. Politics trumped just about everything, even military authority. Rachel saw the finality in his eyes and possibly regret. He couldn't help her. This route was closed to her, but she wasn't going to abandon Max without firing a shot.

Chapter Twenty-three

M ax could sleep anywhere—on a gurney in a dark corner waiting for the OR to be cleaned and the next patient to be wheeled in on a long night of back-to-back emergencies, on the ground behind a swell of sand while her comrades kept watch for the enemies who lurked in the night—almost anywhere except in her rack, where she was supposed to be safe. Maybe the only time she felt safe was when she was actually facing death, one-on-one. She wasn't safe with Carmody, but since she'd been left alone in a bare room with nothing but two metal chairs and a steel table, she'd rather sleep than stare at the blank walls and know she was being watched and probably recorded. Besides, closing her eyes was as near as she could get to flipping off whoever was trying to rattle her.

The instant she closed her eyes, she thought of Rachel and pictured the man and woman who'd shown up outside her CLU looking for Rachel. They weren't military. They were more likely of Carmody's brand, maybe even working with him. They might be friend or foe. Rachel could handle herself, but she'd probably never run up against people like these before. People who thought nothing of using any tactic at their disposal to get what they wanted. People who thought their mission was somehow more vital than that of those who put their bodies on the line every day. People who seemed to have forgotten what the enemy looked like. Rachel didn't belong anywhere near this snake pit of suspicion and accusation.

Max would have given almost anything to know Rachel was far away from all of this, but she hadn't asked. Giving Carmody any indication Rachel mattered to her would be like handing him a loaded weapon and pointing it at her own head. He'd already asked the same questions as he had the night before all over again, as if expecting the answers to be different this time. Who were the insurgents who attacked the camp? How did they know the timing of the rescue operation? What was their target? *Who* was their target? Who had Max told about the operation? Who had someone else told? Who had she met in the jungle? Every time he asked, she answered him the same way she had the first time, and after he'd grown tired of questioning or perhaps thought if he left her alone she'd panic or bargain, he walked out. After a few hours he came back and started again. Keeping track of time was difficult after so many days without sleep in a barren space with nothing to orient her. No windows, no clock, no voices outside the room. They hadn't taken her to HQ as she'd first expected, but to a nondescript building at the far edge of the base. She hadn't seen any base personnel at all when she'd climbed out of the Humvee. Maybe no one even knew she was there. She considered who might miss her if she didn't arrive back in the States anytime soon.

No one.

She hadn't notified the hospital of her pending return, since her position was secure—ERs always had trouble keeping surgeons willing to take in-house call to cover emergencies—and she hadn't been sure when she'd arrive stateside. Her fellow docs would be glad to see her—another body to take call and lighten everyone's load. Maybe the OR nurse she'd spent a night with would give her an extra-special welcome-back smile. But if she never returned? No one would inquire. She hadn't talked to anyone in her family in over a decade. They hadn't shown any interest in her plans when she'd been young—in fact, her father had made it clear she was on her own when she hit eighteen. She'd researched how best to pay her way through college and medical school and settled on the Navy. The day after her eighteenth birthday she was on a bus south to Cornell on an ROTC scholarship. She'd never looked back and doubted she'd crossed their minds in years. No girlfriend. No friends. Not even a fucking cat.

Carmody held all the cards except one—she didn't care what he did to her. And his brand of power depended on fear.

The second time he left her alone she'd slept. And the third. That felt like a couple of hours each time. He hadn't brought her any food, but he'd left a plastic bottle of water on the table, which she drank. She could use another one. She could use two or three cups of coffee and a big meal.

What she really needed was to see Rachel. Just to know that she was somewhere safe and out of whatever was happening here. When the hunger kept her from sleeping and her mind started to wander a little bit from fatigue and stress and anger, and her tight, iron control started to slip, she thought back to the moments before the Masters at Arms had come for her. Rachel had appeared out of nowhere, standing there on the steps of her CLU, refusing to be turned away or ignored or put off by Max's wall of silence. Max smiled to herself. Stubborn as she was beautiful. And then somehow, the barriers had crumbled and her resolve had vanished under the soft caress of Rachel's mouth. She couldn't push her away, she'd needed her too much. She needed the incredible sensation of being with Rachel—as if they were alone in the universe, standing in a pure mountain glade with the sun shining down and the breeze, so cool, blowing over her skin. As if they had stripped naked and stepped into a crystal lake and the only heat came from Rachel's skin against her skin, driving the chill away, warming her deep inside. Body to body, she'd run her hands over silky skin and tangled her fingers in thick red-gold hair glowing in the sun. Rachel's eyes were the color of the evergreens that formed a shield around them. There'd been no death, no dying, no pain. She couldn't think back to a time when there hadn't been pain—of rejection, of being on the outside, of never quite being enough to matter. She smiled to herself, thinking of Rachel astride her, wild and free. She'd been enough then. She'd given everything she had and for those few moments, she had been enough.

The door opened and Carmody walked in. "Something amusing, Commander de Milles?"

Max slowly opened her eyes and focused on him. He'd shaved and showered and wore a fresh uniform. She could smell the aftershave still wafting from his skin. Ate too, probably, the bastard.

She said nothing and carefully blanked her mind. She didn't want him in the room with even the memory of Rachel. He carried a laptop computer that he set on the table between them as he settled into the other chair. He opened it unhurriedly, pushed a few buttons, and turned it toward her.

"I wonder if you could help me out with this."

Max stared at the laptop as a video played. There was no sound and it was very dark—a night scene—and a little bit grainy, but she instantly recognized the base, the landing field, and a line of Black Hawks tethered to the tarmac. Every few seconds a vehicle passed by on an access road and the headlights cut a swath of light through the darkness, illuminating the birds as if a spotlight shone on them. A shadowy figure leaned over or…she squinted…maybe reached under the open bay of one of the birds. The view panned away as the slowly swiveling security camera made its circuits. More vehicles passed, red and white lights flickered in the air from departing and returning aircraft, and then another view of the Black Hawks shot into the foreground. This time the light shone inside one of them from the bird's interior running lights, and she recognized the figure leaning into the bird. She recognized herself, checking out the med supplies before the mission. The video went on for a few more minutes showing the same sweep, the same random base activity, but this time when it showed the Black Hawk again, the bay was dark and empty. When the image came to an end, Carmody turned the computer around and closed the screen.

"Would you like to interpret that for me?" he asked.

Max had no idea if Carmody knew the figure in the second sweep was her or not. If she'd trusted him, she would have told him. She'd had every right to be there and hadn't been doing anything she hadn't done a hundred times before. The only one who knew for sure she'd been there was Grif. He might be awake by now, and they could've questioned him. He wouldn't have had any reason not to tell them he'd seen her there. Carmody might already know that was her in the video—but then why was he asking her? If she denied it, she could be walking into a trap. But he didn't strike her as the subtle type. If he had a weapon, he'd use it. He'd get too much pleasure out of watching the bullet penetrate flesh not to. She said nothing.

"Funny, the timing," he said conversationally. "I just don't like coincidences, do you?"

Max thought about closing her eyes and going back to sleep.

"Of course, there is another possibility." He smiled, and if she'd been a dog, her hackles would've been up and her teeth would've been bared. He'd be the kind of animal to attack from the back, slashing at your hindquarters when you weren't looking.

"Someone else did know. I mean, outside of us."

Max didn't like the little bit of triumph in his voice. She kept her hands flat on the table so she wouldn't clench her fists. She wondered if she could lunge across the table and get her hands around his throat before someone came through the door to restrain her. If she did, she'd probably be looking at a prison cell. That might almost be worth it.

"It appears Ms. Winslow received a communication the night before the operation was to take place. So there was someone out there who might have"—he waggled his hand—"alerted someone. If she had friends in the area or if her friends had friends."

Max took a second for her vision to clear and her temper to edge down a notch. "Seems odd to me, but then, it's not my job to weave fairy tales. But…I'm not seeing why someone would want to arrange for their own attack."

A spark of fire flared in Carmody's flat, dead eyes, giving Max a little burst of pleasure. He didn't like being challenged. He probably didn't like that she wasn't afraid, either.

"There's plenty of places to hide a transponder on a Black Hawk," Carmody said.

So that was that his working hypothesis—that the rebels had tracked one of the birds after a sympathizer had put a transponder on one. That might even be true. Thousands of people, troops and civilians, moved about the base every day. Base security was focused on entry points for vehicles that might be carrying bombs and the heavily populated areas that might be a target for suicide attacks. A single unarmed individual walking about was not likely to raise an alarm. Anyone might have put a tracer on the bird, although she still wasn't buying it. Carmody wanted a scapegoat really badly. She wished she knew why.

He pushed the laptop to one side and leaned forward, probably thinking he'd appear more intimidating. "Tell me about Rachel Winslow."

Two feet between them now. She could almost feel his flesh beneath her fingers, feel her thumbs pressing into his hyoid, hear the satisfying crack of the tiny bone when she squeezed. She leaned forward too, her hands still flat on the table. She looked into his eyes, watched his pupils flare.

A sharp rap sounded at the door and Carmody's brows twitched. A muscle in his jaw tightened, and he leaned back in his chair. Max took a deep breath, let the vision of choking him to death slide out of her mind. The door swung open and Captain Pettit walked in.

"We're done here," Pettit said.

"We'll talk again," Carmody said softly. He stood, picked up the laptop, and walked out.

Max struggled not to slump in her chair. She was a lot more tired than she'd thought. Her arm ached beneath the bandage. Other places ached too. Her rib cage where she'd taken the weight of the SEAL when he'd tackled her at the aid camp, her hip where she'd landed on a rock, her shoulders from digging the foxhole and burying the dead.

"Let's go, Commander."

Max stood and saluted. "Yes, sir."

He returned her salute perfunctorily. "You'll be escorted back to your CLU. Get some food, get some sleep, get cleaned up. Report to HQ at zero eight hundred in battle BDUs."

"Yes, sir. May I ask why, sir?"

"It seems you have friends with interesting connections, Commander."

He didn't look pleased so she didn't ask anything else. She was just happy to get out of the sweatbox and away from Carmody.

"And, Commander," Pettit added as she followed him outside, "you are confined to your quarters until then."

"Yes, sir." Max judged it to be just a little after sundown. She'd been inside all day.

Pettit vaulted into his vehicle and his Humvee pulled away. A second vehicle idled nearby. Max climbed in and nodded to the ensign, who drove her directly to the DFAC. She filled a tray with mashed potatoes, roast beef, vegetables, and bread and took the tray to a table in the corner. The ensign stood just inside the door at the far end of the room, discreetly watching her. She was too damn tired to run, and besides, where would she go? And why? She hadn't done anything wrong, and she wasn't about to let Carmody hang something on her to cover his own ass, which was what she suspected was at stake.

She ate methodically until her plate was empty. When she rose, she felt a little stronger, but her head was muzzy with fatigue. The next stop was a shower facility, and as the hot water eased some of the aches in her stiff muscles, she tried to come up with a plan. She needed to talk to Grif and the other team members. She wondered if there was any way to find out about Rachel but knew there wasn't. Rachel was really gone this time.

Emptiness hit her harder than a bullet.

Chapter Twenty-four

The CLU was empty when Max stumbled in. CC's half of the unit was neat and tidy as usual. She'd made her bed as she always did, put away her laundry, and neatened up the objects on her storage shelves. Max's portion looked just like she'd left it—her fatigues were in a pile in the corner, her sheets twisted, and the blankets half off on the floor. About as wrecked as her life.

Max stripped and fell face down on her rumpled bed. The pillow smelled like Rachel, the faintest hint of almonds and vanilla. Light and sweet. Some of the weight lifted from her heart. How was it that Rachel always brought peace, even in the throes of chaos? Rachel. Fuck. Rachel was gone. Out of habit, she reached over the side of the bed and felt around for the bottle of whiskey. Her fingers closed around the slick glass and her mind clamored for the cool burn and the dull edge of almost-forgetting. She rolled over and left the bottle where it was. She didn't want to forget. She wanted to remember. She slid her hand under her T-shirt and over the surface of her midsection where Rachel had stroked her. Everywhere Rachel touched had come alive, and even now her skin, her muscles, her very bones tingled with the memory. She pressed her face closer to her pillow, immersing herself in the scent of Rachel, and closed her eyes.

When she woke, the hazy light filtering through the slatted window of her CLU told her it was morning, just after dawn. She sat up despite her body's protest. She was stiff and sore everywhere, inside and out. Her stomach was queasy, her head pounding. She hadn't dreamed, or if she had, she couldn't remember. She felt drugged although she knew she wasn't. She wondered what would be waiting for her at HQ. If she'd be facing another day with Carmody or maybe someone else, for some other kind of inquisition. Maybe Ollie and Dan and the others on the team were locked away in another windowless room going through the same thing. Something had gone wrong somewhere, and blaming the troops on the ground was always better than blaming the brass. The fuckups at the detention centers in Iraq had been proof plenty of that.

Grif ought to be awake by now. If he hadn't been shipped out to the regional hospital, they might have questioned him. She wasn't worried. Grif would always have her back. Her stomach twisted—she didn't want him being browbeaten when he was in no position to defend himself. She checked her watch. Two hours before she needed to report. Time enough to fuel up and check on Grif. Pettit said she was confined to quarters, but unless a Master at Arms stood at her door, she was going to see Grif.

She pulled on clean BDUs, washed up with water from a bottle of drinking water, and broke out an MRE. She swallowed the ham and egg sandwich in three bites and washed it down with the rest of the water. She peered out through the slats and scanned the road in front of her CLU. No vehicles. No escort she could see. Just to be safe, she found a screwdriver and pried off the plywood square they'd nailed over a ventilation port to prevent light from escaping after dark, removed the screws holding the screen in place, and went out the back window.

No one paid any attention to her as she strode through the camp to the hospital. She stopped a hundred feet away and watched for a while. Just the usual stream of troops straggling in for morning sick call. At 0700 everyone in the place would be busy dealing with the walk-ins. At 0705 she skirted around the line, nodded briskly to the ensign handling sign-in, and slipped inside. Everyone knew her, and after the usual quick greeting from harried personnel, no one spared her a second glance. She bet Grif was in the step-down unit—semi critical care—and tried there first.

"Griffin?" she said to the corpsman at the desk.

"Third bay on the right," she said without looking up from the morning report.

"Thanks." Max checked the hall. No one on guard outside Grif's cubicle. She hustled inside. Grif was propped up in bed with a steaming Styrofoam cup in the hand that that wasn't attached to an IV.

He paused, the cup an inch from his mouth. His eyes glinted. "You look like shit, Deuce."

"Then I'm looking twice as good as you." She couldn't stop a grin. "How's the leg?"

"Hurts like a mother."

She reached for the sheet across his lap.

"Hey—commando here," he said quickly, covering his groin.

"Seen it before. Still reeling from amazement."

He laughed and she pushed the sheet aside, keeping his most important parts covered with one corner. The dressings had been removed and the incision was covered with a clear plastic adhesive barrier. Looked nice and clean. No signs of infection. She checked the skin temp of his lower thigh. Color and circulation fine. The pulses in his foot were bounding. "How's the sensation?"

"There's a little numbness just above my knee. The foot's good."

"Cutaneous nerves." She replaced the sheet. "Nothing to worry about."

"I owe you," he said softly. "The surgeon told me he found a major bleeder tied off in the hole in my leg. If you hadn't gotten it I'd be dead."

Max shrugged. "Maybe. Maybe not. Either way, you don't owe me." She met his gaze. "You probably saved Rachel Winslow. I owe you for that."

His eyebrow twitched. "She's...interesting."

"Yeah."

"And hot."

Max narrowed her eyes. "Careful."

"Huh," he said thoughtfully. "Like that?"

"Yeah."

"Huh." He handed her the coffee cup and pushed himself up higher. "What the fuck is going on, then?"

Max set the cup on the table. "No fucking idea. Well, I have some idea, but no facts. Has a guy named Carmody been here?"

"Midday yesterday. I was still pretty groggy."

Carmody must have come over here during one of the times he'd left her alone. Maybe hoping to get some information from Grif to contradict what she had to say. "Then you probably know as much as me."

"Why do they think the mission was sabotaged?" Grif asked.

Max pulled over a chair and sat. "Nobody likes it when a mission objective fails and casualties are involved. You and I had front-row seats to what went on out there—or at least Rachel, Amina, and I did, so they're focusing on us."

"Seems like overkill," Grif muttered.

"I think this is more than the usual assigning of blame—but I can't quite figure out what."

Grif gave her a look. "What about Rachel?"

Max's jaw tightened. "What about her?"

"Down, boy—jeez." Grif grinned. "Maybe she's the unknown factor. What do you know about her?"

Max considered. If she said she knew everything she needed to know that mattered, would he understand? She thought of the photo he carried in his pocket of Laurie and his kids. Yeah, he'd understand.

"Enough to know she's not to blame."

"Don't doubt it," he said instantly. "But she's in it."

"Maybe not. She's gone."

"That doesn't mean she's out."

❖

Rachel stared into the mirror as she put the finishing touches to her makeup. Her face was a blur and she blinked to clear her vision. How fitting that her own face seemed that of a stranger. The Sheraton was a block from the embassy in Djibouti and a universe away from where she'd been just days before. Last night, she'd slept on clean, crisp, cool white sheets. She'd had clothes and shoes delivered by the hotel concierge from an order she'd phoned down. She'd had dinner and breakfast brought to her on a rolling cart with real dishes and silverware, served by deferential hotel staff. All the comforts of home and she'd never felt so displaced in her life. She felt like an imposter. This was not where she belonged. She should be back in the jungle camp or with Max.

She was very good at playing a part—she'd been doing it all her life. Dutiful daughter. Willing bed partner. Even selfless activist. She'd gone along with her father's demands more often than not rather than propagate family unrest. She'd dated women she didn't love because she knew she never would. And even her aid work was as much about her need for validation as it was to help others. She'd been pretty much a fraud until she'd come face-to-face with death and learned from Max what really mattered. Loyalty, honor, love.

Now here she was, playing a role again. But she didn't have a choice, and she'd use whatever resources she had. The clock on her bedside table read a little after seven. She was supposed to meet Kennedy and Smith in the lobby in half an hour. She didn't know what to do with herself. She'd slept on and off during the endless night out of sheer exhaustion, and awakened not feeling rested. Her dreams, what she could recall of them, had been fragmented and filled with clatter and the sour taste of danger. She'd kept the light on in the adjoining bathroom and the door partly ajar. She hadn't wanted to go to sleep in the dark and couldn't help but think if Max had been with her, she wouldn't have cared what nightmares crept into her dreams.

Her hand trembled and she put down the sponge covered in pale pink powder. Max. More than twenty-four hours since she'd seen her. What had they done to her in the last twenty-four hours? Rachel wasn't so innocent as to disbelieve the stories she'd heard of interrogation techniques, but surely not with a United States naval officer?

She couldn't think about it. If she did, panic swelled and her head grew light. She'd felt safer in the jungle, trapped in an empty, decimated camp surrounded by the dead and faceless enemies than she did here in this supposedly civilized world. She'd felt safer because she'd been with Max and they'd stood together, waiting to face whatever was out there. And she'd known with absolute certainty that Max would be beside her, no matter what.

"I'm coming," she said as she turned from the face in the mirror. "I hope you know that. I'm coming."

The phone rang on the small table by the bed and she jumped, the sound so alien she almost couldn't recognize it. She picked it up on the third ring. "Yes?"

"Rachel, it's Amina."

"Amina!" Rachel sank onto the side of the bed. The sound of a friendly voice made her eyes fill. "How are you? Where are you?"

"I am home, with my family. They drove me from the camp yesterday. You got the message I had left, yes?"

"Yes." Kennedy had informed her that Amina was gone as they'd driven Rachel to the embassy. She'd been glad that Amina was safe, even though the loneliness was choking.

"Good. I did not want you to think I had left you."

"I knew you wouldn't."

Amina said. "I also got yours—the one you left at aid headquarters. I called there this morning and they gave me this number."

"I couldn't think how else to reach you," Rachel said. "I knew you'd call there sooner or later."

"How are you?"

Rachel considered the security on her phone line. Anything was possible, but she rather doubted the hotel lines were being monitored. "I've been better. Something strange is happening."

"Many questions," Amina said tentatively.

"Someone talked to you, didn't they?"

"Yes, after you left yesterday morning, Major Newton came back. I'm afraid I might have made a mistake."

"No, whatever is going on, none of this is your fault."

"She asked questions and I was very tired. And…remembering. I didn't think what I was saying."

Rachel's breath grew cold in her chest. Making Amina relive the horror was torture by any name. Rachel wanted an enemy to face, not these nameless shadows. "I know. The remembering is hard."

"I told them about the phone call. I didn't realize it would matter."

For a minute, Rachel couldn't sort out what Amina was saying. Time had become so compressed at the camp—moments became hours and days felt like weeks. She felt as if she'd known Max all her life, maybe because during the time they'd been together her life had been distilled into a series of acute moments where every thought and action mattered. How could it be that a whole lifetime of moments could have less meaning than just those very few? She shuddered and closed her eyes. God, Max. *Where are you?*

"Rachel?"

Rachel opened he eyes. "Phone call? Oh, the night before—"

"Yes, I'm sorry. I thought I should tell you. I didn't think then it mattered, but I've been remembering all those questions. Now that I am not so tired, I am worried I said too much."

"It's all right. Really."

Amina's sigh came through the line. "What about Max and Grif?"

"Grif is going to be all right."

"I'm so glad. He was very brave."

"So are you. He asked me to tell you that. And he said to tell you thank you."

"He remembered?" A lightness filled Amina's voice, a note of pride and happiness amongst so much sadness.

"Yes, he did specifically. And he was right. I don't think I could have held it all together if you hadn't been there."

"Yes, you could have. You became a warrior, like Max."

"No," Rachel said softly. "Not like Max. But thank you."

"She is all right?"

"I don't know," Rachel said softly. She glanced at the clock. "But I will soon."

CHAPTER TWENTY-FIVE

"Commander." The chief saluted Max as she walked into the anteroom of the CO's office. He rose from behind his desk, his broad face implacable as always.

She returned the salute. The clock on the wall behind his desk showed one minute before 0800. Her escort, unofficial guard, had picked her up as she'd walked back to her CLU from the hospital. He hadn't returned her grin when she'd climbed into the Humvee.

"Come with me," the chief said. "They're in the ready room."

They're? Max followed him, a kernel of hope threatening to germinate. Maybe this was just a routine debriefing. After every mission the team got together to reconstruct the events—the timeline, the roles everyone played, the problems, the outcome. Not only did this help provide useful information on mission planning and effectiveness, it provided the additional benefit of letting the team members voice their experiences. The incidence of post-mission stress and anxiety dropped as debriefings became standard. If ever a mission required an after-event review, it was this one. Carmody's face flashed through her mind as she walked down the brightly lit hall. His involvement had changed everything. No one was likely to volunteer any information about the failed attempt to rescue Rachel.

No. She wasn't headed to a debriefing. More likely she'd be facing a panel from JAG—hopefully with a representative from the legal corps on her side. At least if that was the case, she wouldn't have to go up against a group of them one-on-one. She almost smiled. She'd rather go one-on-one against a dozen armed rebels than four lawyers.

At least in the field, she understood the nature of the battle. Somewhere behind all of this was politics, something she understood enough to know she hated. She bumped up against it now and then in medicine but managed to stay clear by refusing advancement into positions where she'd have to play the bureaucratic game in order to achieve her goals. She was much more comfortable going head-to-head against any kind of adversary.

The chief rapped on the door to the ready room, pushed it open, and stood aside for her to enter. She knew the layout—a long table in the center of the room, standard metal folding chairs around it. With luck, fresh coffee in the big pot on a stand in one corner. She stepped inside, the door closed behind her, and she tried to register what she was seeing. Nothing made sense. All she could see was Rachel.

She stopped breathing, a cannon barrage filling her head, driving out thought. Rachel sat on the far side of the table, her hands folded on top, looking back at Max. She looked…different. Beautiful in an entirely different way than Max had ever seen her before. Beautiful in the way of women she would have automatically discounted as anyone she might have anything in common with. Rachel's hair shone in lustrous red-brown waves that fell around her shoulders and feathered on her neck. Her green eyes were clear, without smudges beneath or shadows within. Her face was elegantly composed, every line and angle accentuated to perfection. The laceration Max had closed beneath her eye was invisible—expertly covered with makeup. Her mouth glistened with a light gloss—apricot or peach. Max could almost taste the sweetness. Her smile was a subtle stroke, appraising or secretly seductive. Her shirt was a deeper green than her eyes, silk or some other sleek fabric that clung just enough to show the outline of her breasts. Only the glint of fire behind the cool surface of her gaze hinted at the woman Max had discovered in the jungle. The one she'd held astride her.

Rachel didn't greet her and Max felt the ground shift under her boots. Another hot zone, new rules of engagement.

Max pulled her attention away and looked at the man seated beside Rachel. About Rachel's age, he wore a white shirt open at the throat, his cuffs casually rolled back to mid-forearm. His skin was tanned, the muscles corded. His hands were smooth and regular, not the scarred, bruised, rough hands of a soldier. His black hair curled slightly around his ears and at the back of his neck, surprisingly soft-looking in stark contrast to the chiseled planes of his face. He resembled a marble Michelangelo come to life, and he sat very close to Rachel.

Less than twenty seconds had passed. Max pivoted to Pettit and saluted. "Sir."

Pettit sat at the head of the table looking moderately annoyed. He saluted and gestured to a chair opposite Rachel and the other civilian. "Have a seat, Commander."

Max pulled out a chair and sat down, her gaze returning to Rachel. She couldn't look anywhere else. This woman was contained and controlled, as Max imagined Rachel had been before the assault on the camp. Maybe this was the real Rachel, not the woman who had taken her pleasure with abandon, wild and carefree. Maybe the woman she'd held in her arms had only existed in the aftermath of shared horror and had faded into the shadows of forgotten memory.

Pettit's voice cut through her reverie.

"I believe you know Ms. Winslow. Mr. Benedict is with Reuters."

Max focused on Benedict. A journalist. What the hell?

Benedict reached across the table and held out his hand. "Commander, very happy to meet you."

"Mr. Benedict." Max couldn't quite figure out what this guy was doing here. Journalists and photographers were familiar figures around the base. They were embedded with a lot of the units, and she'd flown with some on board. But what was he doing here, and what did he want with her?

"Before we get started, I just wanted to add a personal note of thanks."

"Oh?"

"For saving my future sister-in-law…and the others, of course."

"Tommy," Rachel said softly, laying a hand on his arm. "This isn't—"

"Sorry, Rachel, but it's true." Benedict glanced at her, his expression earnest and charmingly intense, before turning back to Max. "My sister Christie would've been devastated if anything had happened to Rachel. We all would have been."

Pettit cleared his throat. "Commander, Mr. Benedict is here to do a story about the rescue of Ms. Winslow and her associates. I think you understand our position on these things."

Max was still trying to process what Benedict had said about Rachel being his future sister-in-law. Rachel and Benedict's sister, Christie, engaged? Why was she surprised? A woman like Rachel wouldn't be unattached.

Icy calm settled through her. Whatever had happened out there in the jungle was over and done. Now she had to focus on what was in front of her—she didn't know why Rachel was here with this reporter, but she'd go along with it if it kept her out of the box with Carmody. This was just another mission to be gotten through. At least this time, no one would end up bleeding.

She glanced at her CO. "Yes, sir. I understand."

He didn't have to tell her that anything said to the press must represent the corps in a good light. When the press was around, no one complained about the duty. No one criticized policy. No one ever revealed the truth of what they saw or did or how they felt about it.

"We're happy to cooperate with the press, of course." Pettit stood. "The American public needs to know that the Navy is here to protect the citizens of Somalia and our international civilian allies everywhere in the region. That's what you and your fellow troops came here to do, and that's what you did. Your duty."

Every word sounded as if it was being pulled out of his intestines with pliers. Most military personnel, especially the brass, viewed the press as having a different and often opposing agenda. The press was looking for news—and sometimes the news was not to the benefit of the military. But good PR was as important to the military as to any other group jockeying for money and power, and they couldn't be seen as uncooperative or adversarial.

Max understood what was expected of her. "I don't know that I'm the best one to represent—"

"Of course you are," Benedict said. "You were there on the ground with Rachel and the others. If it weren't for you, as I understand it," he glanced at Rachel, "none of them would have survived."

Max regarded Rachel. "Ms. Winslow exaggerates. I was only doing what any other troop would have done."

His smile suggested he didn't really believe her. "Well, let's talk about that, so we can tell the world just how important it is that you're all here."

"Right." Max shifted her gaze away from Rachel. Just another mission.

❖

Tommy clicked off the tape recorder. "Thank you, Commander. I...well. Like I said before. That's a remarkable story, and I'm sure the Sec—"

"Tommy," Rachel said before Tommy revealed any more personal details she hadn't wanted Max to find out this way, "I'm sure the commander knows how much we all appreciate what she and the whole team did out there."

Max stood. She looked gaunt and worn, but her shoulders were back and her voice clear and strong, as it had been through the seemingly endless interview. "Please be sure to include the other members of the team when you write your story, Mr. Benedict. Because no one out here makes it on their own, and no mission is ever successful just because of one person."

"I'll be talking to the others," Tommy replied.

"Good." Max nodded to Rachel, her expression as remote as if they were strangers. "Good-bye, Ms. Winslow. I hope you have a safe trip home."

Rachel rose, but she didn't have time to protest before Max spun around and left. She only had a minute to make a decision as she started after her. "Tommy, go ahead without me. I'll find my own way back."

"Are you sure?"

"Yes. Go ahead. I know you want to file your story."

"Where are you going?"

"I've got some unfinished business." Impatiently Rachel hitched her shoulder bag higher and opened the door. If she didn't hurry, Max would be gone.

Tommy grasped her arm, his brow furrowed. "What about the security people? Aren't they supposed to drive us back to the hotel?"

"Damn it, yes." Rachel spun back to him. "Tommy, I need a favor. Tell Kennedy—that's the woman—"

Tommy grinned his devil-may-care grin. "I noticed."

"Tell her I'll be here a while but that you need to file your story right away. Ask them to drive you to the motor pool or somewhere so you can catch a ride back to the hotel."

"Ah—where will you be?"

"I'll be back here in an hour. Tell Kennedy that's how long I'll be with the CO."

"Why do I feel like we're back at Yale and I'm about to get busted again for sneaking into the sorority house?"

"You *did* sneak in, and I covered for you so you wouldn't get suspended. I told you my roommate wasn't interested, but you wouldn't listen. That part wasn't my fault."

He fingered his jaw. "She didn't have to deck me."

"Yes, she did. Now go run a screen for me—I really have to get out of here."

He kissed her cheek. "All right. But I want to do a follow-up story in Mogadishu and maybe a longer exposé when we get back to the States. You agree?"

"Yes, all right. But get this one filed first. It's important."

"It's a great story. I'll talk to you soon. Dinner tonight?"

"Yes, of course, if I can." She just wanted to get away. She wanted, needed, to find Max.

Tommy gathered his briefcase, recorder, and notebooks and left. Rachel forced herself to wait five minutes before searching for an exit that would let her avoid the main entrance in case Kennedy or Smith didn't buy Tommy's story and were still outside. She slipped out a side door and hurried toward the road, angling between the adjacent buildings until she was far enough away not to be seen. She hoped.

The last two hours had been hell. She'd known reliving her experiences out in the jungle for Tommy would be difficult, but watching Max withdraw behind a shield of remote indifference had been harder. Max had answered Tommy's questions, she'd been polite and, as Rachel had expected, had downplayed her own role in the events. But Max had never looked her in the eye after those first seconds when she'd stared at Rachel in confusion, then anger, and finally dismissal. The distance between them was agonizing. Damn Tommy.

Not that he was to blame for his assumptions about her relationship status, but she'd have to make things clearer to quite a few people. First she needed to find Max. She stopped at an intersection and didn't recognize anything. She'd been walking so fast she hadn't paid any attention to where she was. Rows and rows of CLUs stretched in every direction. The place was a maze. God, was she lost? She couldn't be lost. She didn't have *time* to be lost. She had to find Max. She half laughed, a painful sound that caught in her chest and tore at her. She was lost and she needed to find Max. Why had it never occurred to her she'd spent so much time avoiding the paths other people laid out for her, she hadn't been able to see where *she* wanted to go?

She took a breath, looked around, and picked out a larger building she remembered seeing when she'd been standing on the steps of Max's CLU. Please let that be the same one. She headed in that direction, checking the markings on the CLUs as she passed. Finally she reached the series of letters she recognized and found Max's. It looked as it had the first day. Closed and shuttered. Like Max had been when they'd first met. Like she'd been that morning.

Rachel wet her lips, stepped up, and knocked. The silence was so oppressive she had trouble drawing a breath. Sweat misted her temples. Her heart ricocheted around in her chest. She pushed back her hair with both hands and rapped again, louder. "Max, please. Open up."

The door opened. An African American woman with wary dark eyes and a cautious smile looked out. Her dark green T-shirt and boxers were wrinkled. Her face was creased as if she'd just gotten out of bed.

"Sorry," Rachel said. "I'm looking for Max."

The woman tilted her head and squinted against the sun, studying Rachel as if she were an alien presence. "How'd you get here?"

"What? I walked." Rachel waved behind her. "From—over there."

"Come on in and get some water. You'll cook out there."

The woman held the door and Rachel climbed inside. A blast of cool air hit her and she sighed. "Thanks."

"Here." The woman opened a bottle of water and handed it to her. "I'm CC, by the way."

"Rachel. Sorry if I woke you." Rachel peered down the length of the CLU, looking for Max.

"You missed her by about fifteen minutes."

Rachel's throat tightened. "Where is she?"

"Probably at thirty thousand feet."

"I'm sorry?"

"Orders came this morning while she wasn't here. She was due to fly out at ten forty. I helped her pack. Took us under a minute, and she had five to make the airfield. Knowing Max, she did."

"Fly where?" Rachel said, an ominous stillness seeping through her.

CC grinned. "Stateside."

Chapter Twenty-six

Stateside?" Rachel stared at CC, certain she'd heard her wrong. "But...I just saw her. Not even half an hour ago."

CC shook her head, her wide expressive mouth turning down for an instant at the corners. "Half an hour out here could be a lifetime."

A chill rippled through Rachel's chest. A *minute* out here was a lifetime—or at least life changing. "Are you sure she's left? Is there any chance I could catch her?"

"I doubt it. When orders come through, sometimes you don't even have time to pack. And with something like this..." She shrugged. "If there's a seat on a transport with your name on it, you'll do anything to fill it. Max probably flagged down someone from the motor pool and caught a ride over to the airfield. I'm sorry."

"You wouldn't happen to know where she's going?" Rachel's thoughts whirled as if in the vortex of a tornado, jumbled fragments spinning around randomly, banging into each other or missing by inches. Making no sense. She'd been running disaster scenarios for the last twenty-four hours—worrying about Max facing Carmody alone, afraid her plan to use Tommy to make Max a public hero would backfire somehow, terrified she couldn't pull it all off in time. When Max had walked into the room that morning, she'd had to use every bit of her control to maintain her composed façade. All she'd wanted was to jump up and touch her. Instead she'd had to sit there while Tommy interviewed them, pretending to be calm while all the while dying to be alone with Max. Her stomach was on the verge of revolt by the time they'd finished, and then Max had bolted before she could explain.

"If she grabbed a spot on a C-130 she might get a ride straight through to Lejeune or Norfolk." CC drained a bottle of water and dropped the plastic container into a bucket by her bed along with half a dozen other empties.

"I really need to talk to her." Rachel hugged her midsection. The thought of never seeing Max again sent a sliver of pain slicing through her.

"She'll probably be a day or two in transit and then a few more until she's done with all the separation details. Your best bet is to try tracking her down by phone."

"Thanks," Rachel said, her energy finally draining away. She didn't have a number for her. The idea was almost laughable. She'd put her life in Max's hands a dozen times. She'd made love with her, for God's sake, and now Max had vanished and she had no idea where she'd gone. She could find her—she had the connections to do it, if Max even wanted to speak to her after Tommy's cock-up. She should have told Max everything before…Before what? Before they spent every second working to stay alive, before they fell on each other out of desperation and wild need, before Carmody and his slimy accusations put them in another kind of firefight? Could she possibly have screwed things up more?

Rachel went to the door. "Sorry I got you up."

"No problem. When you catch up to Deuce in the States," CC said, "tell her hi for me."

"Yes," Rachel said, wondering if that would ever happen. At least Max was safe. Away from whatever quagmire of political blame-placing and manipulation was going on here. She was glad for that. Glad that Max was out of the line of fire. But the emptiness ached more brutally than anything she'd ever known. "I will."

Steeling herself for the long, hot walk back to headquarters, she stepped outside. A Humvee blocked the road directly in front of the CLU. Kennedy climbed out, a scowl replacing her usual bland expression. Her mouth was set in a tight line, and her brows knotted in the center, creasing her perfect forehead. She jammed her hands on her hips.

"Ms. Winslow." Kennedy's voice vibrated with annoyance.

Rachel narrowed her eyes. "I shouldn't have to remind you I don't work for you *or* answer to you, so I won't."

Silently, Kennedy opened the rear door for her and held it while Rachel slid in. The door slammed and the Humvee lurched forward. She leaned her head back and stared at the roof. She couldn't remember ever being so tired, and the last thing she wanted to do was sleep. If she slept, she might dream. If she dreamed, she might remember. The memories were clear enough—terrible enough—while awake. In dreams the horrors took on new life, towering above reason and reality. She wasn't prepared to risk it—not just yet. If she thought she could close her eyes and dream of Max, she would sleep right there. But she didn't need to sleep to dream of her either. Her face, her voice, the lingering press of her hands and heat of her mouth surrounded her. God, she wanted her.

Kennedy said from the front seat, "Where would you like to go?"

"The hotel." Rachel looked out the window as the CLUs faded into a blur of indistinct desert tan. "I'm done here."

❖

Max braced her back against the shuddering side of the C-130's cavernous belly, closed her eyes, and tried to sleep. The white noise from the droning engine ought to have been enough to drown out her thoughts, but her mind wouldn't settle. She hadn't had time to think about anything since she'd gotten back to the CLU and CC had handed her the departure orders, the last thing she'd expected after Carmody's questions. But her training was ingrained and orders were orders. She didn't think, she acted, and now here she was rattling around in the dark confines of a cargo plane headed for home. The word didn't mean much, only a destination, and she didn't give it much thought. Everything that mattered was behind her and growing more distant by the second.

Her brain struggled to make sense of things. Getting out of Carmody's sights was a bonus, but she couldn't quite figure out the how and why of it. A guy like Carmody didn't quit, and since he hadn't gotten anything out of her, he couldn't be done. Her blood chilled. If he was still looking for a scapegoat, that left Grif. No, not Grif. Grif had been unconscious—that was verified and unarguable. That left Rachel.

And she was leaving Rachel behind. Rachel and everything else that had been her life for over a year. Like stepping into a time machine and being instantly transported from one world to another, because that's what it amounted to. The next time she woke up in her own bed, she wouldn't be facing the possibility of death at every turn. She wouldn't be trusting her life to a handful of people—friends—when she set out to do her job. She'd be alone again.

For an instant she wondered if another tour might be the answer. She knew plenty of Joes who re-upped almost as soon as they were stateside. And not just for the reasons the newspapers liked to highlight—the lack of jobs, the strained relationships, the PTSD. Back in the desert, you knew your worth. And when you faced death and won, you were worth plenty.

Heading back to the Iraqi desert or the mountains of Afghanistan wouldn't get her what she really wanted. Rachel didn't need her to fight for her. She recalled the way Rachel had looked that morning—comfortable, in control, self-assured. Rachel had already slipped back into her world, her real world. In the jungle, Rachel had been transformed—changed into a different person by the necessity to survive. But they weren't in the jungle now, and the Rachel Max had known didn't exist in the world she was headed toward.

❖

Somehow, Rachel fell asleep on the bumpy ride back to Djibouti. When the Humvee pulled in beneath the canopy shading the hotel's large front doors, the change in the engine sound alerted her, and she opened her eyes. Kennedy jumped out and opened her door before she could. Smith joined them and they walked through the lobby together in silence. Smith punched the elevator button and Rachel entered the car automatically. Strange, how everything around her had become monochrome, a world filled with grays. Maybe she was still asleep—sleepwalking, more like it. She leaned against the back wall of the elevator and watched the numbers on the elevator panel flash. She frowned as they sped upward. "I'm on six."

The elevator was not stopping at any of the other floors. They rode straight to the top and the doors opened. "Where are we going?"

Kennedy stepped out, looked right and left, and said, "Right this way, Ms. Winslow."

Rachel debated jumping back in the elevator and realized Smith had used a key. She hadn't really taken note of it at the time. She wouldn't be able to send the elevator down without it. Lovely.

Kennedy and Smith waited for her to join them. She walked between them down the wide carpeted hall to a door at the end. A Smith clone stood by the door, an earpiece curling behind his left ear. He murmured something into a wrist mic, nodded to Smith, and the door opened from the inside. Kennedy gestured her in.

Half expecting Carmody, Rachel steeled herself and entered a huge suite with French doors opening onto a balcony overlooking the city. She glanced around and her breath caught when she saw the man sitting on a love seat in the lounge area, a table for two laid out in front of him. "Dad?"

CHAPTER TWENTY-SEVEN

Stateside

Max had been back on US soil for ten days, back in New York City half that time, and back to work for close to twenty-four hours. She could have put off returning to the hospital for a few weeks, but why would she? What would she do with herself if she wasn't working? Her studio apartment in the Village had a reasonable-sized galley kitchen, a bathroom with decent water pressure, and a small living room-sleeping area combined. Perfectly suited to her needs, but not a place where she wanted to spend a lot of time. She slept there, when she slept. When she returned there after a shift, she showered, reheated whatever takeout she'd had for the last meal, slept if she could or went for a run if she couldn't, and headed back to work. Her real home was the emergency room. She was more at ease in those halls than any place she'd called home except the dirt streets of CLUville. The people were closer to her than any family except her fellow troops. Sure, she wasn't really *close* with any of the doctors and nurses and techs she saw every day, but she knew them and they knew her enough to say hello and pass the time in casual conversation. She had human contact. She had a community. She had something to take her mind off what she didn't have. So she'd called to arrange to return to work even before she'd completed her separation procedures at Lejeune.

Now, at the end of her first shift, part of her at least felt she'd come home. The night had been busy. They usually were with trauma and the emergencies people put off until darkness fell and brought with it the pain and fear that light and activity held at bay. She'd been occupied, body and mind, for long stretches when she didn't have time to think of anything else. On the off times, when she stopped for coffee or to wait for the next patient to be readied for her, she thought about those she'd left behind. Grif and Amina. And Rachel. And the dark crept into her soul too and brought pain with it.

Pushing aside thoughts of what she couldn't change, she signed off on the facial laceration she'd just repaired and dropped the chart into the to-be-filed box. She checked the whiteboard for other surgically related cases and saw they'd brought in a gunshot wound while she'd been in the treatment room suturing. The wound must be superficial if they'd triaged the patient to the ER and not directly to trauma. She noted the room number and headed that way. The curtain was partially open and she glanced inside. A young Hispanic male, eighteen according to his chart, lay on the white sheets with his left arm elevated and a bloody bandage wrapped around his hand. No one else was in the room.

"Mr. Diaz," she said, closing the curtain behind her as she entered. "I'm Dr. de Milles. What happened?"

"Nothing," he said, eyeing her suspiciously.

She raised an eyebrow and gestured with a tilt of her head to his hand. "I'm guessing something did."

"Bad luck. Wrong place, wrong time."

"I know how that is," she murmured. "Is that the only place you're hit?"

"Yeah. Ain't that enough?"

"Mind if I take a look?"

"You the one is gonna fix it?"

"Maybe. Depends on how bad it is."

He blew out air. "Sure. Why not."

She pulled gloves from a cardboard box on the counter next to the sink, put them on, and unwrapped his dressing. As she got closer to the ball of loose gauze in the palm of his hand, she said, "This'll probably hurt a little bit. You ready?"

"Sure," he said in an almost bored voice, but his body tensed beneath the sheets.

She gently eased the gauze away and inspected the wound. A neat round hole was centered in his palm, blood caked around the edges. His thumb and fingers were posed in a natural position as if he were holding a bottle. That was good. If the tendons or nerves had been severed, the fingers would be lax, as if the strings of a marionette had been cut, making the limbs hang flaccidly. She lifted his wrist and turned his hand over. The exit wound on top was considerably larger, almost twice as big as a quarter, and the edges ragged. With a clean gauze she teased away some of the clot. White tendons like thin rubber bands were visible in the depth of the wound.

"Can you straighten your fingers?"

"Hurts like a mother." His fingers didn't move.

"I'm not surprised. But if those tendons aren't cut, we can clean it out down here and get you out of here. If you've got nerve or tendon damage, you need a trip to the OR. And then you'll be here a while."

"Fuck that," he muttered and slowly straightened his fingers.

"Good. Can you close them? Just go slow."

Once again, he slowly flexed his fingers toward his palm.

"That's good enough." She tested sensation in his fingertips and thought as she did about luck. His injury had all the markings of a defensive wound, as if he'd put his hand up to stop the bullet. And perhaps he had. But the bullet did not go through his hand and into his head or his chest or some other vital part of his body. It appeared to have passed through his hand without striking him anywhere else at all. Not only that, none of the critical structures in the incredibly complex anatomy of his hand had been damaged. The wound was no more dangerous than a deep laceration—painful, but neither life-threatening nor debilitating in the long term. He'd been lucky. She'd been sitting next to men who had suddenly fallen over dead from a bullet that skirted beneath their helmets and exploded their heads. She'd seen troops blown into a bloody mist with one misstep on a supposedly safe road that had been cleared by bomb dogs and sweepers. Just bad luck. She'd flown into fire, jumped into hot zones, been feet away from vehicles pulverized by IEDs and here she was, as if she'd never gone away. Unharmed, but changed nonetheless.

"So it's gonna be all right?" he said, uncertainty thinning his voice.

Max dragged herself out of the desert, out of the jungle, and back to the brightly lit room. The dark receded with a howl and a promise to return.

"Yeah. It's gonna be okay. First, we'll put your hand in a basin with some Betadine and get this cleaned up. The nurses will give you something for pain before we get started. Then we'll wash it out and clean it up a little bit and send you out on antibiotics."

"So—how long will it be before it's better?"

"Are you left- or right-handed?"

"Left," he said, indicating the injured hand.

She wondered what he was thinking about holding again—a gun, a violin, a child? She didn't know him, not like she'd known Grif and Rachel. The pain of remembering made an end run and she shoved it back again. They didn't need her now. Grif was probably in a stateside hospital with Laurie holding his hand. And Rachel—Rachel was living her life far away from danger. Max regarded the anxious boy, her responsibility now. "The wound will be healed in a couple of weeks. You'll be stiff and sore, but the more you use it once the soft tissue is healed, the better."

"Yeah, okay." He relaxed against the pillows and closed his eyes. "You do it, man. I'm good."

"Yeah. You are." Max went out to find a nurse to medicate him so she could irrigate and debride the wound and get it closed.

What was left of the night was uneventful, and at seven she met her replacement, a big man with the personality of a teddy bear, in the coffee room.

"So I saw the article in the newspaper the other day," Ben Markowitz said after Max finished filling him in on the patients who were waiting for X-rays to be read, lab tests to come back, or for the OR to open up for their urgent but noncritical surgeries.

"Uh-huh," she said, hoping that would be the end of it.

"Seriously, that was an incredible story. I…I don't want to say the wrong thing, but I don't know—I feel like I should say thank you."

Max put the charts down and looked into his well-meaning face. His blue eyes were soft and compassionate, his broad, soft features gentle. A wave of anger passed through, surprising her with its heat. No one would have known what she'd done if Tom Benedict hadn't written about the rescue, and he wouldn't have known about that if Rachel hadn't needed to bail her out. She spoke with measured calm. "It's not necessary. I didn't do anything that thousands of others haven't done."

"I'm sure that's true, but your story makes it real, Max. To me, to a lot of people. And that's important." He leaned forward earnestly. "It's important to put a human face on the cost of it all. That's what makes it real."

"Real," Max murmured. She'd looked at the story, saw the pictures that Benedict's photographer had taken at the end of the interview of her and Rachel posed together. She'd read the account of what had happened in the jungle, but the telling of it—no matter how accurate Benedict had been—sanitized the events. Even the descriptions of the dead were impotent compared to the truth of it. Rachel, she discovered in the article, was Rachel Winslow Harriman, daughter of the Secretary of State. That put the pieces together, finally, of why the Black Hawks had been deployed to extract the aid workers, particularly Rachel. Her father's surprise visit to the Middle East was probably related to the timing. And now Rachel was traveling with her father while he toured the war zone, assessing the need for retracting troops or redistributing them or simply boosting morale.

Max hadn't known any of that when she and Rachel had spent those hours together preparing for another attack. She hadn't known when Rachel had come to her CLU and taken solace in her arms and pleasure in her body. The article didn't make it real for her because none of that had anything to do with what mattered to her.

"Like I said," Max said, "things like that happen all the time out there. There are thousands of heroes. I don't deserve anything special."

He nodded solemnly. "Okay. Well, I'm glad you're back."

She took a breath and said what he needed to hear. "Thanks. So am I."

Maybe one day it would be true.

Max wished Ben a quiet shift, collected her gear, and walked out into the morning. She blinked in the sunlight, surprised as she always was to realize another day had begun while she had spent the night locked away in a world that might have been a galaxy away from the life that passed outside the hospital. She was forty blocks from home, but she liked the walk and headed in that direction.

"Max?"

Max stopped, not certain she'd actually heard her name. She turned and watched as Rachel handed money to a cabbie, picked up a suitcase, and walked toward her.

"Rachel?" Max waited, breathing slowly and carefully, afraid to disturb the air and dispel the apparition.

"Yes." Rachel set down the suitcase a few feet from Max and pushed hair out of her eyes. Her hand shook. She was pale, circles under her eyes, weariness in the lines around her mouth. She looked thinner, haunted, like a ghost figure from one of Max's dreams.

"Are you okay?" Max grimaced. "Dumb question. Sorry. I just didn't expect to see you." *Ever.*

"Yes," Rachel said. "Sorry about that. I've just spent eighteen hours on a couple of airplanes. Sorry to barge in on you like this. But—I had to see you."

"I thought you were still in Mogadishu."

People walked by, streaming around them as if they were an island in the midst of a fast-running river. Max feared Rachel might be caught up by the current and swept away at any second. She wanted to hold on to her—to keep her close.

"I was until last night. I couldn't get away before then. My father—"

"Yes, I saw in the paper about his surprise visit to the forward bases. You traveled with him, it said."

Rachel's gaze roamed Max's face. "Part of the trip. He wanted me along. PR. I don't suppose I need to explain." She winced, shook her head. "Well, not that at least. A lot of other things."

Max slid her hands into the pockets of her black cargo pants. "Rachel, you don't need to explain anything to me."

Rachel's eyes looked older than Max remembered. Wounded in a way they hadn't even in the midst of all the terror. She wanted to brush her thumbs over the bruises below Rachel's eyes and whisper them away. She wanted to heal her the way she sometimes healed others, only this need to erase the pain touched her so much more deeply than ever before.

"Please, Max." Rachel took a step closer and clasped Max's arm, her fingers warm and soft. "I know it's not something you even want to hear, but if you would just let me explain—"

"You're not going to do any explaining until you've eaten and slept." Max couldn't bear the sadness in Rachel's eyes. She cupped Rachel's jaw. "How about I make you breakfast."

Rachel smiled and made a small sound that was half laughter and half sob. "Are you still taking care of me, Commander de Milles?"

Max picked up Rachel's suitcase. "As much as you'll allow, maybe."

"I could have gone home," Rachel said, not moving. "My apartment is uptown, but I came here because it's the only place I knew you might be. I haven't been sleeping well."

"No, neither have I. Let's get a cab."

"All right," Rachel said.

Max stepped to the curb, waved down a cab, and as it pulled over, returned to Rachel. She hefted the suitcase and slid her arm around Rachel's waist. Holding her was the first thing that felt totally right since she'd left Djibouti. "My place okay with you?"

"Perfect."

CHAPTER TWENTY-EIGHT

The cab bumped along in the stop-and-go morning traffic. Rachel caught herself about to lean against Max's shoulder, knowing she shouldn't, *couldn't*...but she was so very tired and Max was there. After so long, after what felt like forever, Max was there. She hadn't really expected her to be. She'd thought when she arrived at the hospital, Max would be gone. That when she asked for her, the people inside would say they'd never even heard of her. As if Max was all an illusion, born out of terror and hope and desire. If Max hadn't been there, she would have dragged her suitcase back out to the street and gone home. She would have pulled down the shades, crawled into bed, and prayed that when she woke, her world would have righted itself. That when she woke she would be in control again, that her heart would have stopped aching. That she would know how to find Max.

She could smell her. Different than before. The earthy, sun-drenched scent was gone. In its place was a hint of spice—shampoo, maybe, or hand soap—and the underlying bite of something medicinal and stark. Her hair was a little longer. She needed a cut, but the shagginess suited her all the same. A little defiant and wild, like Max. Her maroon scrub shirt hung outside her black pants. Her black boots laced up, like combat boots, and she still wore no jewelry. The chain around her neck was gone, but the dog tags might as well still have been there. Max was still on duty, maybe still at war.

"You're just coming from work," Rachel said, her brain functioning again. "You must need to sleep. This is a bad idea."

Max shifted on the seat until her knee touched Rachel's and their eyes met. Max's eyes hadn't changed. Still that electric blue deeper than any Rachel had ever known. She'd expected anger or distance or cold dismissal, but Max's eyes were tender, the way they had been the first time the two of them had touched on the edge of the jungle. Absurdly, Rachel wished they were still there, standing under the hot sun with Max's hand on her waist, steadying her, Max's eyes gentle and warm. When had she become so desperately needy? She tried to escape the pull of Max's gaze, but she couldn't. Not when she'd come so far to be near her.

"Tell the cabbie to take me home when we get to your place. You can call me or—"

"No," Max said. Just that. No. "I have to run out to get some food. I don't think there's anything except maybe some leftover Chinese."

"That sounds wonderful to me." Rachel didn't want Max to go anywhere, afraid if she left, disappeared from sight, she'd be gone again. Maybe forever. "I don't need you to do anything special. I'm just...glad to see you."

Max took Rachel's hand. Her fingers were as warm as Rachel remembered. She squeezed gently and let go. Rachel wanted to cry out when the contact slipped away.

"It's good to see you too. But the Chinese is way too left-over to be safe." Max smiled a crooked smile and moved her knee.

Silence filled the cab until it pulled up before an apartment building in a long row of them on a narrow street dotted with the occasional maple and lined with cars parked bumper to bumper. Three steps led up to each wooden double front door.

Max handed over money, climbed out, and while Rachel followed, grabbed her luggage from the trunk. Max's building was brown stone, with tall narrow windows on every floor and nothing else to distinguish it.

"It's the third floor," Max said, leading the way inside.

Rachel entered a tiny foyer and climbed a twisting set of stairs, through hallways smelling of disinfectant past closed doors that echoed with emptiness. Max fumbled a key from the backpack she'd slung over one shoulder, opened the door that said *3B*, and held it wide. Rachel stepped in past her and stopped in the center of a single large room with a kitchen tucked into one corner, a sofa under the tall front window, a plain oak coffee table in front of that, several bookcases filled with books on the wall by the door, and a medium-sized television on a stand that needed dusting. No dishes in the sink, no magazines and newspapers lying around. Neat and Spartan, like Max's CLU had been. There was even a pile of clothes next to the sofa, which she guessed was Max's bed. Functional and nothing else. The door closed behind her, the suitcase thumped to the floor, and they were alone again. She was almost afraid to turn around, she wanted Max so desperately. The hot glide of her flesh, the cool oasis of her mouth, the steady strength of her arms. Everything she needed. She wrapped her arms around her waist and kept facing the window.

The silence was still and heavy.

Max wasn't yet completely sure Rachel was real, standing there in the middle of her barren life, not sure she wouldn't wake from a dream to find Rachel gone and herself caught in another form of nightmare where the loss would be more than she could bear. Rachel was battered and bruised now, and Max was the only one who really knew why—they shared the same haunted memories. In time, Rachel would heal and Max might be a reminder of what she'd rather forget. Rachel was not only too strong to need anyone to slay her demons, she also had another life far different than anything she shared with Max.

And none of it mattered—not the risk, not the pain, not the empty place her life would become if she let Rachel in and Rachel walked out again. Nothing mattered except Rachel, and she was here. Nothing else had mattered since the moment she'd run toward the rising Black Hawk, taking fire from every direction, jumped into its belly, and turned to see Rachel waiting for her. Rachel was here now, and she looked on the verge of collapse.

"I'll get you a towel and you can grab a shower," Max said. "I'll pick up some food and be back before you're done."

"Yes, all right," Rachel said softly.

Max rummaged in the single closet and found clean towels. "It's in here."

Rachel followed into the small bathroom.

"Take as long as you need," Max said. The space between the sink and the wall was just large enough to turn around in, and with two of them, the fit was tight. Rachel was an inch away, so still and vulnerable Max's heart bled. She cupped her face, ran her thumb over the arch of Rachel's cheek. Rachel drew a breath that quavered.

"Then you sleep," Max whispered.

Rachel's fingers closed around Max's wrist, sending a surge of fire through her.

"I need to tell you things."

"Maybe," Max murmured, "but that can wait."

"I'm afraid," Rachel said so softly Max wasn't sure she heard her. "Afraid if you walk out, I won't see you again."

Max cradled her head in both hands and kissed her gently, not with the passion that roared inside her, but with all the tenderness and reassurance she could put into it. "I won't. I told you that before."

Rachel's hands fisted in Max's shirt and she rested her forehead against Max's. She laughed unsteadily. "I seem to keep losing you."

"No, you don't." Max closed her eyes, drew in the light scent that clung to her hair, the same vanilla that had lingered on her pillow. Her heart raced so fast she was dizzy. "You never have."

"If you say you'll be back, I believe you." Rachel raised her eyes. "I always have."

Max forced herself to break away. She wanted to be inside her, lost in the scent and taste of her. But that wasn't what Rachel needed. Maybe not even what she needed. She took another step away while every inch of her protested. "I'll be here."

"Thank you." Rachel smiled wanly and reached for the buttons on her shirt.

Max fled.

She grabbed her keys, checked her wallet to be sure she had money, and raced down the stairs to the street. In the twenty-four-hour market on the corner, she hastily gathered juice and bread and eggs and whatever else she thought Rachel might want to eat, waited impatiently while two people in front of her checked out, and sprinted back. When she let herself into the apartment, the water was still running in the bathroom. The tightness in her chest eased. She didn't want Rachel to think she wouldn't be there for her.

She poured some juice and popped bread in the toaster. When she turned around with the juice in her hand, Rachel stood in the bathroom door, the plain white bath towel Max had given her wrapped around her chest beneath her arms. It fell to midthigh, a V opening along the outer aspect of her left hip. Her thigh was smooth and long and sleek. Her hair was wet and hung in tangles to her shoulders. She was barefoot. She was beautiful.

"I made toast," Max said inanely.

Rachel smiled. "I can smell it. I didn't think I was hungry, but it smells wonderful."

"Eggs?"

Rachel shook her head. "Maybe later. I think right now just the toast."

Max nodded, realized she was still holding the glass of orange juice. She set it down on the coffee table, aware of Rachel moving closer. She carried the heat of the shower with her, the scent of soap and shampoo. Max's hands trembled.

"Max."

Max straightened and Rachel was there, inches away. She groaned, the wanting a beast that tore through her, shredding sanity and reason. "I'm having trouble thinking of anything except touching you."

"I'm glad."

Max shook her head. "Sorry."

Rachel slid her arms around Max's neck and the heat of her skin wafted over Max. "Don't be."

Max tugged the towel free and pulled Rachel the rest of the way to her. Rachel was naked and warm and fit perfectly in her arms. Max held her tightly and kissed her with everything she'd held back earlier, ripping aside every barrier she'd ever made to take her in, needing her taste more than water in the desert. Rachel whimpered and fisted her hands in Max's hair, wrapping one leg around Max's to join them more closely. Max kissed her for a long time, their bodies locked, stroking the length of Rachel's smooth back, over the curve of her ass, up her sides until her thumbs brushed the full swell of Rachel's breasts. Rachel whimpered again, her hips circling beneath Max's hands.

"The couch," Max gasped. "I have to open it."

"Hurry."

Max shoved the coffee table aside and flipped open the bed. She hadn't slept in it much and the sheets were neat and regulation tight. She ripped down the top one, yanked her scrub shirt off over her head, and shoved free of her pants and boots. She grabbed Rachel's hand and pulled her down onto the bed. Sunlight streamed through the window over their heads, painting Rachel's skin golden. Max leaned over her and kissed her again, running her hands over her breasts and belly and the arch of her hip. Rachel's legs parted and her hips rose. Max eased back to look into Rachel's eyes as she caressed her. Rachel's lips parted on a sigh and her eyes went liquid.

"I dreamed this," Rachel whispered.

"So did I." Gently, Max filled her. She shuddered, feeling as if she was holding back a tidal wave. She wanted to drive inside her, to take her and take her over and drown in her pleasure. She pressed her forehead to Rachel's shoulder and fought to catch her breath, to find her control.

Rachel's fingers came around her wrist, pushed her deeper. "Don't go slow. Not this time."

Max kissed her and followed the call of Rachel's rising and falling hips. Gliding deep and long and smooth, circling her clit with every stroke. Rachel's nails dug into her shoulders, urging, demanding. Max let go of her last restraint and sped up. Rachel came with a sharp cry, her mouth pressed to Max's neck. Max kept going, heeding the pulse of desire tight around her.

"Yes, yes," Rachel cried, lifting to take her deeper. She came again, and again when Max slid down and put her mouth where her thumb had been, teasing and stroking until Rachel gripped her head and came in her mouth.

Max would have stayed as she was forever, but Rachel pushed at her shoulder, the other hand tangled in her hair. "Enough. God. I'm done. I'm finished."

Max rested her cheek on the inside of Rachel's leg, smiling as she caught her breath. "Temporarily."

Rachel's fingers tugged feebly at her hair. "Like temporarily for a week. I can't believe what you do to me."

Max kissed the soft skin on the inside of Rachel's thigh and sat up next to her. She caressed her breast, cupped her warm fullness. "I'm not done."

Rachel stroked her face, her eyes hazy and satisfied. "Good."

Max stretched out beside her and drew Rachel's head to her shoulder. Rachel kissed her breast, fingers playing over her chest and down her belly. Max jerked and Rachel laughed, a predatory sound that sent Max's heart thundering in her chest.

"No, not done at all," Rachel said.

Rachel's fingers slipped between Max's thighs and her vision blurred. All the need she'd set aside, intent on pleasing Rachel, came roaring back. She rocketed toward the peak. "Fuck, wait."

"Oh, I don't think so," Rachel murmured.

Fingers closed around Max's clit and her muscles turned to jelly. Her breath heaved from her chest and her legs went tight as iron bands. Rachel's mouth was at her breast, her throat, and all the while she was stroking and stroking, and Max could only groan.

Rachel's lips skimmed over her ear. "I love your body. I love touching you."

Max struggled to focus on her face. She was helpless and Rachel was there.

"You're beautiful." Rachel circled and stroked and squeezed.

Max exploded with an astonished cry, gripping the sheets and shaking with the blast. Rachel slid on top of her, still stroking, and rocked against her thigh, coming again as the last tremors coursed through Max's body.

Rachel collapsed on top of her, still inside her. Max held her close and pulled the sheet over them. She closed her eyes, her mind completely blank, and knew she would not dream.

CHAPTER TWENTY-NINE

Rachel woke naked with Max's arm circling her waist, a hand cupping her breast, and warm breath wafting softly against the back of her neck. The sheets were tangled around her feet and a faint breeze blew through the open window. Max must've gotten up to open it sometime after Rachel had fallen asleep. She couldn't tell how long she'd been asleep, but it felt like a long time. Outside the street noises were a jumble of car engines, horns, and muted voices. By the feel of the air, it was late afternoon—the air carried the moist, warm thickness of summer in the city, so different from the punishing dryness of the desert. Her sleep had been deep and dreamless, or if she'd dreamed, she couldn't remember.

She lay still, absorbing the happiness stirred by Max's nearness. She'd always wanted to live her life on her own terms and prided herself on charting her own course, certain of what she wanted—and didn't want. She'd made her own way without games, without pretense or politics, and had created a life with purpose, with a goal that had meaning beyond her own gain or ego. Most of those she helped never even knew her name. Her work satisfied her, and she'd relegated relationships to a distant part of her psyche and her soul. She socialized with women, she had sex with women, she moved within the world they had in common—the society they'd been born to—and she kept what mattered most private. She hadn't needed or wanted more.

Lying in the afternoon sun, her body still flushed from passion and pleasure, she revisited the images of the past hours. Desire like a hunger she'd never imagined, excitement so sharp she feared she might die from it, satisfaction so sweet she could never have enough. She covered Max's hand where it covered her breast, and Max's fingers slid through hers. She'd been content before, but she wanted more now. Much, much more.

Rachel lifted Max's hand and kissed her palm.

Max's lips moved over her neck.

"Hi," Rachel whispered.

"Hey."

Max's voice was throaty, heavy with sleep and languorous with satisfaction. Rachel recognized the sound of a woman well-pleasured but had never been so pleased to hear it. Max was always so well defended, so strong and self-sufficient, she seemed always in control. To feel Max open to her hands and her mouth and give herself so completely was a gift Rachel feared she didn't deserve and wanted over and over. She wanted her now with an ache in her bones. Her loins were heavy and full and pounding. Her nipples tightened and she pressed Max's fingers to her breast again.

"Do you need to go to work or—"

"No," Max said.

"I don't think I'm nearly finished yet."

Max made a low growling sound in her throat and pressed her hips against Rachel's ass. Rachel pushed back, ready for Max's fingers. For her mouth.

"I could go on like this forever," Rachel murmured.

"Done."

Rachel's heart soared but she knew it wouldn't be that easy. The past stood between them as much as it united them. She turned onto her back to say what she needed to say to Max's face before her body ran away with her brain. Max gave a protesting grumble but shifted onto her elbow, leaned over Rachel, and kissed her.

"You look beautiful," Max said.

Rachel laughed in protest, feeling shy when she never had been before. "I couldn't possibly be. I think I fell asleep without even combing my hair."

"You did. I like the tangled look." Max grinned, a satisfied glint in her eyes. "And *I* promised to feed you, and I still haven't done that."

Rachel gripped Max's hand before she could move away. "Don't go."

Max's eyes darkened and she kissed her again. "I'm not going anywhere."

But she might, Rachel knew. In a few minutes, a few hours, tomorrow.

"There were things I needed to say back in Djibouti. I should have said them earlier." Rachel faltered. What if Max didn't want the woman she really was—here in this world?

"Rachel," Max said, "whatever you need to say, say it. There's nothing you can tell me that will erase what we've shared."

"I know." Rachel took a breath. "I'm more afraid about the future."

"Tell me about Christie."

"I would have sooner, if I'd thought there was anything to tell. Tommy blindsided me, but it was hardly his fault," Rachel said, equal parts relief and anxiety rushing through her. "Christie is Tommy's sister. I was seeing her for about six months before I left for Africa."

Max's expression never changed, her gaze never wavered. She waited and watched. She was good at that. Good at confronting whatever needed taking care of head-on. Her hand on Rachel's belly was warm and possessive, and Rachel loved the way it felt.

"No promises were made," Rachel said, "and before I left for Somalia, we both agreed there were no restrictions on either of us."

"Benedict didn't get the memo."

Rachel sighed. "Yes, well, our families have known each other for a long time. Tommy and I were in school together. Christie is a few years younger. Our fathers are colleagues, our mothers are friends. Everyone thinks it's a wonderful match."

"Is it?"

Rachel laughed. "No. For a million reasons, the most important one being I don't love her. She doesn't love me either, but I don't think that matters quite as much to her."

"I can't see you agreeing to something just to please your family." Max's brows drew down. "And I can't see you settling for anything."

Rachel caressed Max's forearm, tracing the taut muscles down to Max's hand on her belly. No, she wouldn't settle. Not when she knew what she wanted. What she'd always wanted but been afraid to admit. "Christie might think we'll just pick up where we left off when I get home. We won't."

Max's eyes darkened, and she slowly leaned down and nipped Rachel's lower lip. "Good. Anything else?"

"Where to start?" Rachel closed her eyes, wishing she could just begin her life with the day she met Max, but she couldn't. "I'm only telling you because sometimes it's hard to keep one's private life private."

"For the daughter of the Secretary of State?"

Rachel's face grew hot. "That and the fact that my family is… well-known in some circles."

Max's eyebrow rose. "Meaning it's news if you get a parking ticket?"

"Something like that."

"Is that why you don't use your full name?"

Rachel had known when she'd asked Tommy to file his article Max would see it sooner or later. She'd planned to explain everything after the interview, but Max was gone. She hadn't wanted her to find out the things she'd kept from her that way, even though when they'd been together none of it seemed important. Not what her father did, not who her family was, not Christie and their relationship—none of it had mattered out there where life was minute to minute. Out there, she was Rachel Winslow, Red Cross worker, just as right here in this small, quiet apartment, she was only Rachel, stripped of everything except what truly mattered—what was in her heart.

"I love my family," Rachel said, "but they can be—stifling. I've always struggled not to get pulled under, not to get caught up in the plans other people made for me. For that and other reasons…security"—she grimaced—"it's been easier to use my middle name."

"I like it," Max said. "Winslow."

Rachel laughed. "Me too."

Max didn't care about Rachel's high-profile family or her past girlfriends, but she was happy to listen if Rachel needed to tell her, especially when the shadows began to leave Rachel's eyes. Rachel's laughter was like a light turning on in the dark, illuminating passages long forgotten, igniting hope as fears retreated. A day ago Max had never expected to see her again, and now she held her. A fierce urge to protect her, to possess her, to *keep* her, made her shudder with its force. She caressed Rachel's face. "Your trust means everything. I hope you always feel safe telling me what matters to you. But none of this changes anything." Max pulled her close. "None of this changes what happened out there between us."

"What about here, Max? It will change things here."

Max shrugged. "I don't see how."

"It's my fault Carmody went after you."

"How so?" Max narrowed her gaze. "Are you a secret CIA agent?"

"Would that be a deal breaker?"

"I'd rather you be FBI."

Rachel laughed again and pressed a kiss to Max's throat. "Sorry. I don't have any other secret lives."

"So how is it you're responsible for Carmody?"

"That would be because I'm my father's daughter. My being at the aid camp brought your whole operation to the attention of a lot of important people."

"Important, or powerful?"

"Yes. Well. People who could send Carmody to Wichita apparently, or so my father explained it."

"Your being at the aid camp was why we were there at all," Max said.

"I hope that's not true," Rachel said, her voice uncertain. "I hope you would have been sent to help no matter who was out there."

"Do you know what happened?"

"Some." Rachel snorted softly. "I browbeat my father into telling me what he could. Or what he wanted. I told him I wouldn't go with him on his tour if he didn't explain what was going on."

"Is Carmody his man?"

"He says no. The two he sent to *accompany* me—Kennedy and Smith—were, though. Part of his advance team from State. That's how they got to me so fast."

"Did you know your father was coming?"

"No. His visit really was supposed to be a surprise trip." Rachel sat up against the pillows. Max shifted and slid an arm around her shoulders.

"Advance intelligence got wind of a pending raid on the camp, and he was advised. He called me—he wanted to be sure I didn't resist leaving."

Max rubbed her arm. "He seems to know you."

"Ha-ha." Rachel nuzzled Max's neck. "I probably would have argued against leaving, especially if you just showed up the way you did and couldn't take everyone."

"Why were you—or the camp—a target to begin with? I don't get it. You're a humanitarian group."

"Enter Carmody." Rachel made a disgusted sound. "He was running an operative in our camp, one of our Somali guards who had infiltrated the rebel organization. As part of the guard's cover, he was arranging for weapons to be smuggled in along with the supplies we were receiving."

"The transport trucks," Max said.

"Yes."

Rage simmered in Max's belly. "Carmody was helping to arm the rebels so his operative could gather intelligence?"

"Yes. I guess he figured the trade-off was worth it."

Max thought of Grif nearly dying from a bullet Carmody might have put into the hands of the enemy. If she'd known, she would have gone through with her fantasy of choking Carmody to death. "Prick."

"Comes with the territory."

"Yeah," Max said. "So when the operation went south, Carmody had to answer to someone, and he was looking to shift the blame."

"Getting anything out of my father was not easy, but apparently Carmody's operative was compromised somehow and Carmody either didn't know or didn't act fast enough to pull him out. He lost his man, his link to the rebels, and I was almost killed or captured. His ass was on the line."

"I wish I could have seen his face when Benedict's story hit the wire."

Rachel grinned. "Me too."

"What made you call Benedict?"

"I had to do something," Rachel said. "I had to get Carmody away from you, and I couldn't shoot him."

Max kissed her. "Thank you for that. For not shooting him, and for getting him off my back."

"I knew Tommy was embedded, and I thought if the public knew what you and the others did out there, Carmody couldn't railroad you into anything."

"You got me fast-tracked home because Carmody didn't want Tommy or someone else digging around."

"I hadn't planned on them shipping you out so soon." Rachel took Max's hand. "I didn't want…"

"What?"

"I didn't want to lose you."

Max's throat closed. She hadn't been afraid of dying in the jungle. She hadn't thought she'd had all that much to lose. Now she did. "You couldn't have."

Rachel braced her hands on Max's shoulders. Her face was very near, so near Max got lost in the green of her eyes. "I don't want this afternoon to be the end."

"Neither do I."

"I wouldn't mind if we never left this room, if we never saw anyone else again." Rachel sighed. "But I don't think either one of us can walk away from our lives."

"No, and I don't think you want to." Max let herself imagine a life with Rachel in it. The possibility was almost as terrifying as the idea of endless days without her. "You know where I live. There's no one in my life. There won't be."

Rachel studied her, a small frown line appearing between her brows. "Is that what you think? That I want to stop in from time to time, between trips?"

"I don't think anything. I think I want to see you again."

"Our relationship won't be completely private," Rachel warned.

"Because the Benedicts of the world are always looking for a story?"

"Worse, I'm afraid. Tommy is a serious journalist who was willing to put his life in danger to tell the truth. I respect him for that."

"Yes, so do I."

"There are reporters, a lot of them, who would rather sell copy that's a little more popular, and celebrity sells."

"Listen," Max said, "there's nothing reporters can do or say that would mean anything to me after the places I've been and the things I've seen. The things I've done."

"You're sure?"

"Totally."

Rachel smiled. "Then how do you feel about a trip to DC? My father mentioned he wants to meet you, and I'd like the rest of my family to meet you too."

Max stared. "Is that because of Somalia? Or something else?"

Rachel's smile faded. "Everyone loves good press—including the State Department. I can't promise there won't be a reporter or two around."

Max swung out of bed and crossed to the kitchen to give herself time to regroup. Everything was coming at her so fast. Rachel couldn't know what she was getting into. "I'm not relationship material, Rachel—not the meet-the-family kind."

"Oh?" Rachel said from close behind her. "What kind of relationship material are you, then? Just good for sex now and then?"

"I'm not...I'm not what you're looking for."

"You were perfectly willing to keep seeing me a few minutes ago."

"I thought—"

"You thought we'd just bump into each other now and then and fuck?" Rachel's voice was calm. "I understand."

Max spun around. Rachel was searching on the floor for her clothes. "Where are you going?"

"You must have things to do."

"Damn it." Max had fucked up.

CHAPTER THIRTY

R achel picked up her suitcase from where Max had left it just inside
the door and let herself out, being careful not to slam the door.
She wasn't angry, at least not at Max. None of this was Max's fault.
She'd shown up with no warning, had made assumptions, or maybe
just wishes, that Max felt what she felt. Max had every right to want
nothing more than an as-long-as-we're-having-fun relationship. She'd
had more than a few of those herself.

But not this time. She knew how she felt about Max, and for the
first time in her life, she knew what she wanted with a woman, what she
wanted for herself beyond her job and obligations. She couldn't have
the kind of affair with Max she'd had with every other woman she'd
been with. She couldn't pretend that being with Max didn't touch her
on every level, that she didn't want Max in every part of her life. In
every part of her. If Max didn't feel the same, at least she was honest
enough to say so.

The pain would come later, she knew, but for now, she needed
distance. She couldn't be in the same room with Max and not want her.
And if she stayed too long, she might let herself believe she could do
with less. She pulled her suitcase to the curb and stepped out into the
street, searching for a cab.

A window creaked up behind her.

"Rachel, we should talk," Max called down.

Rachel turned and shielded her eyes as she looked up. Max leaned
out the window, her hands curled around the stone sill. She'd pulled on
a T-shirt and it stretched across her chest the way Rachel remembered
her camo shirt doing when Max had taken off her jacket in the jungle to

dig in the dry, hard earth. She couldn't look at her without remembering so many moments, every one of them leading her here. "It's all right, Max."

"No, it isn't." Even from three stories up, Max's eyes burned fiercely. "I don't want this."

"What *do* you want, Max?"

"I don't know. I've never let myself think about it." Max leaned out farther, looking as if she might jump down. "I never imagined you."

"You need to think about it now," Rachel said. "I'm not going to settle. I can't, not where you're concerned."

Max's smile was crooked. "You shouldn't settle for anything with anyone."

"So. I'll be waiting." Rachel had to turn away. Max was so beautiful it hurt to look at her.

A cab slid to the curb and Rachel picked up her suitcase. She slid into the back and gave him the address. He pulled away, and she closed her eyes. Walking away from what she wanted with every breath was worse than a nightmare. She'd feared losing Max so many times as they'd fought enemies who attacked with guns and power, but she'd never imagined letting her go.

Chapter Thirty-one

With the same care that she usually reserved for inspecting her equipment before a mission, Max fastened the last stud on her pleated white shirt and checked to see that her black tie was straight. Details mattered, and tonight more than ever.

She'd thought at first there'd been a mistake. The invitation—really, more like an order couched in fancy language embossed on pretty stationery—had arrived just hours before the phone call from the CO of her naval reserve unit. She was to appear at a State Department function to meet with members of the press, DOS officials, and other dignitaries to honor her service in the remarkable rescue of Rachel Winslow Harriman and other members of the Red Cross team.

"Did you get the message?" Captain Yoon said when he called.

"Am I to take this as official?" Max wasn't ready to see Rachel yet. She knew what Rachel wanted—what Rachel deserved, and couldn't imagine herself being enough. She'd never been enough for anyone she'd wanted to care about her. She'd only been enough in the ER or in the field of fire, and even then she'd failed so many. Rachel's world was so much larger than hers. And Rachel was so much braver.

"You're to take it as a *request* from command." Yoon's tone told her the Navy couldn't order her to attend unless she was an official representative of the corps. Then whatever she said would be the Navy's responsibility. But they were making it clear she was to go *un*officially—and if she found herself in a tight place, the Navy could and probably would cut her loose. Just like they'd done with Carmody.

"I got it," Max said.

"So what the hell's going on?" Yoon's curiosity rang down the line.

She couldn't very well tell him what she didn't know herself. The invitation might be exactly what it appeared to be—the press wanting more of a story and the State Department wanting to capitalize on a situation that made them look good for a change. Maybe Carmody and his ilk had nothing to do with it. Maybe no one was watching her. Or Rachel. Questions she couldn't answer and even if she could, it wouldn't matter. She owed it to Rachel to appear.

"I'll be there. What about Grif and the others?"

"Griffin just arrived at Bethesda for rehab. The others are all still deployed. You're the poster girl for this op."

"Great."

Yoon laughed. "Good luck. And remember, the Navy never questions our mission, and we never make mistakes."

"Ooh-rah," she murmured and disconnected.

Now, three days later, she stood in front of the mirror in a hotel in Foggy Bottom a few blocks from the Harry S. Truman Building where the function was to kick off with a reception at 1900 hours. She wasn't nervous about talking to the press or rubbing shoulders with statesmen and other political types. They meant nothing to her. But Rachel would be there. And when she thought of her, her hands shook.

She'd passed the Red Cross building in the cab on the way to the hotel and wondered if Rachel had settled back into her life by now. Returned to work, reconnected with friends and family and…other relationships. Max had resumed her life as much as she ever could, working twenty-four on and thirty-six off. But she hadn't quite been able to return to the insular world she'd inhabited before Rachel. Work still consumed her in the moment, but as soon as a crisis was past, other thoughts crept in. Memories, fragments of conversations, glimpses of Rachel. The ache in her chest never went away. She'd been on the verge of tracking down Rachel's phone number a dozen times, but nothing she wanted to say to her could have been said over the phone even if she had known what to say. And now she'd be seeing her for the first time since she'd watched her drive away in a cab almost two weeks before.

She snapped the cuffs of the dress blue jacket, took the elevator down to the street, and walked to the Harry S. Truman Building. She told the guard at the door why she was there; he ID'd her and directed her through security to the elevators. She stepped off onto a massive, brightly lit two-story lobby with stone colonnades, marble floors, and rows of crystal chandeliers. A wall of sound slapped at her, reverberating like the hum of a dozen birds with rotors churning getting ready to lift off. The noise—distinguishable as voices now—grew louder the farther she walked until she found herself in the midst of a crowd of men and women in black tie, evening dresses, and uniforms from every branch of the armed forces. A bar was set up along one side with rows of white-linen-covered tables and a dozen bartenders in white jackets, white shirts, and black bow ties pouring drinks. She made her way over and asked for a soda water. Wineglass in hand, she turned and surveyed the room, ice cubes clinking as she sipped. She didn't know anyone and hadn't expected to. She hadn't taken a second sip before a brunette who didn't look more than twenty, in a deep burgundy dress and low functional heels, pushed through the crowd and gave her a bright smile. "Commander de Milles?"

"That's right," Max said.

"I'm Shelley Carpenter, one of Secretary Harriman's interns. If you'd come with me, please."

"Sure."

She followed the young woman through the crowd to an archway where a small group of men and women stood conversing, drinks in hand. The intern rushed over—double time seeming to be her normal speed—and spoke to a tall, broad-shouldered, dark-haired man who turned in Max's direction and gave her a steady look of appraisal. She looked back. Rachel had his strong features, but her eyes were warm where his were cool, even at a distance.

Max stepped forward and squared her shoulders.

Rachel's father held out his hand. "Commander, Christopher Harriman."

"Sir," she said as she returned his firm grip, "it's a pleasure to meet you."

"I want to thank you for taking care of my daughter out there. And the others, of course."

"No thanks are needed, sir."

"I won't argue the point, but the thanks stand." He smiled wryly, and his gaze swept the gathering. "Now for the other matters. The *Post* wants to do a series of articles on the impact of the ongoing unrest in Somalia and elsewhere on civilians caught up in all of this, and this story is right up their alley."

"I'm sure Ms. Winslow and her team can shed much more light on that than I."

"The press are always looking for a story to grab the public's attention, and this one has all the right angles—humanitarian workers at risk, the daughter of a cabinet member under attack, a daring rescue by America's finest. We need the public to know the military's mission is to secure civilian liberties and aid in rebuilding these nations."

"I was just one—"

"Tom Benedict made you the face of the Navy in all of this. I'm afraid you'll have to play the part."

"I understand." Max did. This was payback time for getting Carmody off her back. "Of course I'll be happy to do whatever is necessary."

"I'm sure you will. I've read the statements you gave Tom Benedict. Well done, considering."

"Sir?"

He regarded her a moment longer in silence.

Max waited. She had no agenda, and if he did, he'd have to spell it out. She had plenty of practice waiting.

"I'm afraid events unfolded rather too rapidly for us to contain, and you suffered some of the fallout. Despite some regrettable avenues of investigation, you demonstrated remarkable restraint with the press."

"I was just doing my job, sir."

"Yes. Well, we all have a job to do." Harriman set his rocks glass on the silver tray of a passing waiter. "My daughter speaks very highly of you."

Max held his gaze. "Your daughter is quite exceptional."

"Yes. And very single-minded."

"That's part of what makes her exceptional." Max smiled.

"We're in agreement on that." He gestured to Shelley Carpenter, who rushed to his side. He murmured something, and she hurried away again. "You won't be bothered with inappropriate questions in the future. And I'm sure you'll handle the press with your usual skill."

"I'll do my best, Mr. Secretary."

"Ms. Carpenter will provide you with the details. Good night, Commander."

Harriman turned back to his companions just as Shelley appeared with another drink and handed it to him. That duty done, she turned to Max with her eager smile.

"If you'll allow me, I'll escort you around, Commander."

"That would be fine. Thank you, Ms. Carpenter."

She blushed and Max wondered how often anyone thanked her.

She followed Shelley dutifully in a circuit through the crowd, nodding at introductions, offering the standard line every time someone told her how remarkable the rescue in Somalia had been. They'd almost reached the bar again when Rachel materialized out of the crowd. One instant she wasn't there, the next she was. Max stopped walking. She needed all her energy just to keep her legs under her.

Rachel wore an emerald-green dress that hugged her torso and flared at the hips in soft flowing folds. Her hair fell about her shoulders, glowing red-gold in the light from the chandeliers that seemed focused on only her. She was thinner than when Max had last seen her, and her smile appeared strained. A blonde stood by her side, laughing as she sipped from a champagne flute. Her ivory gown accentuated a willowy figure, and her sculpted nails, painted a darker shade of red than her lipstick, gleamed where one hand rested on Rachel's forearm.

"If you'll excuse me," Max said to Shelley without looking away from Rachel.

"What? Do you need somethi—"

"No, I'm fine. I'll be back in a minute."

Max didn't wait for a response, cutting through the crowd as individual faces blurred and faded. Rachel was all she could see. Well before she reached her, Rachel saw her coming and her mouth curved into a soft smile that was hard to interpret. Welcome? Polite greeting? When Max was a few feet away, the blonde seemed to notice Rachel wasn't paying her any attention and looked around. Her playful expression hardened when she saw Max drawing near.

Max's heart hammered as she took Rachel's hand, leaned close, and kissed her on the cheek. "Hello, Ms. Winslow."

"Commander." Rachel's hand was warm in hers, her fingers fitting perfectly into hers. "You look"—her gaze drifted down and then back to Max's face—"good."

"And you look beautiful as always."

The blonde made a soft coughing sound and inched closer to Rachel. "Do introduce us, Rachel darling."

Rachel continued to look at Max. "Commander Max de Milles. Christie Benedict."

Max nodded to the blonde. "Ms. Benedict."

"Oh. You're the soldier Tommy wrote about."

"Sailor."

Christie frowned, her perfectly arched blond brows flattening in consternation. "I'm sorry. I thought that you were the one who rescued our Rachel in the jungle."

"I was one of the team. Most of us were Navy and Marines." Max spoke into Rachel's eyes. "Rachel, however, pretty much rescued herself. I've never met anyone less in need of saving. In fact, I'm pretty sure she saved me."

Christie's full red lips made an O shape. "How interesting." She tugged Rachel's hand from Max's. "Really, darling, you've been keeping secrets."

"No, Christie, I haven't. You just haven't been listening." Rachel spared Christie a fleeting glance. Max was so close, so very close and all she wanted to do was keep touching her. No, not just touch her, keep her, and the way Max was devouring her with her eyes said she wanted something similar. But then they'd always had heat. Always had passion. What she needed, what she wanted, was more now.

"I know how stressful—how awful it was for you over…there," Christie went on as if Rachel hadn't spoken, her tone solicitous. "I'm sure when you've had time to recover, you'll feel differently about a lot of things. Including us."

"I appreciate your support, but I don't need to recover or forget." Rachel carefully let go of Max's hand. "And I won't change my mind."

Max caught Christie's expression before she covered it with a fake smile. For a second, her face had twisted into a grimace of annoyance, insult, and suspicion. More than a few people nearby were watching them. Rachel hadn't exaggerated when she'd said she was often the object of unwanted attention. She'd almost rather be back in the jungle—at least then she could be alone with Rachel. Her breath caught.

That's what she wanted. To be with Rachel. Nothing else mattered. "I take it there will be another meeting with the press?"

"Yes, tomorrow." Rachel's voice had grown husky, her eyes more intense. "I'll see you then."

Shelley Carpenter magically appeared at Max's side. The woman had some kind of radar. "Commander, the Secretary of the Navy is here. If you'll come with me."

"Yes." Max couldn't find any other words, at least none she could say here. She bowed slightly, unable to look away from Rachel. "Good night, Rachel. Ms. Benedict."

CHAPTER THIRTY-TWO

Rachel slid her arm through Christie's and guided her into the cab line. When their turn came, she opened the rear door of the yellow cab and helped Christie in. "I'll call Sara to let her know you're on the way. She'll answer if I call the house, won't she?"

"I'm really fine," Christie said, enunciating each word very carefully. "You can take me to the hotel. Come up with me."

"No, I can't. I'm sending you to your parents. Then I'll know you're home safely."

"You can still come with me. Sara is very discreet—she always covered for Tommy and me when we got home late."

"I remember." Rachel smiled and shook her head. "But I meant it earlier—I care for you, but that part is over."

"All right, for now." Christie leaned back and closed her eyes. "But I'm not giving up."

"I'll call you soon." Rachel closed the door, gave the cabbie the Benedicts' address, and paid him the fare along with a generous tip. Back on the sidewalk, she moved away from the surging crowds and dialed Christie's parents' home. Their longtime housekeeper answered, sounding perfectly awake and composed at almost two a.m.

"Sara, it's Rachel Winslow," she said. "Christie's on her way home in a cab. Watch out for her, will you, and make sure she gets up to bed all right?…Considering the traffic, half an hour or so. Thanks, Sara."

She ended the call and was about to dial for the car service to pick her up when she sensed eyes on her. Pausing, she studied the shadows beyond the brightly lit entrance of the building. She'd gotten very good at looking into shadows and discerning what was hidden there. Tonight, she had no trouble at all, and her pulse quickened. Max. An instant later, Max stepped to her side. She had traded her dress uniform for a dark shirt worn outside dark jeans. She looked every inch as good as she had earlier. Rachel tried hard not to think about just how damn sexy she was.

"Hi," Max said. "All done for the evening?"

"Yes, finally. I noticed you disappeared quite a long time ago."

"Guilty," Max said, laughing softly. "I escaped as soon as I could politely manage it."

"I bet you gave Shelley fits."

Max slid her hands into the pockets of her jeans and lifted one shoulder, a gesture so *Max* that Rachel nearly groaned. She had about sixty seconds of control left before she would have to touch her.

"She's very passionate about her job, you know," Rachel said, thinking *passion* was a tame term for what she felt for Max. Hunger, need, want. For starters.

"I assured her I would keep to the schedule and appear promptly at the appointed hour tomorrow to meet with the press." Max stepped close. "But tonight is off the clock."

"Is it?" Rachel searched behind the intensity in Max's gaze, afraid to hope too much. When she'd left Max's apartment all she'd known was that she couldn't stay, not feeling the way she did and Max being somewhere else altogether. She was afraid she might give in all over again tonight, but then, would that be so bad? Maybe Max couldn't give her everything she wanted, maybe she wanted too much, maybe she could be happy with just… No. She couldn't. "So what are you still doing here?"

"Taking the night watch."

"Really? And who are you watching out for?"

"You."

Rachel's insides were already smoldering. Now heat like a living thing poured through her, desire so potent she ached. "Max. I—"

"I told you we should talk." Max took her hand. "I got that wrong, and you were right to go. *I* should talk."

"You want to talk." Rachel repeated the words like a ventriloquist's dummy and with about as much comprehension. Her brain had checked out and her libido was driving the train. "God, Max. It's the middle of the night."

"Will you come back to my hotel with me?"

"Now?"

"Yes." Max tugged her hand. Started to walk. "I'll buy you a drink. Give me half an hour."

Rachel would've said yes to anything at this point, and given her a hell of a lot more than half an hour. The walk would give her a chance to collect herself, and she'd be safe in the hotel lounge. She wouldn't be able to give in to the clawing need that scored her heart. "All right."

Max's smile blazed as she offered her arm. Rachel linked her arm through Max's and Max pulled her to her side. Their bodies fell into step, the connection instantaneous. The discordance that had plagued Rachel for days—an uneasy niggling in the back of her mind that was something was very wrong—fell away like a discarded cloak. Being with Max, touching Max, was right. With Max, she was herself, all of herself, in a way she'd never been with anyone else. She sighed.

"What?"

"I wasn't sure I'd hear from you again."

"I'm an idiot," Max said. "I missed you. More than that—I couldn't stop thinking about you. No matter what I was doing, you were always on my mind." Max stopped—took both Rachel's hands. A streetlight lit her face, stark and strong and beautiful. "I shouldn't have waited until now to tell you that. To tell you a lot of things. When you walked away I felt like part of me was gone."

Rachel gasped and pressed her fingers to Max's mouth. Her head was whirling, hope and desire and wanting making her weak. "Don't. Not out here. Not until we're alone."

"I can't let you go again," Max said vehemently. She stopped in front of the hotel. "Would you...will you come up to my room? Just to talk?"

"To talk," Rachel said, echoing again. She nodded, a heavy thrumming in her belly warning her she was in trouble.

Max hurried them through a lobby Rachel scarcely noticed, up an elevator, and into a room with a king-sized bed and the usual hotel furnishings, including a small sofa and coffee table in one corner. She took off her coat and sat while Max rummaged in the wet bar. Max's shirt stretched across her back and she remembered clinging to Max's back while she'd come. She bit her lip and tried to focus.

Max handed her a plastic cup of white wine and sat down so close their knees touched. "The vintage is good. Sorry about the glass."

"It's fine."

Max sipped an inch of dark whiskey without ice and set her cup aside.

"I wanted to call," Max said in her right-to-the-point way. "But mostly I was running scared."

Rachel smiled wryly and set her drink down too. "Yes, I'm sorry, I did dump a lot on you, didn't I."

"No, it wasn't you. It was me. *Is* me." Max clasped Rachel's hand in both of hers. "You're an amazing woman—determined, dedicated, willing to do whatever you need to do. You're brave, Rachel, the way it counts. You deserve someone a lot stronger than me, someone who isn't carrying around a lot of broken places."

"I've never met anyone as strong or as brave or as giving." Rachel couldn't not touch her, not when she suffered so much. She stroked Max's face. "I saw what it was like out there, just a little bit of what you've seen, but enough to understand there's no reason, no logic, to who lives and who dies. Only skill and determination and maybe luck. And you, Max. You made a difference."

"I'm not strong," Max said. "What you saw back at the camp was me trying to make up for never being quite brave or strong enough. Every one I didn't save and every one I knew I'd fail the next day or the next haunted me. Still haunts me." She nodded to the drinks on the table. "I spent a lot of time trying to drink away the nightmares. I'm not drinking much these days, but I'll probably always have the nightmares. And the dark places inside me."

"You think I don't understand?" Rachel's heart won the war with caution. She wrapped her arms around Max's shoulders and pulled her close. She would have pulled her inside if she could have, wanting to comfort her so badly, to erase the pain that always rode so close to the surface of Max's eyes. "I have dreams, nightmares, even when I'm awake. I know how easy it is to shut those places away. To close them down. And I know you haven't."

"When I'm with you is the only time I feel alive."

"I know. I feel the same."

Max hadn't known she'd wanted comfort, was certain she hadn't earned it, but Rachel's heart beat full and strong beneath hers, her body and her words stroking her, soothing the broken, bleeding places. She clasped Rachel's hand tightly and kissed her. "I love you. I'm not worthy, but I swear I love you with all my heart and all my soul and always will."

Rachel cupped the back of her neck, deepened the kiss until Max's head went light and all the blood in her body pooled in the pit of her stomach. Rachel's lips slid over hers like silk between her fingers. "I'm in love with you, Max. You're the only one I want. You're all I want."

Max groaned. "I'm starving for you."

"Show me."

Chapter Thirty-three

I wanted to undress you the second I saw you tonight," Max said, drawing Rachel to her feet.

Rachel looped her arms around Max's neck and pressed close. "I've wanted your hands on me since that first afternoon in the jungle."

Max tangled her fingers in Rachel's hair and kissed her, one hand stroking down the silken curves of her outer breast and over her abdomen and hip. She slid her hand beneath the hem of the emerald dress and found silk stockings topped with lace. Silken flesh above.

"You feel like no one I've ever touched," Max breathed.

"I never expected to feel this way about anyone," Rachel said, opening the buttons on Max's shirt. She kissed her throat, the hollow between her collarbones, the shallow valley between her breasts. "I've never wanted to give myself so much, take so much." She cupped Max's breasts beneath the tight tank she'd worn beneath the cotton shirt. "I've never wanted anyone to touch me the way you touch me. Everywhere, inside me, I feel you everywhere."

Max played her fingers lightly up Rachel's thigh from silk to lace to the soft skin above the stockings and higher, to the satin that covered Rachel between her thighs. Rachel surged into her hand as she pressed gently.

Rachel whispered against Max's throat, "God, Max, you keep teasing me like that, you'll make me come."

"That's all right. I want to touch you forever."

"You can, I'm yours."

"Mine," Max whispered, drawing her finger along the satin-covered cleft in long, firm strokes.

Rachel gripped Max's shoulders as her thighs grew weak. She circled her hips, her body guiding Max's touch. Her breath caught as the pleasure brimmed and threatened to spill. "Close, so close."

Max kissed her and stroked faster, forgetting to breathe, forgetting everything except Rachel's soft whimpers and the demanding thrust of her hips. To pleasure her was an honor she didn't deserve and one she craved every waking moment. "I love you."

Rachel jerked in her arms and cried out against her throat. Max held her closer as her orgasm overtook her.

"I love you," Max said again, and nothing had ever been so true.

"I love the way you make me feel. I love the way you know me." Rachel clung to Max until some of her strength returned. "Will you take me to bed so I can touch what's mine?"

"Yours," Max murmured. "Yes, I am."

Max turned Rachel in her arms and lowered the short zipper in the back of her dress. She smoothed the straps down over Rachel's shoulders and the dress pooled at Rachel's feet, the silky green on the pale beige carpet an oasis in the desert. Holding Rachel against her, she kissed Rachel's shoulder and stroked her breasts and down her bare belly. Rachel's head fell back against Max's shoulder.

"This isn't bed," Rachel said with a sigh.

"I'm getting there," Max said. "But undressing you might be one of the world's greatest wonders."

Rachel laughed shakily. "Max. You make me feel so special."

Max kissed her shoulder again and slid her fingers beneath the satin panties. Rachel was wet and swollen, ready for her again. Rachel gripped her forearm, fingers tightening as Max circled the base of her clitoris.

"Max," Rachel breathed, a warning and a plea.

"I know." Max's legs were as wooden as if she'd just marched thirty miles. She could barely breathe, she was so focused on the rising tension in Rachel's body.

"I'm going to come again." Rachel buried her face against Max's neck. "God, Max. Right now."

"I love you," Max whispered again and again as Rachel tensed and shuddered. The words, the reality, freed her from a lifetime of isolation. Rachel was the sunrise, the promise of a new day. Rachel was life.

"I want you on top of me," Rachel gasped. "I want you inside me."

Max swung Rachel into her arms, carried her the short distance to the bed, and laid her down. She stripped and settled atop Rachel, supporting herself on one arm and straddling Rachel's thigh. She slid her hand between Rachel's legs and cupped her. "Here?"

"Yes. Now." Rachel wrapped both arms around Max's back, stroking the planes she loved to look at, and lifted her hips to take Max in deeper until the ache that hadn't left since she'd walked out of Max's apartment faded away. Max looked down at her, her expression fierce, intense, possessive. Rachel pulled her near to kiss her and kept kissing her as Max carried her, stroke by stroke, to the crest of another orgasm. When she was close, so close she was only seconds away, she pushed Max over and straddled her.

"Watch me," Rachel whispered, her knees on either side of Max's hips. She reached behind her to cup Max as Max filled her.

"So beautiful," Max groaned, her dark gaze fixed on Rachel's face.

Rachel squeezed, and the tendons in Max's neck stood out. Gliding up and back, she rode Max's fingers to the peak.

"I'm coming," Rachel whispered, falling at last into the clear dark depths of Max's eyes. Max groaned and bucked beneath her, carried over the edge with her. Boneless with release, Rachel slumped forward, catching herself on Max's shoulders, her hair falling down to curtain Max's face. "Never. Never like this."

"I know." Max cradled her breasts, softly thumbing her nipples. The sensation was erotic and soothing, like Max, always exciting and safe.

"I love you." Rachel gathered her strength and slid down the bed between Max's thighs. She stroked the iron-hard length of her legs and kissed her still-hard clitoris.

"Jesus," Max groaned.

Smiling to herself, Rachel took her time, sucking gently for a few seconds until Max's body tensed and she knew she was close, then easing away. She indulged herself, taking what was hers, one slow stroke at a time.

"Rachel, please." Max cupped the back of Rachel's head and drew her face closer. "I need you."

Rachel's breath stilled and every sense filled with Max. Only Max. She drew her in and pushed her over, holding her while she came in her mouth.

❖

Max ran strands of Rachel's hair through her fingers as she watched the ceiling grow light with the coming dawn. Rachel lay with her head on Max's shoulder, her arm draped around her middle, one thigh over hers. She fit perfectly, as if she'd always been there. If she thought too much about how good Rachel felt in her arms, she'd begin to worry about jinxing what had to be a mistake. She ran a hand down her chest, an automatic gesture looking for her dog tags, her talisman, a reminder of who she was and that she was still alive. The tags were gone. Maybe her luck was too.

"I hear you thinking," Rachel murmured, kissing Max's breast.

"Not so much," Max said. Rachel didn't need to know about her fears. "Just enjoying you."

"Well, you can enjoy all you want." Rachel snuggled a little closer and kissed Max's throat. "Especially when it makes me feel so good. But you're not allowed to worry. Not when everything is fine."

Max laughed and some of the darkness receded. Rachel always managed to do that. "How did you know?"

"I can feel you worrying. You're not concerned about later today, are you?" Rachel said.

Max frowned while her brain tried to engage again with the rest of the world. She didn't want to let the outside in. All she wanted was Rachel. This room, this bed, this moment with no past to haunt her, no failures and fears to torment her. "The press conference? No, but I'd be just as happy to skip it. I guess there's no way we can just stay here?"

"I think Shelley Carpenter would find us," Rachel said.

"I don't want to put her in a bind. And I think you're right. She's determined."

Rachel caressed Max's chest. "I'd be happy staying here except for her too. But, Max—this moment, it doesn't have to end. I don't care what it takes."

Max lifted Rachel's hand and kissed her fingers. Took a breath. "I don't fit in your world."

"Thank God." Rachel raised up. Kissed Max slowly and thoroughly. "I never wanted that world or someone who fit in it."

"Your parents won't approve."

"Max, you might not have noticed, but you are a decorated war hero. Not that it matters to me what my parents think, but they'll have no objections."

"I'm not particularly sociable."

"You seemed to be doing quite well last night. I think Shelley Carpenter is half in love with you."

"That's just because I thanked her."

"You noticed her, Max. You saw her. Like you see me. It's one of the reasons I fell in love with you. That's so much more important than empty words."

"My nightmares probably won't go away."

"Mine might not either. But I'll sleep better in your arms. You have a way of chasing off the monsters."

"You're pretty good at that yourself." Max pulled Rachel on top of her and kissed her. "I love you. I need you."

Rachel caressed Max's jaw. "You won't have to go back there, will you? I'm not sure I'm brave enough to stand you being in combat again."

"Probably not. The troops are being retracted. But medics with field experience are the first called up if troops are sent to battle. So I still might be, one day."

"Okay," Rachel said, her expression firming. "If it happens, we'll deal. I know who you are, Max. And I'm so proud of you. We'll deal."

"My schedule is hard on…family." Max savored the word, almost afraid to use it.

Rachel's smile was radiant. "My schedule is too. I'll have to be away—out of the country sometimes, for a while."

Max cupped her chin, kissed her. "I'm proud of you too. All I care about is that you're mine and I'm yours."

"Max, I love you. I'm yours."

"And I'm yours," Max murmured.

Rachel kissed her. "Then there's nothing else we can't handle."

About the Author

Radclyffe has written over forty-five romance and romantic intrigue novels, dozens of short stories, and, writing as L.L. Raand, has authored a paranormal romance series, The Midnight Hunters.

She is an eight-time Lambda Literary Award finalist in romance, mystery, and erotica—winning in both romance (*Distant Shores, Silent Thunder*) and erotica (*Erotic Interludes 2: Stolen Moments* edited with Stacia Seaman and *In Deep Waters 2: Cruising the Strip* written with Karin Kallmaker). A member of the Saints and Sinners Literary Hall of Fame, she is also an RWA/FF&P Prism Award winner for *Secrets in the Stone*, an RWA FTHRW Lories and RWA HODRW winner for *Firestorm*, an RWA Bean Pot winner for *Crossroads*, and an RWA Laurel Wreath winner for *Blood Hunt*. In 2014 she was awarded the Dr. James Duggins Outstanding Mid-Career Novelist Award by the Lambda Literary Foundation.

She is also the president of Bold Strokes Books, one of the world's largest independent LGBTQ publishing companies.

Find her at facebook.com/Radclyffe.BSB, follow her on Twitter @RadclyffeBSB, and visit her website at Radfic.com.

Books Available From Bold Strokes Books

Kiss The Girl by Melissa Brayden. Sleeping with the enemy has never been so complicated. Brooklyn Campbell and Jessica Lennox face off in love and advertising in fast-paced New York City. (978-1-62639-071-3)

Taking Fire: A First Responders Novel by Radclyffe. Hunted by extremists and under siege by nature's most virulent weapons, Navy medic Max de Milles and Red Cross worker Rachel Winslow join forces to survive and discover something far more lasting. (978-1-62639-072-0)

First Tango in Paris by Shelley Thrasher. When French law student Eva Laroche meets American call girl Brigitte Green in 1970s Paris, they have no idea how their pasts and futures will intersect. (978-1-62639-073-7)

The War Within by Yolanda Wallace. Army nurse Meredith Moser went to Vietnam in 1967 looking to help those in need; she didn't expect to meet the love of her life along the way. (978-1-62639-074-4)

Desire at Dawn by Fiona Zedde. For Kylie, love had always come armed with sharp teeth and claws. But with the human, Olivia, she bares her vampire heart for the very first time, sharing passion, lust, and a tenderness she'd never dared dreamed of before. (978-1-62639-064-5)

Visions by Larkin Rose. Sometimes the mysteries of love reveal themselves when you least expect it. Other times they hide behind a black satin mask. Can Paige unveil her masked stranger this time? (978-1-62639-065-2)

All In by Nell Stark. Internet poker champion Annie Navarro loses everything when the Feds shut down online gambling, and she turns to experienced casino host Vesper Blake for advice—but can Nova convince Vesper to take a gamble on romance? (978-1-62639-066-9)

Vermillion Justice by Sheri Lewis Wohl. What's a vampire to do when Dracula is no longer just a character in a novel? (978-1-62639-067-6)

Switchblade by Carsen Taite. Lines were meant to be crossed. Third in the Luca Bennett Bounty Hunter Series. (978-1-62639-058-4)

Nightingale by Andrea Bramhall. Culture, faith, and duty conspire to tear two young lovers apart, yet fate seems to have different plans for them both. (978-1-62639-059-1)

No Boundaries by Donna K. Ford. A chance meeting and a nightmare from the past threaten more than Andi Massey's solitude as she and Gwen Palmer struggle to understand the complexity of love without boundaries. (978-1-62639-060-7)

Timeless by Rachel Spangler. When Stevie Geller returns to her hometown, will she do things differently the second time around or will she be in such a hurry to leave her past that she misses out on a better future? (978-1-62639-050-8)

Second to None by L.T. Marie. Can a physical therapist and a custom motorcycle designer conquer their pasts and build a future with one another? (978-1-62639-051-5)

Seneca Falls by Jesse Thoma. Together, two women discover love truly can conquer all evil. (978-1-62639-052-2)

A Kingdom Lost by Barbara Ann Wright. Without knowing each other's fates, Princess Katya and her consort Starbride seek to reclaim their kingdom from the magic-wielding madman who seized the throne and is murdering their people. (978-1-62639-053-9)

Season of the Wolf by Robin Summers. Two women running from their pasts are thrust together by an unimaginable evil. Can they overcome the horrors that haunt them in time to save each other? (978-1-62639-043-0)

The Heat of Angels by Lisa Girolami. Fires burn in more than one place in Los Angeles. (978-1-62639-042-3)

Desperate Measures by P. J. Trebelhorn. Homicide detective Kay Griffith and contractor Brenda Jansen meet amidst turmoil neither of them is aware of until murder suspect Tommy Rayne makes his move to exact revenge on Kay. (978-1-62639-044-7)

The Magic Hunt by L.L. Raand. With her Pack being hunted by human extremists and beset by enemies masquerading as friends, can Sylvan protect them and her mate, or will she succumb to the feral rage that threatens to turn her rogue, destroying them all? A Midnight Hunters novel. (978-1-62639-045-4)

Wingspan by Karis Walsh. Wildlife biologist Bailey Chase is content to live at the wild bird sanctuary she has created on Washington's Olympic Peninsula until she is lured beyond the safety of isolation by architect Kendall Pearson. (978-1-60282-983-1)

Night Bound by Winter Pennington. Kass struggles to keep her head, her heart, and her relationships in order. She's still having a difficult time accepting being an Alpha female—but her wolf is certain of what she wants and she's intent on securing her power. (978-1-60282-984-8)

Windigo Thrall by Cate Culpepper. Six women trapped in a mountain cabin by a blizzard, stalked by an ancient cannibal demon bent on stealing their sanity—and their lives. (978-1-60282-950-3)

The Blush Factor by Gun Brooke. Ice-cold business tycoon Eleanor Ashcroft only cares about the three Ps—Power, Profit, and Prosperity—until young Addison Garr makes her doubt both that and the state of her frostbitten heart. (978-1-60282-985-5)

Slash and Burn by Valerie Bronwen. The murder of a roundly despised author at an LGBT writers' conference in New Orleans turns Winter Lovelace's relaxing weekend hobnobbing with her peers into a nightmare of suspense—especially when her ex turns up. (978-1-60282-986-2)

The Quickening: A Sisters of Spirits novel by Yvonne Heidt. Ghosts, visions, and demons are all in a day's work for Tiffany. But when Kat asks for help on a serial killer case, life takes on another dimension altogether. (978-1-60282-975-6)